The Organization

Volume 1: The 7 Deadly Sins

by

Keith Morris

Chapter 1

"Why? I can't understand why I must manifest my own destiny." This is Rico Jones' disposition of life. Rico is a young, handsome Black man who is average height weighing 175 lbs. with brown skin. Man should not have the power of free will, simply because in the heart of man, lies the 7 deadly sins.

- Lust: Rico had desired the finest women and had usually gone out of his way and means to obtain them. To him they were notches under his belt, but he could not find satisfaction without them.

- Extravagance: Rico had constantly wanted and desired the finer things in life. To him, life had no purpose without luxuries and lavish living.

- Gluttony: Rico ate at the finest restaurants and spent hundreds of dollars a night on food rather he ate it all or not. To add to this, once he was finished, he'd dispose of the food that he no longer wanted.

- Greed: Rico had to have as much money as possible. His greed was the most obvious of his actions simply because he was cutthroat. He would go to length's end to obtain money and would make sure that no one else would get any in his pursuit of wealth.

- Sloth: Rico was a genius in every way imaginable. He had an IQ of 140, he was given a scholarship to Stanford, only to drop out after a short period of time, and he had excelled in every venture after his departure from Stanford. Unfortunately, he still never realized his talent.

- Acedia: Rico was never satisfied with his life, no matter what he accomplished. To add to this, when he was doing well financially and mentally, he never took the time to reach back to the people that loved him.

- Despair: On many occasions, Rico contemplated suicide because of his low-self-esteem and the fact that he felt hopeless. Why? No reason, it just comes back from his dissatisfaction with himself.

His committing of the 7 deadly sins, led to his current situation as Federal inmate #59781-024. But, what does a genius such as Rico Jones do to go to prison? Name it, he's probably done it. Because of his intelligent prowess, he was bit too smart to get wrapped up in the drug trade, and murder or robbery was too violent. Rico was a smooth operator, a hustler who always tried to get the upper hand on people by outsmarting them. He started at 15, when his mother viewed him as an intelligent yet conniving young man. "Did you clean your room Rico?" she would ask. "Yes mom" Rico would reply, but truthfully, he had a girlfriend come over and clean up the room after introducing her to some sexual acts that she had never experienced. Rico never looked at the truth; he thought everything had an alternative yes and no answer. Sure, the room was clean, but he hadn't cleaned it himself. This was Rico Jones in a minor capacity. His entire livelihood depended on him manipulating and bending the truth until it could not flex anymore. But his luring prison sentence had shaken the entire world, simply because of the complexity of the case.

Rico had graduated high school with a 4.0 GPA and entered Stanford University in Palo Alto, California on a scholarship. Life in Palo Alto was different from his life in Chicago; he went from weather that changes like clothes to beautiful sunny weather all year long. He went from living in the Windy City's gloom and self-destructing social state within the inner city to a life of exuberance and energy. But, in true Rico form, he looked for the holes and cracks that he could exploit. He met Brandon Schultz, a white kid from Seattle who was just as gifted as Rico. They were roommates on the dorm, and they had several classes together because they were both majoring in the same thing, Computer Science. Even though Brandon was a squeaky-clean white kid who stood about 5'7 with frizzy hair and glasses from Seattle, he had a dark side. For years he had been a hacker who had transferred $10 from different people accounts every week into his own. "No way dude, how is that even possible." Rico asked, "It's simple, all you have to do is crack the security code that the bank has in its system. After that its money in the bank, literally." explained Brandon. "Look dude, I know that you were doing this on a small scale, just enough to put some pennies in your bank account, but I think we can take this thing and blow up!" said Rico. "Hey man, I don't know, you know that is illegal and I don't want to get in any trouble" Brandon said. "Brandon, I'm not trying to back you into a corner, but I am saying that we would maximize profits simply because there is no expense to do this, just time that has to be dedicated to breaking the security codes. But, just imagine, money from interest bearing accounts, merchants accounts for E-commerce, online bets....there are so many avenues to getting money with this plus banks and these online companies are liable for the money that doesn't make it from point A to point B" Rico explained with true remorse for attempting to corrupt Brandon's mind, but, he would stop at nothing to learn the secrets of this operation. "Well, Rico, I think that we can do some things, but I am not going to participate in too much, because we are at one of the finest institutes in the world and we are going places. Why do you feel the need to take part in this risk and we all know the consequences of what could happen?" asked Brandon. "Because, we are smarter than any jack-off law enforcement agent and by the time they catch wind, we'll be long gone" Rico replied.

Things were sweet for a small period, it was so simple, with just the simple push of a button, Rico and Brandon went from "have nots" to "have gots." They started small for precautionary reasons; $100 here, $250 there. But, as time went on, they began to venture into bigger things like online betting. Once they tapped the system, it was like taking candy from a baby. One guy sent a bet through for $10,000; this was the big score for the time being. Rico and Brandon split it $5,000 apiece and went on a shopping spree. Brandon bought sounds for his car and a big screen TV. Since they were roommates, Rico took his money and saved half and spent the other half on more useful things like food, a car of his own, and wiring some to his mother back in Chicago. With the rush of a big score like this, they knew there had to be bigger and better ones out there.

"Hey man, we need to hack into the Federal Reserve Bank in San Francisco." said Brandon. "Why? We just hit another online guy for like $15,000" responded Rico. "Because, this just isn't enough, we need the big score man, fuck this petty shit!" said an excited Brandon who seemed to be a little erratic. "Hey, what's your deal? Are you high?" asked Rico, now seeing the root of Brandon's problem. "Hey, mind your fucking business!" replied an irritated Brandon. Rico now saw what Brandon was really doing with his money. There were some guys on campus who knew the town drug dealers, but Rico never saw any point in getting involved with them simply because he didn't want any parts of drugs. He saw what it had done to his father, uncles, and friends who got involved with selling and using them back in Chicago. "Hey dude, I fucked up, I should have never propositioned this shit to you, and I refuse to get involved with you anymore. As for the coke, you need to lay off before some bad shit happens. But I will not tap into the Fed because their security is strong, and it can be traced back" said Rico with sympathy for the once squeaky-clean Brandon. "Hey man don't be a chicken, anyway, I already did it! That money is going to go into that account any minute now" said a surprisingly calm and happy Brandon. "No way…" Rico started a sentence but, before he finished, he grabbed all his stuff and started packing. "Rico where are you going?" said a high and curious Brandon. "I am getting the fuck out of dodge; this is the Fed we're talking about dude. I don't know where I am going but I am clearing the way before the heat comes. You should have talked to me Brandon; I would have not let you get into this shit. There is something serious about to jump off, so I suggest you get out of

here as well." said Rico as he was running out of the door.

Chapter 2

Special Agent Jack Shapiro of the San Francisco FBI office was shocked about

a phone call that he received the morning that Brandon pulled the trigger on the

interception of a transaction involving the Fed and an international health

organization. Sharon Weinstein, a prominent figure in the banking industry had just

been promoted to Vice President of the Fed in San Francisco and was irate about a

$250,000 transaction that had seemed to vanish into thin air. "Mrs. Weinstein, I want

to assure you that we will get to the bottom of this craziness. There is no such thing

as a disappearing act when it comes to money." said Shapiro. "Thank you Mr.

Shapiro I will be glad when the person who has pulled this off is brought to justice!"

Shapiro was a cold, calculating agent who had spent 15 years with the bureau as a

field agent and had just been promoted 1 year ago to the fraud division. He was an

intimidating figure to see standing 6'4 and weighing 230 lbs. He had spent many

years in the field investigating crimes like racketeering and drug trafficking, but this

was a different beast altogether. Sure, he had spent some time on a few white-collar

cases, but this was no politician corruption or bribery, this would take more time to

trace every little detail to the whereabouts of the money....

Rico and Brandon were now in different arenas based on the transaction. Rico

had got in his car and kept driving all the way until he ended up back in Chicago.

Brandon, who had the money wired to a cousin's friend's cousin's account in

Vancouver, jumped a flight and began to count his riches. He feared crossing the

border taking heed to what Rico had told him, so he stayed. There were APBs put out on the both simply because no one had heard from them in weeks and the residential director of the dorm stormed their room only to find that they both were gone. Though Rico was in Chicago, he hadn't contacted his family yet because he feared what they had been told, plus the Feds could have his mother's house under surveillance.

"Fucking Brandon, we had it sweet until he started doing fucking coke!" said an upset Rico as he stared out of the window. A very attractive young woman named Jordan accompanies him. She is an average height, petite woman who has been a friend of his since elementary school. "What's wrong now?" she asks. "Nothing, I just don't know what is about to happen to me. Yeah, I did something wrong, but am I wrong for wanting some of the finer things in life? Fuck that, life doesn't give you anything you have to take it! If we were meant to be blue-collar middle-class Americans, then the middle class would be the rich" said Rico. "Rico, I know that you're upset, and I really enjoy having you here with me, but don't you think you should go see your mother?" Jordan asks very calmly. "Hell no, the Feds are probably staked outside of my mom's house. There is no way I am going home." he says. "I understand, but don't you think that you should go see someone from your family?" she says as she removes articles of clothing. "Yes, but I can't because I'm with you and will stay with you." They commence in sexual intercourse, but Rico is still getting used to the idea of possibly getting in trouble for his involvement in the scheme. He knows that Brandon will not be able to deal with what will happen to him and he will rat Rico out. To Rico, it's not a matter of if; it's a matter of when.

Agent Shapiro arrived after 2:00 pm to pick up all the disks and records of transactions that had occurred within the last 4 days. Upon his arrival he is greeted by his ambitious, young subordinate who beat him there. Agent Cody Jankowski is there already shuffling through records in the lobby. Jankowski was a frail, younger man in his mid-20s who didn't sleep or eat much; he stood about 6'0 but only weighed 160 lbs. His entire life was based around work and trying to get Shapiro's position when he is promoted again. "What 'ya got?" asked Shapiro in his sarcastic drawl. "Well boss, according to these reports, the money was sent, but never received by the bank, but instead a third party that picked up the transaction. It's like an interception in football, the quarterback, the health organization, threw it to the Fed, but these guys stepped in front like a DB and picked it off" said Jankowski in a very excited voice. "Alright, so basically you just told me what I already knew but thanks. Let's take this stuff to the office and examine it to see if you can tell me something that I don't know" Shapiro said in a near angry voice. Just then, Sharon Weinstein the vice president of the bank appeared, "Agent Shapiro...Agent Shapiro, can I talk to you shortly please?" "Yes, of course, Mrs. Weinstein, wait here Jankowski" said Shapiro. "I have noticed an inconsistency in the data that I would like to point out to you" said Mrs. Weinstein once they entered the office. Mrs. Weinstein was a short woman in her 50s with red hair. "Oh really, and what would that be Mrs. Weinstein, it would help to know before I began to examine the data myself." said Shapiro. "Well" said Mrs. Weinstein, "I would like you to see this withdrawal 1 hour after it was deposited. It seems to me that the hacker grabbed it, put it back, then pulled it out once they got the confidence to pull it off." "Well that is exactly what has happened Mrs. Weinstein, the hacker was nervous about just pulling it out and may have even considered just giving up. But when they saw that they could pull it off without any immediate infraction, they decided to pull the trigger." said Shapiro." Exactly Agent Shapiro, but I want you to see the name of the sender" said Mrs. Weinstein. "Well" said Shapiro "who is it?" Mrs. Weinstein with a very uncomfortable and confused look said, "The International Organization of Health Wellness." "I could be wrong, but to my knowledge, there is no organization of that name" said a now puzzled Shapiro. "Exactly" said Mrs. Weinstein. "Well not to worry for the greater good of the Federal Reserve Bank, I will do everything that I can to recover the funds, and I am really going to start looking into this whole thing about the 'so-called International Organization of Health Wellness'" said Shapiro, who was now compelled to believe that there was something more than a simple fraud going on. "Well thank you Agent Shapiro and good luck in your on-going investigation" said Mrs. Weinstein. As Shapiro exited the building, he knew there was some form of monetary corruption going on but now there was an even more complex issue to deal with. Who is the International Organization of Health Wellness? Did they instrument this whole thing? How did they crack the security network? Where were they based? But what if they weren't connected and this happened to be a weird coincidence? So many scenarios so few answers and so little time before everything got away. Shapiro found Jankowski and they agreed to meet at the office to go over the records. "Is everything okay boss?" asked Jankowski. "Yes, fine, but we are in for the long haul here kid"

Rico had gotten desperate; he is now at a point where he needs money. Though he had finally returned to his mother's home, he was still living on the edge. Cutting a deal with Mookie, a childhood friend and neighborhood drug dealer, he brings them back money. "Dog, I don't know how you're doing this, but I don't care!" said Mookie "here is another $5,000." It's a form of loansharking. Mookie and the other guys around the way give Rico $1,000-$5,000 and Rico goes and hacks a merchant and brings them double the amount in a matter of 4 days. It's simple until Rico starts living too comfortably in this shady lifestyle. Once, very calculating and smart, 6 weeks of stress has brought him into the abyss. His mother eventually found out that he dropped out of school. But he could never tell her why, he only could say that he had good reason, which she did not believe. Even though the Feds are struggling to build a case that still worries him the most. He is depressed about his life simply because he knows that if he wasn't being a corrupt monger for money, then his life would still be good, and he would still be the golden boy of the West Side of Chicago. He could have been the guy who made it out and went on to achieve greatness through his willingness and determination. "Don't worry, there will be more, just make sure you all keep the money coming!" said a darker Rico who have lost himself in this chase of happiness. He goes in the house and scrolls through his phone, 10 different women to call of his choice at any given time and he was always looking to add more. He looks in his drawers, cash everywhere about $60,000 from his recent adventures and some still left over from when he and Brandon had their set-up back in California. He looks in his closet, full to the max with designer clothes and accessories. Rico had everything that a man at 19 could only dream of, money, power, respect, and of course women. Life was good, but there was always a thought that crossed his mind, "where is Brandon?" He knew that Brandon still owed him money and wanted to stop at nothing to find him. Rico had become greedy and even became enraged that Brandon still hadn't resurfaced with his cut of the money. Before Rico could think another thought of Brandon, the Feds were breaking down his front door with a search warrant of the home and arrest warrant for Rico. Rico's mother nearly got a heart attack from the raid and couldn't believe that the son that she had raised to do right and achieve success was now on the FBI's list. Rico jumped out of the window but was caught in the backyard with a blow to the sternum. "Here it is" thought Rico as he was apprehended and taken into custody in the neighborhood, that he had grown up in. Neighbors watched and little kids stopped playing to watch the neighborhood success story turn into the neighborhood heartache. He looked back at his mother to see her crying and screaming how much she was disappointed in him. He yelled "I'm sorry" as he was taken into custody by the FBI.

Chapter 3

"So, Mr. Jones, do you think you're smart" asked Agent Marcus Brown, a Black man in his 40s with gray hair who stood about 5'6. He played no games because he dealt with poverty and escaping gang life, so he was rougher on his own people. "No, sir, that's why I'd like to speak with my lawyer" said Rico, who didn't feel the pressure that was being put on him to dime out Mookie and everyone else he was involved with. Rico thought that the thing with Brandon had finally caught up with him, but to his surprise, it was his recent hacking extravaganzas that led the Feds to him, especially since he had used the same computer to execute the scheme. "Why do you need a lawyer? You're going to prison anyway." said Brown "I know your kind some guy who think he's smarter than everyone else but guess what, you're going to do some hard time if you don't cooperate with us." "Well sir" said Rico "I don't have anything else to say so I'm sorry, if you would like to speak with my lawyer, that is fine." "Fuck your lawyer punk, you will make a nice bitch for Big Bubba." said Brown right before he picked Rico up and punched him in the stomach for not cooperating. "You get your hands off of my client before I have you investigated for brutality" said Justin Stone, Rico's lawyer and certified animal in the court room. Everyone around Chicago has a saying about Stone: "When you get Stone, you'll go home!" Brown walks out and leaves Rico and Stone alone to strategize. "So, is everything ok?" asked Stone. "Yeah, I just need to bond out, when they broke down my door, I hid my money in the gutter on the side of the house right before the other guys came and apprehended me." "Don't worry Mr. Jones, your mother found it and made sure that I was paid, now, as far as bond, they

haven't given you one. We'll have to go to court and ask for it" said Stone.
"Damnit!" screamed Rico "okay, well you stay on top of it, they want to give me
charges that I could get 20 years on! This is crazy." "I know Mr. Jones, but you rest
assured that my firm is going to work to get your case resolved and get you a bond
so that you can go home." said Stone. Rico sat back and realized that this situation
alone could get out of hand and wondered to himself "what the hell am I doing here,
in a murky detention center about to go into lockdown with other inmates, this is not
the life that was meant for me."

"Damnit Jankowski, it's been a month and we still can't figure this shit out!"
shouted Shapiro upset that the investigation has taken forever. "These assholes
robbed the Fed for $250,000 and didn't use a gun! How did it happen, I just don't
understand? This International Organization of Health Wellness has no address, no
phone number, don't register anywhere in the world and don't have any kind of
recognizability." Said Shapiro before he went off into his thoughts. "What can you
do with something like this? How can we help them ensure their money if they are
nowhere to be found?" Questions like this continuously play through his mind, but
he digs through the files and sends it over to the technology department to analyze
the whereabouts of either the sending or receiving of the money. "We've got
something for you sir" said Josh McNamara; a frizzy headed geek who had just
began working with the bureau 2 weeks ago. "Well what do you got?" asked
Shapiro who was now fed up with the nonsense that this case had brought. "We
analyzed the data and moved forward in evaluating the address of the network that
received and sent the deposit through. The sender is incognito, we can't quite

figure that out, but the receiver was some trumped up system that never truly existed, but was piggy-backed off of Stanford's system as if to separate the two systems, but I am really good at what I do so I was able to see right through that" said McNamara who was grinning from ear to ear. "Well kid, looks like you've brought us some very useful information, but what makes you so sure it came from Stanford I mean that is a very respectable college that gives births to CEOs of Fortune 500 companies, what makes you think that one of the guys at Stanford had anything to do with it" asked Shapiro. "Well sir, we took a look at the IP address, once that was done, we checked the listing of all business and public institutes that came close to that IP address and from there we noticed that although it wasn't the same as Stanford's it was very close, and then I discovered that the creators of this separate network had been students at Stanford University once I got a stronghold on the fact that the separated branch had once operated under the Stanford network." McNamara replied. "You're really close kid, any names?" asked a dazed Shapiro. "No sir, but we are working on that now that we have narrowed down the pool of people who could have been involved." McNamara said. Just then Agent Jankowski got a great idea, "hey boss, remember when those two kids from Stanford disappeared?" Shapiro replied, "Yes I do." "Well we need to go and see if we can find out some information about them and see what room they stayed in before their disappearances as well as get a general idea of what they were involved in." "Great idea Jankowski let's head out." replied Shapiro as they were beginning to head towards the door McNamara said to them "If we were able to decode this much information, the sky is the limit in finding that quarter million." "Alright, well you guys do that while Jankowski and I go and see what's going on over here.

Across the country in New York City, in a dark and seemingly vacant office space sits a tall, athletically built Black man in a black suit lost in thought. "Sir, your 5 p.m. has arrived" says the assistant a gorgeous tall woman resembling Naomi Campbell says to the man. "Thank you Amber, why don't you go home, you work a 9-5, not a 9-9" says the man to his assistant. "Sure, I will send them in to you." "Have a great evening, my dear." he says as his 5 p.m. arrives. "You sure have a way with the ladies, don't you?" says Justin Stone, star federal defense attorney. "Stone, you have always had a sense of humor, but I don't like it, if you want to tell jokes go to the fucking Laugh Factory" says the man to Stone who promptly fixes his face and pulls out Rico Jones' case file. "Who the fuck is this?" asks the man. "This is Rico Jones, a genius who boasts a 160 IQ and would be perfect for the recent vacancy in your regime. Normally, these two-bit drug dealers and crooked politicians are just cases, but this guy is a genius, honestly. For months, sloppily by choice might I add, he ripped off online merchants' accounts, gambling, and banks and he was still airtight because the Feds don't even know what to charge him with," said an excited Stone. "Really, you don't say, well we should sign him up right away. Are you out of your fucking mind? Some kid who had some luck with online stealing is good enough for my operation? You have got to be fucking kidding me" says the man in a skeptical and angry manner. "Listen, I know that you only like the top of the line guys to work with you, right? Well why not take chances on a kid who has a high IQ, money earning abilities, learns fast, and was on scholarship to Stanford before some changes in his life happened" said Stone. "Stanford? Where is the kid now" asked

the man. "At the MCC in Chicago, awaiting a bond hearing" said Stone. "Well I

want to him to meet Murphy he's there now, prolong his arraignment and then make

the case go away without him being sentenced, I'll make some calls. If this guy is as

smart as you say we'll test him out and Murphy is the ultimate tester. Oh yeah, don't

allow him to get a bond. I can make things happen at the MCC, but after that,

dealing with the Bureau of Prisons is a bitch" said the man. "You got it, by the way,

there is one more piece of information that you are going to love" said Stone to the

curious man. He replied, "and what is that?" "This is one of the kids that grabbed

the quarter million." said Stone. He froze and asked, "how the fuck do you know

that?" "Because he is one of the kids that the APBs were put out for" replied Stone.

"Well Stone, another one of your wacky ideas may come to light, but I'll have

Murphy check him out and if he is okay, then this can mean major moves for you.

Well, I have another meeting with the Godfather to discuss how we will take over the

world. Get this in motion now Stone, we don't have forever, you never know how far

the heat is away from you." said the man as he exited. Justin Stone had just done

Rico a huge favor without him even realizing it. If Rico ever wanted for power,

success, or fortune he wouldn't have to look too far, so long as he passed the test that

was upcoming.

Chapter 4

"The big buildings, the beautiful girls, the frat houses, college is great" said

Agent Jankowski as they cross the university to get to the main building where the

dean awaits them. "Hello, we are here to see Dean Massey" said Agent Shapiro to

the receptionist. "I'll go and get her sir" she said as she went to get the dean. "Wow

look at this place it's just gorgeous" said Jankowski. "Will you stop babbling on and

on about this darn school? We are here on official business on behalf for the Federal

Bureau of Investigation, remember that" Shapiro told him as Dean Massey emerged.

"Hello gentlemen, I am Barbara Massey, dean of student affairs, please follow me."

Shapiro and Jankowski followed Dean Massey to the office and wasted no time in

inquiring about the two students that had APBs set out on them over 6 weeks ago.

"Well, those two students were quite odd and seem to be the 'talk of the town' as

some of the kids around here said." said Dean Massey as she took a sip from her

coffee mug. "Oh well I assume that this will be an open and shut type of thing" said

Jankowski "who were these guys?" "Well, what I think my partner means to ask is,

can we please have some information regarding the young men who stayed in that

room and perhaps their records to help give us an idea of what type of activities they

were into" Shapiro asked politely as he checked his watch. "Gentlemen, the APBs

were closed on these gentlemen a month ago, they weren't found so the Palo Alto

Police Department shut down the investigation and assumed that these kids ran back

home" said Dean Massey. Jankowski ever so inquisitive asks "so can we assume that

the PAPD would have an idea of who they were?" "Once again, I believe that my

partner would like to say that we are conducting an investigation that involves a quarter million-dollar transaction being intercepted from the Federal Reserve Bank in San Francisco. The interceptor was traced here, to a system that had at one point been linked to your school's system. We would like some information about the two guys who had the APBs put out on them simply because, it happened around the same time as the transaction." said Shapiro. "Well gentlemen, to assist you in your ongoing investigation and to keep the great name of Stanford out of scandal, I will release the records of the two young men who occupied that room" said a now understanding Dean Massey. As she searched information on the records on the two young men, nothing showed. No record of them ever being on campus and no pictures, date of birth, nothing. "Well this is an odd case, gentlemen, hold please my records don't indicate who the two were, maybe the PAPD will still have records of the young men" said a confused Dean Massey. Even when students transferred to other schools, there would be some form of records that would indicate that the students at one point had attended the school in this case, no luck. "Yes, thank you, please continue your search" said Dean Massey to the PAPD on the line. "Well, according to them, they have no records, but you are free to check the newspaper archives for pictures and descriptions of the event. "I have never seen such a horrendous error within our systems" said a shocked Dean Massey. "Well this is shocking to say the least ma'am, a place like this fine institution is supposed to be in the upper echelon as far as intelligence and student reputation, to be quite frank" said an upset Jankowski. "Well sir, if you feel that way then maybe you should just go over the PAPD and see if they have answers and we won't have to have this problem again" said a frustrated Dean Massey "now if you'll excuse me, I have another order of business to attend to." "Dean Massey please forgive my partner for his antics and schoolboy behavior, but this has been a hard case to break into and for the longest, we have been working diligently to connect the dots. Please call me if you happen to come across any information, because we believe that these young men are the link to our case" said a polite and mild-mannered Shapiro. As they all left Jankowski whispered over to Shapiro, "these guys are good." Shapiro leaned over to him and said, "well we're better!"

The small Palo Alto police station was a reminder that in small towns, there is no room for big crimes. Shapiro and Jankowski were surprised to see that the receptionist was sleeping on the job. "Wish we had some down time like this" said Jankowski. "Excuse me sir, we were here to get some information on some APBs that were put out some weeks ago" said Shapiro. "APBs?" said the lazy officer "who wants 'em?" "Well sir I am Special Agent Jack Shapiro and this is Special Agent Cody Janikowski, we are here from the San Francisco FBI office and have reason to believe that two men who mysteriously vanished from Stanford University a few weeks ago could be connected to a crime of wire fraud" said Shapiro not wasting any time. Shocked that FBI would be at their station he diffused the wise guy act "Okay, well if there were APBs then they would be in the system hold..." "No sir, that is just the problem, we were at Stanford earlier and they had no data at all of these two men, but we were hoping that you guys might have stored some hardcopies of the APBs somewhere here in the facility" said Shapiro. "Well I'll go and get the shift commander and you guys can see what he knows" said the lazy officer. Shapiro was still in astonishment because of the irresponsibility of the PAPD as well as the school. Before he could finish his sentence, the shift commander in clean, pressed white shirt and blue slacks approached the two agents. "Hello gentlemen, I am Sgt. Howard Stanton. I was here when the call came through about the APBs for those college students came out and I must say that I am shocked that the system is not registering this information" said the captain. "Well sir," said Shapiro "I believe that it will all come together, over at the office we have those problems as well." "Well, I believe that we will relieve this problem in a short period of time" said Sgt. Stanton, as a younger officer walked up and whispered something to him. "What do you mean, there aren't any archives? You guys better get down there and look harder" demanded Sgt. Stanton. "Sir, with all due respect, we just aren't able to locate them. We looked through the database to see what shelf they were stored, but when we looked, there was no record. Sir, it could take hours, days, or even weeks to find this stuff" said the young officer who had a look on his face as if he was going to be fired for this issue. "Well gentlemen, we are going to put some more men on this case, and I am going to get with Internal Affairs. If these files don't show back up, I will have no choice but to believe that one of my own men is involved with all this madness" yelled the now angry Captain Stanton. "Sir, don't worry we aren't going to jump the gun here, but we are curious to know what could have possibly happened to these files. I know that you have a basic understanding of what is going on but let me further elaborate to help you see the picture clearly. Around the time that these two students disappeared, there was a $250,000 wire transfer that was picked off before it touched the Fed in San Francisco. The problem is that the organization sending the money through didn't exist. Now, with no traces of the organization, the money, or the kids, I am nearly forced to close the case and send it over to the cold case department, because it is going to take a very long time to figure all of this madness out. These two guys are the only link that we have in opening the case. So, I beg you on behalf of my partner and I, as well as the FBI to find these files and help us crack this case so we can at least question these young men. Thank you very much sir" said a disheartened Shapiro. He knew that with no significant leads in a case that has been open way too long, the bureau was going to pull him off the case. "Sir, I promise that we will investigate the disappearances of the kids and the files and get back to you as soon as we know something" said Sgt. Stanton. As Shapiro and Jankowski left, they both looked in the sky and thought to themselves in silence. When they made it to the shiny, new black Crown Victoria, Jankowski asked "now what?" "I don't know kid; guess this was too big for me, back to busting drug dealers, I guess. But even though I know we were so close, we still never got anywhere. This isn't over, but I know the bureau wouldn't put us back on this even if we had more information" said Shapiro. "This kid McNamara discovered a lot of information though. Maybe we can convince Cap to leave us on the case if McNamara can come up with more information" said an optimistic Jankowski. "Well, you know Cap was already bitching about getting some progress on the case and warned us that if we didn't get anything, he would pull us. But I guess it's worth a shot, this is a high-risk case, but if we crack it, we will be respected and promoted to top positions. I might even get a chance to run a branch" said Shapiro who now found more motivation in pursuing the case.

Chapter 5

"All rise" shouted the bailiff of the court "court is now in session, the honorable Marshall Bradley presiding." "Please be seated" said Judge Bradley "the first case on the docket is the United States vs. Rico Jones." "Jones" yelled Stone as he approached bench while Rico sat at the defendant table in a jumpsuit and shackles with a correctional officer standing next to him. Although Rico had felt alone the last few days, he didn't want anyone to see him in this state. He just hoped to secure a bond and be able to see the outside world. Jail wasn't anywhere for a human being. The food tasted like newspaper, the cell smelled of sewage, concrete, and dirty laundry. The phones were of poor quality, the TV had to be shared by the entire wing, as well as the shower. "Your honor, on behalf of my client, I would like to motion to set bond of $10,000 simply because he is a first-time offender who deserves fair due process of any other defendant. Upon the setting of this bond, we would like to move for a continuance, so I have the ability to learn more about this case" Stone said to the judge in his legal jargon. "Your honor" said Assistant District Attorney Michelle Hernandez "the prosecution moves that based on the defendant's capabilities and IQ test results; we fear that he is a flight risk." "So, you think that our officers of the law would allow him to slip through their hands Ms. Hernandez? Please continue with a more detailed explanation" said Judge Bradley. "Your honor, the prosecution feels that Mr. Jones is capable of manipulating more accounts and committing more frauds which is why he shouldn't have access to any computers. The only way to ensure this, is to deny him access to any form of computer system" said Hernandez. "I object, the prosecution is establishing guilt without due process" said Stone, upon hearing this Judge Bradley replied "sustained." "your honor, my client is innocent until proven guilty and is deserving of due process as is stated in the United States Constitution. To deny him his rights would be a direct violation of the Constitution. Furthermore, the prosecution is insinuating that my client has committed a crime which would constitute a ruling of bias. Unfortunately, for the prosecution this is not the case because my client didn't admit any guilt" said Stone. "Your honor, may I remind you that the defendant was indicted on 3 counts of wire fraud and 1 count of larceny by a grand jury? The indictment alone should affirm that the prosecution is at least credible for believing that Mr. Jones should be held before releasing him, or at least until further investigation can be completed" said Hernandez. "Your honor, if I could say one more thing..." said Stone but was promptly refused the opportunity by Judge Bradley. "Councilor, you make a good point, but I do believe that this case requires some further observation before I make a ruling on releasing Mr. Jones on bond. I rule that Mr. Jones is held without bond until further investigation can be conducted. I will set a date 3 weeks from today to see what progress we have, we will check the status of the case and see if Mr. Jones is eligible for bond" said Judge Bradley to the defense as Rico balled his fist up in frustration. "Your honor I feel that this is ill-advised but, I would like to file a motion of discovery so the defense can have a full idea of what is going on with Mr. Jones' case" said Stone as he approached the bench and handed the judge the motion. "Adjourned" said Judge Bradley as Rico was escorted to the back. "Rico, I will be back there to talk to you in a few minutes, let me fill out this paperwork and we will strategize" Stone told Rico as he was being escorted.

Stone left out of the courtroom and found Michelle Hernandez in the hallway. "Ms. Hernandez, could I please see you in the conference room? I have some questions for you" said Stone. "Yes Councilor, you may" she responded. As the door closed, Stone looked to make sure no one was standing by the door. Michelle Hernandez was a beautiful spectacle to say the least. She was a 5-year veteran of the District Attorney's office and was a close friend of Justin Stone, a man that she had secretly been having an affair with. "You're really good, but now it's time to downplay the situation" said Stone as he rubbed her hand. "Look Justin, we have to be careful. This is a dangerous situation, and we can't keep having meetings in the courtroom, the DA could have someone watching us" said a nervous Michelle. "Look babe, my guy has us covered; he has so much pull that it is ridiculous. No one is watching; anyway, remember the plan *ixnay on the flesay*" said Stone speaking in pig Latin as code for "get rid of the files. "We've got a good thing working here. I want you to keep doing what you do, but when it comes time, you know how to handle it, okay babe? I mean I know you love me, so you won't disappoint" said an arrogant Stone. "Yes baby, I will do as I am supposed to, but I want you to be careful" said a worried and antsy Michelle "can you do that for me?" "Yes Michelle, but don't worry, now what do you want, black or white diamonds? Plus, our arrangement will meet at about 7:00 pm tonight" said Stone referring to a bribe that they arranged. "Okay, and I like black diamonds, they're more expensive" said Michelle smiling as she left the conference room.

Stone sat back and smiled for a minute. He had a gorgeous mistress, beautiful wife and was flying high on a wave of success. Not bad for a guy from the suburbs who was too slow and injury-prone for sports and too nerdy to be cool in school. Now he was the coolest guy in the world. He was a link to the outside world of sorts for his partner back in New York, and an orchestrator for the members of the partner's organization. He had partnered with his boss as a law school student and took a liking to him immediately. The firm that he was interning with had represented him and Stone was taken aback by the slick, professional, yet stern and harsh demeanor of the client; Rashan Gaden. Gaden was a different type of individual; evil but good because he took care of his organization. Rich, yet he didn't look down on people because they were poor. Charismatic, yet partially anti-social this was strange because it just added to the fact that Gaden was a walking talking contradiction. He originally was the leader of a criminal organization that robbed drug dealers, pimps, and other criminals. The law firm that he worked for took on his case when he was accused of murdering a police officer. Once he was cleared, he made good friends with that law firm and Stone because he saw a lot of himself in Stone; young, brilliant, and good with words. Unfortunately for Gaden, he wasn't afforded the same opportunities as Stone. Because of this they formed the ultimate alliance and used each other's influence as the catalyst to create a major force, a world power. Stone, who had taken a liking to Rico, was going to put him in position to operate with Gaden, catapulting him from small time crook to well respected diplomat and businessman. Stone couldn't quite figure out what it was about Rico, but he knew that he would be a perfect fit, which would make him a millionaire in a matter of months.

Upon exiting the conference room, Stone was approached by a beautiful young Black woman wearing a dress with her hair tied up. "Hi, Mr. Stone, my name is Jordan Riley. I just wanted to know would be going to see Rico" she inquired. "Yes ma'am, how can I help you" asked Stone. "Well, can you pass this to him? By the way, tell him that I love him very much" upon saying this, the beautiful woman walked down the hall in a somber manner. Stone watched her as she walked and thought to himself, "lucky ass kid." At 19, Stone could have only dreamed of having a gorgeous woman give so much of her for a guy who was in a tricky situation. But on the flip side, it could give Rico more edge as to succeed. Whatever way it affected Rico, Stone would use it to capitalize and deliver Rico to Gaden. Even if he had to hint to Rico about the test that Murphy was going to deliver to him.

"Hello Mr. Jones, I am sorry about the debauchery in the courtroom. Let me assure you that I am going to be working my ass off to get you out of here on that date" said a determined Stone, even though he knew Rico would be out. "Well just do what you can, I am a realist Stone. I know that you are a great attorney to have, but you are only human just like me; full of mistakes and mishaps. Perfection is not human nature because if it was, no one would be in prison nor would anyone be dead" said Rico. "Whoa man, you surely have gotten philosophical in here haven't you? Don't worry, perfect I may not be, but I am the closest to it in attorneys that you're going to find. Now it seems that the indictment apparently had no witnesses come in, it makes me question the credibility. Indictment means nothing, you want to know why? Because its these fucking prosecutors talking to 23 other prosecutors, clerks, and other court employees. To me, it is the most biased form of charging an individual that you will ever hear of, but that's America for you" said Stone. "Well

how is it looking besides that, you know the prosecutor will find a way to prove that

what they are saying makes a lot of sense while what we say makes none, just like

she did today" said Rico, who was totally unaware that Stone orchestrated the whole

bond hearing, but that was good. "Mr. Jones, that is true, but I also want you to know

that they don't have any substantial evidence. They just raised enough suspicion to

secure a search warrant, but it wasn't enough evidence to be signed off by a judge

and that is a fourth amendment violation. Finally, I'd like to add that their whole case

is theory, nothing that can really be proven. This isn't like a bank robbery where

you smacked someone upside the head and cleaned out the safe like a grunt. This is

a white-collar crime that takes intelligence and precision to solve and that is

something that they don't have in the DA's office, hell the DA is a dimwit" said Stone,

who was passionate about his disposition. "Okay Stone, sounds good, but I need

you to get on top of this stuff. I need to get out of here and then I will be able to think

clearer and not feel like I am going to die every day of the week" said Rico being

adamant about getting away from the conditions he was subjected to at MCC. "Rico

Jones, I guarantee that I will be on my job, but you need to be on yours" said Stone,

beginning to hint about the upcoming test. Rico stared at him for a moment in

confusion and finally asked "my job? Stone what are you talking about?" Stone

calmly looked at Rico and said "look, I can't tell you much, but I can say to be careful

about who you associate with and make sure that, if you do associate with anyone,

that it is worth your time, got it?" "Yeah, of course, I don't want any more trouble

and I will only keep positive energy flowing my way" said Rico in a semi-joking manner. "Oh, and one more thing" said Stone as he pulled out the letter from Jordan "she says she loves you very much and misses you." Rico was truly appreciative of Stone bringing the letter to him and instantly began smiling "thanks Stone you're a stand-up guy." Rico motioned for the guard to take him back to the cell block and Stone motioned to be taken back to the courthouse. Stone knew that this would pull Rico out of the dumps and that it would motivate him to not get wrapped up in any non-sense. He had no idea what Gaden had in mind but certainly, it would be one hell of a test for a man incarcerated in federal prison. Stone couldn't quite figure out why but was taking a liking to Rico and had a good feeling that he would pass the test and be able to work in the organization.

Chapter 6

"No fucking way am I going to sign off on you two idiots continuing on this case" said Captain Wade Nicholson, head of the FBI branch in San Francisco. "You guys have better gathered some damning evidence or at least a good reason why I shouldn't have both of you demoted to the evidence room or shipped out to the office in Fargo" screamed Captain Nicholson. "Well sir, I know things haven't quite produced the way that we originally thought they would, but we have an x-factor" said a confident Jankowski. "Oh, really and what is this 'x-factor' that you speak of Agent Jankowski" said Captain Nicholson who felt that this whole operation was a mockery of law enforcement. "Agent Josh McNamara, sir. He has gotten us a lot of information that has been helpful in the investigation and if we keep him on the investigation with us, then I know that we will discover a lot of information that only a technological expert like himself can find" said Jankowski who now was holding his chest because conversations with the captain had always intimidated him. Shapiro was fed up with the captain's ranting and intervened "Well captain, if I may? I will bring up the fact that this case is not going to solve itself. We have been working diligently and now with the addition of Agent McNamara, we know that we will be able to get to the bottom of this case." "Well Agent Shapiro, that is nice to know, you know what else would be nice? Knowing when results will spawn from this investigation. In my 26 years with the bureau, I have never been part of an investigation that has stretched this long and still haven't generated any results. Shapiro, I don't know about you, but me as the captain of this branch will have to say no, plain and simple. But without this kid trying to explain to me about the unnecessary junk that I don't want to hear, I will give you one chance Shapiro. Your one chance to produce some results and bring me some form of information that will show me that the case is going somewhere. But I am going to have to put a cap on the time limit of some result" said Captain Nicholson. An excited Shapiro responded "okay, sir, how much time will we be able to secure on this case?" "5 days" said Captain Nicholson "5 days to bring me some information, and I mean the whole enchilada here pals. I need pictures, profile, motive, and proof that they could have pulled off this extreme crime. After 5 days, not only will you not be able to work that case again, but you will be put back on the SWAT team. That goes for both of you, so make sure that you two are willing to bet your current positions on obtaining information." "Yes sir, we will definitely get our necessary information and not only that, we will retain our positions and make you proud to call us your subordinates" said an excited Jankowski. "Agent Jankowski can be quite erratic at times, sir, but we are going to get to work and we will let you know what we find within 5 days" said a calmer and more focused Shapiro. As they left the captain's office, Shapiro had no choice but to wonder, who is this greater power that is pulling fast ones on them left and right? What about this McNamara kid? For a guy that they didn't even know was an FBI agent, he sure has become important. "Let's get to work Jankowski, our jobs are on the line" said Shapiro as they walked into McNamara's cubicle.

"What ya got kid? I know it's got to be some good news" said Shapiro as McNamara looked like he was researching the information he had found earlier. Yes, I actually have found some small detail on the roommates' identity" said

McNamara. "What do we have kid? Is it useful? I can take it in to Cap right now"

said an anxious Shapiro. "Well, it isn't very significant, but if you want to that's fine"

said McNamara. Shapiro looked at the screen and saw general information like

height, weight, and birthplace. But something that they had found was very

significant, names. "Rico Jones and Brandon Schultz were their names" said

McNamara scanning the screen for more significant information. "Rico was Black,

and Brandon was White. But I am certain you can tell that from their names" said

McNamara jokingly. "That's funny but what about them what were they into, where

are their pictures? Social security numbers? Without that information this is very

hard to capitalize on" said Shapiro "we can check the population index in Illinois and

California for Rico Jones and check Washington and California for Brandon Schultz.

If these were the guys, they must be somewhere around. If that turns up nothing,

then call the Census Bureau, and if that doesn't work call Stanford and see if they can

account for students by those names. We only got 5 days guys, hopefully no one has

a family to go home to, because there is a lot at stake here, let's get to work!

"Alright, everybody shut the fuck up and sit down right now" said the guard

as he was taking inventory on the prisoners who were in the holding tank awaiting

transfer from the courthouse back to their units. Prison was the human equivalent of

the dog pound to Rico. They throw you in a cage, lock you in there, and throw bones

for you to eat on their terms. "When you hear your names say here" ordered the

other guard. "For these guys to be in charge of monitoring notorious criminals, they

sure are stupid" thought Rico as they began shouting names off. When he heard his

name, he answered and could step out of the holding tank and stand in line to be taken back to his cell. Even though there was so much wrong with prison, Rico made use of the time away from society to clear his head. Though there were major charges against him, he just used his time to think about his future. If he was able to get out of this situation, returning to college would be great. Rico had excelled back at Stanford and enjoyed reading and writing now that he was forced to make use of his time with limited and scarce resources. Upon arriving to his cell, he noticed that his old cellmate had been transferred out. No big thing, except this guy was doing 15 years for racketeering. "Where could they possibly have taken him?" Rico thought to himself before another man walked in. Rico seeing all the prison movies in the past thought that he was about to be murdered. "What up young blood? I'm your new celly, T-Dog" said the new cellmate. "What's up man? I'm not going to lie, I thought you were here to kill me" said a now relieved Rico. "What I want to kill you for? I don't even know you" said T-Dog. "Sorry about that, they call me Rico just got in a few days ago" said Rico now weary about the man's background. "Oh ok, well I been in the Fed system for 4 years. They just shipped me here to transition me to a lighter environment. Say they want to send me out to Leavenworth out in Kansas, you know the place Michael Vick was at" said T-Dog. "Cool well good luck with that my man" said a nonchalant Rico. "Say young blood, want to make some money? I got some people up in here that's got a connection on weed and heroin. Their girls smuggle it in, and we sell it around the compound. Easy money, plus you ain't gotta be callin momma and girlfriend to send you nothing" said T-Dog who began laughing. "That sound like a good opportunity my friend, but I don't want no part of that. I just want to do this time until I go to trial and then see what happen from there" said Rico who now was even more wary about T-Dog then before. "Say, look here man, I am not trying to dictate to you what you should do, or how you should do it. But I am trying to plug you into something real serious and heavy here baby. Now if you can't get down, you might have to lay down and that's for real" said an aggressive T-Dog. Rico stood there, caught off guard by T-Dog's shrewd remarks. "Are you threatening me bro? It can't be that because I am from a place where I have been prepared for this for a long time. Now if you wanna bang, then we can do that, but if that is how you want it then we have nothing else to talk about" Rico took a step back and sized up T-Dog, a short but stocky guy who looks like he have spent his last 4 years in prison, lifting weights and jogging the whole time, but Rico wasn't fazed. "Hold on now young blood, I ain't threating you, but it's not me that you gotta worry about. It's these gangs that are looking to recruit. It's these other guys in here that have it in for a young, green guy like yourself and figure that they can use you as a pawn in their game" said T-Dog. "Ok, just watch how you say things next time and we will be okay. As far as the rest of these guys in here, I'll deal with them on a case by case basis. In the meantime, if I have to fight then that is what I will do, but I will say this much, Rico doesn't run from anything" said a passionately furious Rico who paced and looked down the hall of his cellblock. It was the daytime so for 6 hours a day, the inmates could freely move up and down the cellblock. "What have you heard? I mean something has to have you thinking this way" said Rico. "Well, some of these guys have been talking about that they wanted to hurt you because they said that you're not a gangster" said T-Dog who had gained a new level of respect for Rico. "Well I appreciate it because you never know whose out to get you so keep me posted if you hear anything and I will definitely stay on my Ps and Qs" said Rico.

The next day, Rico went through his daily routines while being held at the Federal Detention Center in Chicago; brush teeth, wash face, push-ups, sit-ups, eat some honey buns, more push-ups, more sit-ups, coffee, newspaper, news on the cell block's television, and listening to the latest word around the prison from other inmates with movement. "Yeah man, they say that this dude really got it out for you man" said T-Dog who looked a little worried. "That's it, I'm tired of this shit, who the fuck is this asshole who keeps putting nonsense about me out to everyone" said an infuriated Rico who was pacing the floors. "Word has it that it's this one fella, big mean ugly fella too" said T-Dog who now was nervous about revealing the information. "Ok, so this big, mean ugly fella got a name" asked Rico, who was now happy to be closer to figuring out who this prospective adversary was. "They call him Reck very dangerous guy who is known as the top dog around here" said T-Dog who was becoming sick by looking at the grin on Rico's face. "Okay, well where the fuck is Reck and how do I get at him? Does he come to the yard?" Asked Rico who was highly upset by the fact that some guy who wasn't on the cell block wanted to challenge him. "No, that's the thing Rico, he is some dude who doesn't go to yard with us on our time" said T-Dog. The yard was a place where inmates of different cellblocks could meet up. Unfortunately, Reck's cellblock didn't come out at the same time as Rico's. "So, let me get this straight; This big scary gangster that everybody in the joint fears is talking shit about a guy he doesn't know? What the fuck is wrong with this coward, I mean how does he even know about me?" Said

Rico in a very discontent mood about the news that he has just received. "Well" said T-Dog "there is an opportunity for you to see him, it will be in the chow hall." The chow hall was the cafeteria that inmates of all different cellblocks came to eat. "What can I do in the chow hall? I mean there are so many guards there that if I even look at this dude too many times, I will get escorted out of the building" said Rico now cautious because to him, there was nothing worse than being put into isolation. For his time, Rico had vowed not to go to isolation, just because being thrown in cell alone with no socialization along with no TV, commissary, or phone calls just made him want to vomit. "I know it is not the most conventional way to do things, plus I know that you are smarter than any one of these guys in here so it's time for you to put together a plan. I am not trying to encourage you to kill this guy, but he has to be confronted one way or another" said T-Dog. "Well" said Rico "how can we put this thing together I mean look at it; I have spent all of my time avoiding people, now I am forced to put something together quick, fast, and in a hurry because someone is after me? No way, I will plan this out perfectly, and it won't be in the damn chow hall. It will be at neutral ground that we can all agree on. Tell me about his crew, I mean, a guy who is talking so reckless in this place must have some guys around him that are very weak and don't want to get their asses kicked, so they kick ass for him" said Rico who now seemed to be devising a plan. "He does have a crew, that much you can bank on" said T-Dog "his crew is very strong and powerful, matter of fact, they run the entire prison. There is the Sorcerer, a guy who makes thing appear and disappear at the snap of a finger; money, drugs, people" said T-Dog. "Okay, so who else? I mean there has to be more than one guy for this prick" said Rico who was now giving his undivided attention. "Well then there is Mercury, he is the errand boy, he runs the dope that Reck sells at breakneck speed. On top of that he stashes the weapons and plays lookout just in case something is going down" said T-Dog who was now getting in the spirit of being Rico's word man. "Okay, what else? Because there has to be some muscle in all these slicksters who call themselves working with him" said an inquisitive Rico. "Okay, well that's when it gets interesting. There is Lysol, aka the clean-up man. He is a specialist at dealing with stabbing a man to death and then cleaning all the blood and delivering the body to the Sorcerer. There is also Rocky, they named him that after the movie for his strength and brute force. He can literally beat a man to death with his bare hands and leave him there on the floor while he dances around. It's entertaining, but sick" said T-Dog who was now scared because he felt that the inevitable was on the horizon. "Well T, is there anyone else? I mean this guy seems to have his whole crew in order ready to pick an unsuspecting bastard apart" said Rico. "Well" said T-Dog "there is a couple of more guys, but now we are out of our jurisdiction. There is Motley and Brasham, two CO's that help him conceal all his violence and dirty work. These two guys are reckless and will help in killing you if Reck can't get to you. You ask why? Because apparently Reck was a huge drug dealer and has plenty of money to make sure that this place goes how he wants. If not, then he buys his way to that feeling" said T-Dog. "Well, you know what? It is time for me to have a word with Reck. I don't like violence and maybe, just maybe, if he is a good businessman, he will feel the same way" said Rico.

Chapter 7

Two have days gone by, and Jankowski and Shapiro are at a disadvantage.
McNamara have found the names of these guys, but no relevant information. "What
can we do about finding these guys? Apparently, no one knows where they are"
said Shapiro. He and Jankowski had been on a rampage calling every known phone
number that Rico and Brandon have had in the past to no avail. They both had been
in contact with the FBI offices in Chicago and Seattle to find these two young men
and they weren't successful. Brandon's parents honestly hadn't seen him since the
disappearances and Rico's mother had been so heartbroken about Rico's recent
incarceration that she just wouldn't deal with more police contact. In the Chicago
office, there had been speculation that Rico had been jailed, but no records of him
existed. Matter of fact, Rico's recent arrest didn't even register to the FBI. "In my 15
years with the bureau, I have never heard of anyone rumored to be in jail and not be
in jail. I swear this case is turning into a soap opera the more time pass said Shapiro
who just couldn't believe that all these leads were turning into dead ends. As he
looked out of the window, McNamara came running into the office. "You'll never
believe it; we have a lead on Brandon Schultz" said McNamara. "Where? I mean we
have been looking for this guy for days and still haven't heard anything. His own
mother doesn't know where he is, yet you do? I don't know kid; it seems to me that
you're overzealously finding these leads" said a skeptical Jankowski. "His mother
doesn't know where he is because he doesn't want her to know where he is at. Plus,
he isn't in Seattle or nowhere close to it" said McNamara who was upset that
Jankowski seemed to doubt his credibility. "Look kid, I know that you are working

hard just like we are, but we need solid leads. You have found some people that might know where they are, but nothing has come through. It's not your fault, and you might have to pardon Jankowski, but we are running out of time" said Shapiro who was beginning to worry about his future in his current position. "Look, according to the database a man by the name of Brandon Schultz made a purchase at a furniture rental place and scheduled a delivery. That seems to not mean anything, but here is the catch" McNamara proceeds to show video stills of Schultz with a baseball cap on and all of his hair shaved off. "Based off this high school picture of Schultz that I got from the Seattle school system, this is our guy. There is only one problem" said McNamara. "Really? Why don't you break down what this problem is 'Whiz Kid'" said Jankowski. "The purchase was made near Billings, Montana" said McNamara. "Let me get this straight, this guy is from Seattle, went to school at Stanford, and now lives in a boondocks town outside, of all places, Billings, Montana? This guy is either stupid or think that he is smart because he knows there is no field office in Montana. We have to contact the Salt Lake City office, and get some guys on the case if necessary, in the meantime, I'll put a call over to the Billings PD and the Yellowstone County Sheriff to go and check this lead out." said Shapiro. "No office in Montana? Well, it would sure pay in these kinds of situations" said Jankowski. "I'll contact them and see what they can get out of this whole ordeal, which by the way, seems shaky to say the least but we'll make it work somehow, and if we get him, I know we'll get the other guy and we'll figure out what the hell is going on" said a more upbeat Shapiro.

Lt. Jed Lee, a man of honor and respect, had spent his entire life in Montana. Growing up in Missoula, he was raised to be in fear of the Lord, and to love his family. His family values encouraged him to become a police officer at 18 and by 35, become the 3rd in command at the Billings Police Department. This would seem like a cushy job, but Lee took it very seriously and took on a lot of high-profile cases himself, leading the charge against the suspects as they were brought in. "Lt. Lee, sir" said Officer Lisa Cooper, a young woman new on the force who admired Lee. "Yes, Officer Cooper" there is a call from the San Francisco FBI field office, an Agent Shapiro" said Cooper. "Thanks Hun, I'll take it and please close the door" said Lee, a man who was a gentleman first and an officer of the law second. "Yes sir" said Officer Cooper. "Lt. Major Jed Lee, Billings Police Department, how may I help you" said Lee. "Good afternoon sir, and, how are you? This is Special Agent Jack Shapiro of the FBI's San Francisco field office. We have a situation going on and I want to give you some background. First, some time ago there was a transaction that was electronically being transferred to the Fed in San Francisco. Well, it was intercepted by a hacker, but the most interesting part is that the sender was an organization that didn't exist. So, we have been looking for the two guys that seem to have intercepted the transaction, but neither one of them are nowhere to be found, and everything about them has seemingly been erased from every imaginable tracing index. We have a lead about one of the guys, and they are supposed to be close to your town. He recently made a purchase from a furniture rental place on the edge of your town and we have pictures and an address from the store that my partner is in the process of e-mailing you now. All we ask is that a few of your men investigate to see if this guy is there, if he is, we will ask you to detain him and our agents will get him promptly. I have my partner calling the Yellowstone County Sheriff as we speak as well" said Shapiro in a very professional, informative matter. "We don't need the Yellowbelly County Sheriff helping us, I can assure you Agent Shapiro that if this man is going to be found by anybody it will be the Billings PD. With my assistance and innovations, we are the top in the state at fighting crime, and a simple manhunt for some computer hacker shouldn't be any problem" said a confident Lee. "Lt. make no assumptions, based on this person's accessibility to many resources and the possibility of knowing that he is wanted, he could easily become a violent fugitive, willing to do anything and everything to avoid capture" said Shapiro warning Lee of possible danger. "Sir, let me assure you that this isn't San Francisco, we encourage marksmanship amongst our ranks, if this guy think he is going to escape, or as you put it, avoid capture, he's got another thing coming. My assistants will obtain the e-mail on this guy, and we will be moving out within the next 15 minutes. See there Mr. FBI, your case is as important to us as it is to you, plus, I plan to be the chief of this department in the next few years so I will definitely turn to you guys to help me convince the mayor, county president, and governor to make this happen. I'll call you when we got him" said Lee as he hung up the phone. "Hello, hello" said Shapiro "what an arrogant jerk, I sure hope all of these guys out in the boonies don't talk like this guy!" "Well" said Jankowski as he walked into the office, "they do, and I sure hope they find this guy, because this guy has really driven me nuts! And what is the story with this supposed rivalry between Billings PD and the County Sheriff? It sounds like a Hatfield-McCoy feud." "Yeah, tell me about it, but let's just hope that these bumpkins can find this guy, if it's him oh boy will this save our asses" said Shapiro.

"Alright men, here is the detail of the mission" yelled out Sheriff Henry Wallace "Brandon Schultz is this man's name. He is a computer terrorist; he steals and makes a mockery of all of you because he thinks he is one step ahead of all of you. I'll tell you what, if this kid think that he is going to rip off money from our beloved government and then come and hide in our towns, then he's got another thing coming. We've got the address, he is staying up in a house in the woods, that I know hasn't been occupied in 3 years. Now, we're going to go up there and arrest him, kick his tail, and hand him over to the FBI. I've got a message that the Billings PD is going to handle this, sounds like a joke to me, but we will effectively collaborate with them by the blessing of the governor. Now, let's lock and load and get this guy before he does what he does best; take off like a thief in the night." Sheriff Wallace hated to have to deal with the Billings PD and their Lt. Major Jed Lee. Wallace and Lee were in the academy together and were the two top scorers of any graduate. They were partners on the beat together, but Lee received a promotion before Wallace who sought out more opportunities for advancement with the Yellowstone County Sheriff's office. The rivalry between the two began when Wallace and his men snuck in and apprehended members of the Hell's Angels who at the time had been involved in the biggest indictment that the state had ever seen. This group of men had been charged with everything from drug trafficking to murder, armed robbery, assault and battery, and arson. Wallace led the team that apprehended them, propelling him to win a landslide victory for Sheriff and slowing

Lee's growth with the Billings PD, as he and his team were second on the scene. Lee made sure that Wallace would never undermine him again, as he now kept a mole within the Sheriff's department and stayed a step ahead or moving the same as Wallace. As Lee and his men arrived at the house, he noticed that there was a white pick-up truck sitting in a driveway. Just then, Wallace and his men pulled up right next to them. "Men, hold your fire" said Wallace "well Jed, look at you, seems that you have gained a few since the last time I seen you." "Well, Henry it looks like you've lost more hair since the last time I saw you." Wallace turned his lip up at Lee and then they both demanded quiet as a group of the men approached the front door quietly. "Police, we have a warrant for a Brandon Schultz, please come out with your hands up" yelled out the head of the tactics team. Before he yelled out his command, there were other teams surrounding the premises. "Police, we have a warrant, open the door or we will kick it down" yelled the officer again before the men knocked the door down with the battering ram. Now there were groups of men surrounding the outside and two teams were inside scattering the house and methodically searching for the suspect. "Come out with your hands up now" yelled Wallace who couldn't believe that after approximately 3 minutes of searching the suspect hadn't turned up, just then he heard one of his men outside yelling. "Sheriff you have to see this" said the officer. Lee and a few of his top ranked detectives followed suit to see what the officer had discovered. "I'll be, this looks like a door to the basement" said Lee. "Well, Jed, I reckon that that's what it is" said a sarcastic Wallace. The officers proceeded to break the door down, and they all proceeded down. "Keep up the search guys, you're doing great, my perimeter team, stay alert" said Lee to his officers through the walkie-talkie. As they all entered the basement, they felt a damp, cold air that was colder than the breeze outside. "What is that smell? It has the presence of a chemical of sorts" said Wallace. As they took cautious steps forward, they noticed that there were bottles of chemicals stored on shelves along with a workstation where it seemed that bomb-making activities had occurred. "Oh, my Lord" said Lee, "is this what I think it is?" He noticed what seemed to be a tunnel that had been made as a form of escape passage; it was deep, dark, and narrow. "Hold fast, I am going to run and get my bomb squad to be careful" said Lee. As he was heading through the entrance, he heard Wallace yell "what the hell!" At that very second there was an explosion that threw Lee several feet ahead and tore the house to shreds. Lee seemingly was knocked out while his protégée, Officer Cooper observed from the outside, screaming helplessly as she felt the impact of the blast herself "AHHHHHHHHHHHH...!" As Lee, came back to, he saw the house on fire, he heard people screaming, some on fire, and he realized that his bravado and aggressive tactics had gotten a lot of his team killed, as well as the Sheriff's. That's when he realized that the Sheriff was still inside, and he began screaming "Henry! Henry!" Though he and the Sheriff had not seen eye to eye in a long time, he had never wished any ill will to him. He and Cooper began running around to see who survived the blast. There were a few of his men, who had now been resuscitated from the flames and a few of the Sheriff's men, but no sign of Wallace. He found the Sheriff's lead man on the scene and asked him, "where is Henry?" "Sir, I can't be sure if the Sheriff has survived the blast, this much will be determined once the Fire Department arrives" said the lead man. "Oh no" said a concerned and shaken up Lee. The Fire Department had just arrived on the scene

and fighters began putting the fire out and going into part of the house that they

were able to. "Lt." said the lead fireman on the scene, "I believe that you need

medical attention." Lee hadn't noticed but he himself had suffered burns from the

blast, but he was more worried about seeing about his dear friend and rival. "What

about the Sheriff? Did he survive" asked Lee, as the lead fireman put his head down

and took a deep breath. "No sir, I am sorry to inform you that Sheriff Henry Wallace

has been pronounced dead" said the fireman as Lee was escorted to an ambulance

to be treated. After so many years of rivalry between Lee and Wallace, they were

always cordial to one another and still respected one another. Lee knew that

Wallace was as dedicated to his job as he was, and now, with the intrusion of some

computer hacker, he was gone. This would not go easily thought Lee to himself as

he was prepped to go to the hospital. On the ride, he vowed to avenge the death of

his good comrade, Sheriff Henry Wallace.

Chapter 8

"Okay, so if you can really set this up, what do I have to watch out for? This guy is no walk in the park I've heard" said Rico to Jesse, an older Black man who helped Reck and his crew become acquaintances with CO's Motley and Brasham. "That he is not Rico, Reck is one of the most dangerous guys in this prison, hell, maybe the world" said Jesse who warned Rico of all the dangers of stepping up to Reck. "Look I am not here to be a tough guy, I want to have a sit-down, let him air out his problems and we go from there. I am a man who needs peace in my life, and I will have it no other way. I am not opening myself up for extortion, but I will come to an agreement with him about some things" said Rico. "Like what? Joining his crew? Reck only uses the most dangerous people in the world, and you're a smart guy, he won't want you because that would relinquish some of the control that he has" said Jesse. "Alright, it seems that we need some guards on our side, or, try and get Motley and Brasham to work with us too, or, switch sides" said a cunning Rico who was putting together a new plan. "Motley and Brasham? There is no way in hell they will pledge allegiance to you over Reck, there is too much money at stake" said a skeptical Jesse. "Before we go any further, I need to know are you at least willing to hear me out, or do you pledge your allegiance to Reck. If this is the case, just let him know what I said. Otherwise, its strategy time" said Rico, trying to figure out exactly what was Jesse's aim. "Young man, I am an independent contractor of sorts, I pledge my allegiance to myself and only myself simply because it is the only way I survive in this place. I have been here for 8 years and I am up for release next year, I don't want to do anything that will jeopardize that, but if you are trying to go about doing this in a calm, reasonable manner, I can be of assistance; for the right price of course" said Jesse. "Money, is that it? Look man, what do you want? I will fill your commissary up and guarantee that you will no way be traced to any of this" said Rico. "Okay, well, let's map it out" said Jesse now ready to get to work in assisting Rico in his plan. "Cool, so we know that Brasham and Motley are working for him for a good price and will more than likely stop working for him if some heat comes from Reck's way that the warden catches wind of. Well, to beat this 3 headed monster, two of the heads must be cut" said Rico. "How do you plan to do that? They work for him" said Jesse. "T-Dog can get his hands on some bleach and other chemicals. Since he works for the chow hall, he will sneak some drops into the food of Reck's enemies with another concentrate that will mask the smell. This will excite a riot because nearly instantly because guys are going to pass out, get sick, or even die right in the chow hall. Brasham and Motley will get nervous, because the Sorcerer won't have time to make anything disappear. Me and T have also been in contact with a lifer, who for the same pay you're getting, is willing to kill one of the crew members and tell authorities that Reck paid him to do it to get sent out of here. He said he is tired of this joint anyway" said Rico who had thoroughly orchestrated a portion of the plan. "Well, all of this sounds good, but if you have this all figured out, then why do you need me? Sounds like you got it all working" said Jesse. "Simple" said Rico, "because you know the people in higher places. Once all this drama starts happening around Reck and his crew, I know that Motley and Brasham will want to find an exigent strategy. But they won't have to look far because there you will be to bring them in my direction. At that point, they can figure out how loyal

Reck's boys are to him and maybe, just maybe, we can get some of those guys over here. Though I don't care to run this place, I will have peace of mind knowing that these guys are out of my hair and I can continue to stay low key. I do want to send a message to the entire place that if you fuck with me, you'll have to outsmart me, and in my life, it has only happened when I have allowed it to" said a confident Rico that his plan was superior to all. "What if anything goes wrong? You will have to reconfigure the entire plan" said an uncertain Jesse, who knew that it was a good plan but really hoped that Brasham and Motley would be willing to turn on Reck. "Well if not, then it's back to the drawing board" said Rico who had begun contemplating a plan B.

"This is great" said Shapiro as he shook his head in disbelief of the events that transpired in Montana. In one manner, he felt responsible for putting these men in the line of fire. On another note, he was enticed by the notion of catching this suspect. The man obviously knew that the heat was closing in on him, but how? How could a man who was just purchasing some furniture from some rental place suddenly hatch such a disaster, one of the worst that state had ever seen? Even more, how could a non-violent case of man who possibly took part in a conspiracy to funnel a quarter of a million dollars through the Fed, now become a homicidal maniac? Desperation was the only thing that Shapiro could come up with. But if this guy was so tight with his plan, how did he even let the heat come so close to him to force his hand in this matter? One lead to finding out who this guy was to investigate where he bought the explosion material from and go from there. After the explosion, this guy was nowhere to be found, his evacuation had been planned, but why so many innocent lives? Shapiro's last question that ran through his mind was simple; what next?

Captain Nicholson was furious that this investigation had gotten out of hand, but it might have been the best thing for the case. "Now we've got something bigger than some faulty transaction that went through a computer system, now we've got a capital homicide against peace officers" said Nicholson. "Sir, this is a very unfortunate situation, but believe me, we are working diligently to figure this situation out. We had the perp, there was no question about it, why would he wreak havoc on the policemen and women in Montana if he wasn't afraid of capture" said Jankowski. "Well guys," said Nicholson "I think that you two have a case on your hands, this has to be solved. The press is going to have a field day knowing that the FBI ordered the capture of this lunatic for questioning. But what he doesn't realize is that he is now a fugitive of the law and it is going to be an all-out manhunt for him!" Jankowski pleased, asked the captain "What about this Rico Jones character? Do you think that he may have accompanied him in this horrendous crime sir?" "Well Agent, that much has not been discovered. Even if he was, we can't prove it. I believe that Jones stays on status for questioning, but Schultz's case is sent up for indictment, and we can put the homicide warrant out on him" said Nicholson. "Well sir, we will do everything in our power to crack this case" said Shapiro. "You're damn right you will or it's your ass, this started as some career maker for you Shapiro, but now it's life or death! Now get the hell out of here and go find this animal" demanded Nicholson. As Shapiro and Jankowski walked out of the office, they looked at each other and gave each other a nod. This nod indicated that they would have to go into overdrive to find out where this creep was. "Guys, I've gotten

in contact with a man that saw this Brandon Schultz character at his store" said an

overly ambitious McNamara. "How did you find that out kid? We thought we were

going to have to call some of the Montana State Police in for more aid and

assistance" said Shapiro. "Well, that won't be a bad idea. But I figured this out by

going through a database of places that sell this kind of material through the state.

Most of it is usually only brought by demolition crews and in a wide-open state like

Montana, there isn't much demolition taking place" said McNamara. "Well kid, what

did you find? Now I'm curious" said Jankowski. "Well, it seems that there are only

two places that sell those kinds of materials, one in Billings and one in Helena" said

McNamara. Jankowski nodded his head and asked, "so can I assume that Schultz

was at one of these facilities?" "Yes, you would be absolutely correct. The place is

called Harden's Warehouse and they have video surveillance. Over the last month

or so, he says that a guy who fits Schultz's description has been frequenting there

and usually came in to buy different chemical compounds. According to the guy, he

said that he bought different items in intervals and usually was dressed in a

completely different way than the last time. The first time, he came in donning a suit

and tie, the next time a cap and beard with a dirty jean jacket. All the way down to

the last time when he came in with a biker's get-up on. It took some time to figure it

all out but once he connected the dots, he realized that all of these different get-ups

were one guy" said McNamara. "Well, I think that the State Police should be

advised that this guy possibly knew what was going on. I mean, when he figured out

what was going on, why didn't he notify authorities? This guy definitely needs to be questioned" said Jankowski. "Well, not to worry, the State Police are on their way to

him and will investigate him. According to them, Lt. Lee of the Billings Police

Department will not take time off and is still actively participating in the investigation

as well" said McNamara. "Okay, well I know one thing, we need to get to the bottom

of this ourselves. I am going to have Cap contact the guys in Washington and try to

get us to Montana. If getting some answers are the best way to get everything

rolling on our original investigation, then we will have to be the reps for the bureau

investigating all of this activity, you know it's a shame, these guys in Montana live to

serve for the greater good and now there has been a tragedy. The least we can do is

saddle up and go help them out" said a determined Shapiro.

Chapter 9

The next day in New York City, Gaden was excited, for once. He had hatched a grand scheme to cover up his dirty work. Too bad it had to be at the expense of those cops, like he gave a damn. Amber walked in with a sexy switch and handed him his mail. "Mr. Gaden, if you don't mind me asking, why is a handsome and successful man like yourself not married?" She asked him as he shuffled through his mail, he smiled looked up at her and said "my dear, are you propositioning me? Amber you are a beautiful girl and I enjoy you working here with me because you're smart and efficient. So, before I answer that question, what makes you ask?" "Well, it's hard living in this city all alone trying to survive, and those modeling gigs aren't coming through like they should" she said with a sound of disappointment in her voice. He thought to himself for a minute looking at her up and down. She was gorgeous, hands down. The things he wanted to do to her could only be replayed in XXX videos. But Gaden knew not to mix business with pleasure, and this girl was ambitious so he wouldn't risk the dangers that could come with becoming intimate with her. "Could I offer you a raise my dear? 20% as of today" said Gaden who hated to turn down her advancement. "Well Mr. Gaden, I am honored and proud to accept the raise, thank you. And um…. if there is anything that I could ever do for you, and I do mean anything, give me a ring" Amber said to him as she sashayed out of the room. Perhaps if he didn't have too many different ventures going on, he could afford to risk such a taboo. But for now, he was getting ready for a big meeting with some friends in Turkey. To Amber and the few others that knew, Gaden was a respected owner of a manufacturing company. But a girl like Amber wouldn't ask too many questions. In her free time, she was more worried about drinking, doing coke, and getting laid than bringing up her occupation amongst social circles. No one outside of the immediate circle knew that Gaden was the biggest weapons dealer in the world. Not only that, no one knew his operation existed. How is he able to be the broker of wars and go under the radar, and live in the United States? Sometimes, it surprised him how he could pull off such a feat. But time was ticking; he was going to have to find a new place to set up operations. Gaden was accustomed to moving. Though he is from New York, he had been away for many years getting started on building his illustrious career. He was connected; those connections have kept him on his Ps and Qs in times of trouble. A knock at the door took him out of his deep gaze out onto the Atlantic Ocean. "You ready to do this? I got a feeling that this is going to be a sweet deal" said Frank Houston, Gaden's best friend and most trusted confidant. Frank was a short, stocky light-skinned Black man who was willing to die for Gaden, the man who took him from poverty to private jets. "Yeah, I am ready brother, where the fuck is Stone? I told him 3 o'clock on the dot" said Gaden, displeased that Stone was running late. Just then Stone walked into the room and motioned for Gaden and Houston to close the door. "Stone, what's up man? What the hell are you doing? We got to get there by 4 or..." said Houston before he was cut off. "Frank, I promise this is going to be quick" said Stone turning his focus to Gaden "this Rico Jones thing is huge, the kid is a fucking genius, he has plans set up today to take care of things, and I know he is going to pass the test!" "Wow Stone, if I didn't know any better, I'd think that you were fucking him" said Gaden in a skeptic manner, "look; we'll wait to see if he passes this test. Murphy is keeping me posted so don't worry, everything that you're telling me is already known. You're pretty excited about this I see." "Of course, he is exactly what we need for North Korea" said Stone. "Well, don't worry; if he passes, we will do initiation. Until then, let's get on the jet, have some drinks, relax, take care of our business, and then go and get some Turkish hookers" said Gaden, excited about taking another trip around the world. As they walked out of the office, Gaden made sure that Amber had left and cut out the lights. To the unsuspecting eye, they looked like three businessmen leaving the office, but what Gaden loved the most about New York, was that as soon as you got down through the lobby and out of the doors, you disappear into a 9 million person jungle of people, and with this many people covering, he couldn't be seen.

As all these plans were manifesting for Rico, T-Dog, and Jesse, Rico got a surprise letter from Jordan. In the letter, she explained how much sympathy she had for him and told him how much of a shining star he was to everyone, but especially her. So, it was only right to schedule a visit when part 1 and 2 of the plan unfolded. With him being out of sight and out of mind, the plan would go perfectly and Reck's crew would crumble while he was holding Jordan's hand and inhaling the enticing scent of her perfume. Rico was more nervous than excited. With everything going on, he had just realized that it had been some time since he had been around a woman. Furthermore, he had done Jordan so wrong in his quest for self-satisfaction. "You ready big dog? Big day for you, me, and everybody" said T-Dog, as they woke up around 5:00 a.m. "Bro, I finally get to see a woman, you know it has been forever since I've done that" said an excited Rico. "At least it's only been a week for you, shit, it's been years for me dog" said T-Dog before he prepared for the rundown of the plan "so here we go, Jesse, will come and holler at you to let you know if everything is still in place. I'm going over to the kitchen in a few minutes to help with set-up and I will be able to hand him some information through the wire. He'll come through there at about 9, and at that time I can tell him that everything is straight. Your visit won't be able to start before 11 so between 9 and 11 Jesse will be bringing some info back to you. Chow starts at 11:15 so you will already be in the visit while everything is happening. If all goes well, there will be a code going across the CO's walkie-talkie to let everyone know to be on standby in case things get worse. If things get worse, they'll be a code red, the joint will be locked down, and your visit will get cut short, but that's the rules of this shit, you take the good, the bad, and the ugly." "Alright, well then there's nothing to it, but to do it" said Rico, as the cell door opened and a CO escorted T-Dog to the kitchen. Rico set back and reminisced on the sweet essence of Jordan, she was gorgeous hands down. She was the perfect height, at least for Rico since he only stood 5'10. She always was well dressed and always smelled good. Even though there was a big plan on the horizon that could shake the foundation of the MCC, Rico could care less, because right now, the only thing that he could think about was Jordan.

"8:56" T-Dog said to himself as he slows and steadily turned the stew that was being served for the day. He looked up again and heard some people talking outside, but figured it was some of the other inmates who worked in the kitchen with him. He turned the giant pot full of stew again and looked and saw the infamous Murphy, a CO who was a major player and was part of the elaborate scheme that

Rico had come up with, the only thing was Rico had no idea. "Yes sir, Mr. Murphy, I been waiting to do this for a long time" said T-Dog in a sadistic manner. Rico didn't know that Reck had no idea who he was; matter of fact, Reck didn't handle business in the manner that T-Dog had let on. Reck was a big-time drug dealer on the streets, but he also had once been on T-Dog's boss' payroll. He was arrested for drug charges, but as a precautionary way of getting less time, he offered to testify for the government and to the Justice Department about T-Dog's boss. He was moved to the Metropolitan Correctional Center in Chicago, but little did he know. T-Dog's boss had influences in nearly every state and every city. He was pinpointed and now was about to be handed the death sentence that he thought he would never see. Murphy passed a tiny vile to T-Dog to mix into the first tray that T-Dog put together. Rather than make a lot of noise, T-Dog and Murphy had agreed to change the plan. Murphy would take Reck to a secluded area and pretend that some lawyers for government were there to talk to him about T-Dog's boss. He would take him to a holding cell and give him food, but it would be the last time he would eat anything. At this point, Rico could smoothly coerce Reck's crew to join forces with him as well as the CO's that Reck had on his payroll. "Time to rock and roll" said Murphy as he took the tray and began heading to Reck's cell. Simultaneously, Jesse was coming by to make sure that everything was still in good standings. Jesse looked at T-Dog and watched Murphy go out the door and asked, "is everything still cool?" "Well, there has been a slight change in plans, you see, Reck is going to disappear but it'll take some time before anyone misses him, this way he's out of the way and Rico can pick his crew apart before anyone knows what happens. Before it's all said and done, we'll be running this place" said T-Dog. "There you go again with that bullshit; you know damn well that this is going to make it hot for anybody to eat and the kid might get scared" said Jesse. "See there you go again Jesse, you're always getting scared when we need you to man the fuck up, this faggot was going to rat on the Boss, we can't let him do no shit like that. We livin' large and it's all because of the Boss, now respect this shit and accept this shit dog" said T-Dog who pledges allegiance to the orders that are sent down from the Boss. "Aight, man, but I'll tell u what, the shit might get ugly" said Jesse. "Man, look, it has to get ugly before it can be beautiful" said T-Dog with a look of concern on his face "look man, I know you ain't getting scared we came too far for this shit, we got work to do, now let's get to it so we can get the fuck out of this shit hole." T-Dog walked off and began fixing more trays, while Jesse walked out into the hallway pushing a mop.

Jesse headed back down to Rico's cell to inform him of what was going on. It was 10:30 so he had made it with just enough time to break some things down to him. "You won't believe this, but Reck has been taken to isolation" said Jesse. "What! This is going to ruin everything; we must reschedule this whole thing. How can we pin anything on him if he isn't anywhere around to orchestrate an attack? This is not going to work" said Rico who now was putting his plan B back into use, "okay, here is what we're going to do; don't change the plans, but I want you to let dude in the barber shop know what is going down and he can decide what he wants to do from there. If he won't do it, then we'll have to use more smooth and subtle ways of doing things. Or, we might simply have to get our hands dirty ourselves. Whatever the case is, the show must go on, but we will see what happens with phase 1." Jesse nodded his head in agreement and asked Rico "how long have you been prepared for a mishap?" "Since we put plan A together" said Rico who was happy that he had put a plan B in the air. As they set up the final touches to the plan, a CO came through the cellblock and called for Rico. "Alright, that's my beat, be smooth and if anything goes wrong, I need you to step in and fix it as quickly as possible" said Rico as he was heading towards the front of the cellblock. "   You got it man, ay, you a smart guy Rico, I have faith that this plan will come together just fine" said Jesse as Rico met the CO at the front and was escorted to the visiting room. Jesse was astonished by the young man Rico. He was bright, wise, and far ahead of his time in comparison to any other young man his age. It was unbelievable how he had an all-out need to be the alpha male in any situation that he was in, and it was now clear that this kid wasn't any ordinary guy and would fit perfectly into the big picture. He reminded him of the Boss when they were all younger, he was always plotting on a way to stay on top, and if he stayed on top, everyone around him was on top with him. That was the motivation to stay disciplined and loyal to him; money, power, respect. Those three things are the key to the good life, and Jesse and had had his share of it and would continue if everything went according to plan.

Chapter 10

Around 11:00 a.m., Shapiro, Jankowski, McNamara, and Captain Nicholson all arrived in Billings, MT via private jet provided by the bureau. Shapiro's idea of flying to assist in the investigation was a hit, and Captain Nicholson was ordered to go out and get an idea of what was going on. From that point, the bureau would fly some guys from a few different field offices, and Captain Nicholson would anoint Shapiro as the lead agent in the investigation, relieving him and allowing him to go back to San Francisco. Upon arrival they were met by an injured Lt. Lee holding his arm in a sling. "Well, gentlemen, welcome to Montana. Hope you rested well on the flight here, because we got some work to do" said Lt. Lee, flanked by Officer Cooper and a few men who stood with their arms folded. "Lt. Lee, I'd like to send my condolences to the men and women who lost their lives in the blast and hope a speedy recovery for you and the injured officers as well" said Captain Nicholson. Lt. Lee looked at the men with an angry look on his face and said "Well sir, this twisted arm of mine isn't going to stop me from conducting this investigation with y'all. The Sheriff of this county was executed in that blast and I personally knew him to be a fine lawman and outstanding citizen as well as the men and women who lost their lives. I tell you, if I get my hands on this perp..." "Lt., you need not to express your dismay for what is going on, if the Major gets word of this, he'll have you yanked off of this case" said Officer Cooper warning the Lt. to be careful of his words. "You're right officer" said Lee as he turned to Captain Nicholson "so I hear that you are not going to be staying throughout the entire investigation." "No, I won't Lieutenant; Agent Shapiro will take over as lead agent once all of the other men from the bureau arrive" said Captain Nicholson. "Well, that's fine, I just hope that you are capable of handling what is about to take place agent, why don't we head out to the scene of the crime and look at what we were able to gather. I have some crime scene investigators, as well as some forensic people out there gathering what they can, and quite a bit of it has already been examined. We also have some fire marshals and explosion experts to help us understand how all of this happened" said Lee as everyone gathered towards the unmarked vehicles that were near the landing strip. "Alright, gentlemen, let's head over there and look. From that point we can determine which approach we need to take" said Shapiro as everyone got into a vehicle and proceeded to head to the scene of the crime.

"As you can see here, it was definitely C-4 and few other chemicals used to put this all together" said the crime scene investigator. "C-4? That is a very high-profile explosive. No wonder the flames were so hard to put out. But where could it have come from? That is some stuff that is usually only found through the military" said Jankowski who had a look of disbelief that something so powerful could be used. "Yes, but it's not hard to get your hands on these items especially when there are places to go get this stuff from" said McNamara. "That's right! Hey Jack, I think we need to go and pay that place a visit, you know Harden's Warehouse" said Jankowski. "I'll tell you what, why don't you and Josh go down there and see what's going on, me and Cap will stay here and help analyze the information that we see here. Tell me everything that you guys find out" said Shapiro. "Sure thing" said Jankowski as he turned his attention to Lt. Lee "sir, is it possible that me and my partner can borrow one of your vehicles to go check out a lead? We might have some information on where the supplies came from." "Ya don't say," said Lt. Lee rubbing his chin "of course you can take the vehicle as long as one of my officers can go with you... Cooper come here" sounded off Lee. "Yes sir, Lt." said an obliging Officer Cooper. "I want you to take a ride with these two gentlemen to a lead they are investigating. Said there is a possibility that this lead was the seller of the supplies to make this explosive. Find out as much as you can please" said Lee to Cooper who carefully followed the instructions of Lt. Lee. "You got it sir; I am all over this thing" said Cooper in her mountaineer twang. Jankowski almost made a sarcastic remark, but digressed and said "alright, now that all of that is said and done, let's get to work, do you mind driving Officer Cooper; I mean I am sure that you know these roads better than me or my partner." "Don't worry agent, I wasn't going to let you surfer boys drive anyways" said Cooper in a joking manner.

Upon arrival to the facility, Jankowski observed the area and said "this place is in the middle of nowhere, literally. There is nothing around here, no residences, no other businesses, nothing. It would have been the perfect place to come and buy this kind of stuff. I am interested to see what kind of guy this Harden claims to be." They walked in and were attacked by Harden who stood by with a shotgun. Harden lowered his weapon and said, "who the hell are you supposed to be?" Officer Cooper stepped up and announced who they were "sir, good afternoon to you. I am Officer Cooper of the Billings Police Department and these two gentlemen with me are Agents Jankowski and McNamara of the Federal Bureau of Investigation. I have been told that the agents have informed you of our purpose for coming to you. Is that correct? "Well, yes, they called me a yesterday and talked to me. I am sorry, but this whole thing has me scared out of my mind. The locals have been trying to get me shut down for years and with this happening, I have recently had my store vandalized as well as my pick-up. All of the locals seem to think that if my store was closed, none of this debacle would have happened" said Harden. "Well sir, that is the whole thing" said Jankowski walking closer "out of a lot of different things that you could sell here, why chemicals? I mean seeing how there are only two in the state, what would make you get into this type of business?" "Well" said Harden "I will start from the beginning. My father passed away 10 years ago; leaving me a $250,000 inheritance. I had never been anything more than an inspector for the local oil and gas company. Because of that, I didn't know too much to do with the money except maybe open up a little convenience store." "Well, sir, if you were so unknowledgeable about chemicals what made you change your mind? I mean it's not every day that some guy who was wearing a hard hat wants to venture into a business containing dangerous chemicals" said Jankowski while Cooper looked at him with a deep gaze. "Well, that's where I was going with all of this. I met a man who said he was an executive for a major chemical corporation that was looking to expand into Montana, based on the new developments and infrastructure that was getting ready to take place" said Harden. "So, I can assume that you always sold mainly to construction companies that would take the chemicals for demolition" said Jankowski. "Yes, and that's why this guy was strange to me, because he said he was a scientific researcher that was using the chemicals to conduct experiments. He even showed me his scientific license to from the NSW to conduct experiments on the environment. He convinced me that these same chemicals were being used for demolition purposes, could be stripped and broken down to be used for different purposes. He was in suit and tie and seemed to have a lot of knowledge about what was going on, so I sold these things to him" said Harden. Cooper thought on the whole thing for a quick moment and calmly asked "Sir, is it safe to say that you had no clue about what was going on with this guy, and that you would sign a sworn statement as well as turn over anything that we need for our investigations?" "Yes ma'am, anything that you need I will surrender" said Harden with a look of fear on his face. "Well, sir, let us conduct our investigation, we need surveillance tapes of this guy. We also need you to open your books so we will have an idea of how much he bought. We also will need to monitor all your traffic in and out of the store for the purpose of him sneaking back in with a disguise of some sorts" said McNamara who had unofficially become the technological innovator of the case. "Oh, and there is one more thing" said Jankowski adding one more stipulation to these rules "we need a list of all of your employees as well as records of deliveries and what companies deliver and pickup. We will also need you to hang around, I get the feeling that we will still need other information from you." "You got it sir follow me" said Harden.

They all went back and began collecting all the information that they needed, when Cooper had remembered that Harden hadn't finished the story from earlier. "So, finish telling us about this major corporation that introduced you to the chemical business" said Cooper as she dropped what she was doing. "Well, there were two guys, one Black and one White, but the White one said that he was the CEO. They gave me a lot of information and explained that the profit that I would turn from my investment would make me a millionaire" said Harden. "Well sir, it sounds like you have partners" said Cooper. "No, they were my suppliers. They would sell this stuff to me for a discount and in turn, they sent a few clients my way to help get me started" said Harden. "Well that was awfully friendly of these guys considering they didn't know you Mr. Harden" said Jankowski now weary of Harden. "I thought the same thing sir, but they said they really wanted to expand into Montana, and they felt that with my recent acquisition of the inheritance, they could help me, and I could help them" said Harden who was now becoming nervous. Jankowski now started contemplating about this corporation and how they were able to learn of the inheritance, so he asked "well, Mr. Harden, how many people did you tell about your inheritance? Is it possible that an acquaintance could have told them about your inheritance?" "You know something sir? I never asked them, but I assumed that maybe it was made public through the newspaper or something. I never was too much into reading the newspaper so I wouldn't know." McNamara looked over and asked, "does this company still supply you?" "Actually, they sold to this other company called Gresham. Supposedly, they are the biggest chemical supplier in the world. I haven't seen any representatives from the new company yet, but I can tell you that the original supplier sold to them about 5 years ago" said Harden." "So, there might be some things going on with all of this that we're not seeing right now. Do you have the information to the closest Gresham? They are based out of Australia, but there are some offices in the states" said Jankowski." So, some mysterious people from some mysterious corporation approached you with an offer to sell dangerous chemicals, they in turn, sell the supplying company to some major corporation to avoid the heat. This is too amazing even for me to" said McNamara.

"That's what it sounds like to me gentlemen" said Cooper as she stood back analyzing the conversation. "Well, whatever is going on, you can bet your bottom dollar that we are going to get to the bottom of this whole thing" said Jankowski who now felt even more compelled to figure out all of this. They continued to gather all the information necessary to continue in their investigation, including documents of Gresham and the third-party vendors used to deliver the chemicals. They also gathered surveillance of Brandon and other customers who may all play a role in this. The officers gathered everything and put it all in boxes and bags and carried it all out to the vehicle that they had arrived in. Upon leaving, Jankowski gave Harden one last message "call us if anything else happens." "I most certainly will Agent Jankowski" said Harden as he walked back into the store. Harden looked out of the window as they left and drove about a ¼ mile down the road. Upon them getting that far away, a shadow appeared out of back of the warehouse. "So, you like cooperating with police I see Harden" said the mysterious person. "Hey, you! You son of a bitch…" these were the last words Harden could speak before the person shot him 10 times in the chest, stomach, and finally in the head. A grizzly crime scene like this could bring a lot of attention on the guy who appeared to be Brandon Schultz, so he used a silencer on his weapon and immediately locked every door as he cleaned up the blood and rolled Harden's body into an old rug he had with him. "Hey, are you finished? It's taking forever for you to this" asked the accomplice as he grabbed the other side of the rug when he saw his partner rolling up the rug. "I cleaned up good, it'll take a day or two before anyone gets suspicious" said the killer as they walked out the door carrying the rug to a black van. They threw the body into a mix of several other rugs and began heading to the woods. They were initially very quiet, but the partner looked at the killer and asked "hey, how much you think we'll get for this one?" "I don't know, but I know one thing, it better be more than $20,000 this time!" "I am with you on that" said the partner. They sped down the highway until they reached the woods, there they commenced in throwing his body in a pre-buried ditch and covered it up.

Chapter 11

Rico couldn't be more excited. When they opened that door and escorted him to the table that Jordan was at, he smiled uncontrollably. The prison's rule for embrace was only a few seconds, so Rico maximized it when he hugged and kissed her until the guard told him to release. He obliged and he and Jordan began to catch up on what has been going on. "Rico, I can't believe that I am here with you right now. You don't understand how much I missed you" said Jordan who herself was smiling from ear to ear. "Baby, you don't know what it meant to me when that lawyer brought me that letter. It was like a breath of fresh air considering everything that I am going through" said Rico who was now holding hands with her. "What the hell were you thinking" said Jordan who now switched focus into the life he was living "I mean I know times were hard, but you were doing so well for yourself and now it seems like you're going downhill. Rico, you must stop living the life that you are living. It's dangerous and I know that this time in here has made you look at life much differently." "Yes, it has, I mean I guess I thought I was too smart for the system. Not only that, I thought that I was never going to get caught, but now that I have, I don't know what it will take for me to overcome this situation" said Rico who had become disheartened with the decisions he had made. "Rico, don't worry, I'll be here for you, but you have to promise me one thing" said Jordan. Rico had an idea of what it was going to be but instead asked "what's that?" "You will have to promise me that you will never get wrapped up in this situation again and that you use that beautiful mind of yours for the greater good" said Jordan looking deep into Rico's eyes. "Yes Jordan, I can promise that to you" said Rico with sincerity. Just then, a CO walked into the visiting room as if he was searching for someone, he walked by and gave a thumbs up to Rico, as if it was a signal of some sorts. Rico, always aware of his surroundings picked up on the signal. "Rico" said Jordan wondering if he was still paying her any attention. "Yes sweetheart" said Rico assuring her that he was still listening. She looked curious about something, so she asked "So what do you think of me? I know any guy in your situation would accept letters and a visit, but what is your honest opinion of me?" "Jordan, you are a wonderful woman and I would love to have you around all of the time" said Rico. She blushed and asked, "do you really mean that?" "Of course, I do" said Rico "you have been what have kept me grounded while I have gone through this situation. I fell from glory, but with a queen like you on my side, I will surely ascend back to the top of the mountain." "Rico…" said Jordan as she blushed some more and squeezed his hand. Rico could hear something being said over the walkie-talkie and assumed that T-Dog and Jesse had sprung his plan. As he and Jordan talked more about how their relationship would grow and develop, the CO came around and told him it was a situation that had arisen, and the entire visiting room had to be evacuated. He and Jordan said their goodbyes and before they separated the two, Jordan yelled out "I love you Rico, I swear I'm not going anywhere." Rico yelled, "I love you too, don't forget about me" as he was dragged into the inmate evacuation room. But he was put into another room by the CO who was there to inform him of who he was and what was going on.

"Hey, why are you putting me over here? Everyone else is in that room" said Rico to the CO who had forcefully thrown Rico into the dark room where he could barely see the man. "Shut the fuck up! I am here for you jackass, the plan went smooth, except Reck is dead but no one knows because it happened in solitaire" said the CO. Rico, now puzzled, looked at the man and said, "who and the hell are you?" "Murphy, I am here to help you. Now look, you came up with a genius plan to handle this shit, now I am going to need you to do one more thing. Get Reck's crew on our side, but the catch is; if they don't join up, they die" said Murphy. Rico was now really confused so he asked "what the hell? So, what do I get out of all of this?" "An opportunity of a lifetime" said Murphy "I can't tell you too much, all I can say is how would you like to get the fuck out of here free and clear of all charges; make a shitload of money; and fly around the world? "How is any of this possible? I know you make pretty good money as a CO, but it's going to take a little bit more than $50,000 a year to do all of that" said Rico sarcastically. "Oh, you are very clever aren't you, look it's the moment of truth; either yes or no. If it's no, then I hope you enjoy doing time for the rest of your life" said Murphy with a sadistic grin on his face. Rico now feeling threatened asked "what the fuck is that supposed to mean?" "In jail with nothing else to do and you don't even watch the news. Well, your buddy Brandon just blew up a house full of cops in Montana because they were hot on his trail. Not to mention that you are wanted for questioning in connection with this whole thing" said Murphy who could tell he was getting Rico's attention. Rico was once again puzzled so he asked "Brandon! How the hell do you know who he is, and another thing, how can they charge me with something that I didn't do?" "I want you to take this bit of advice with you for the rest of your life; everything isn't always how it seems. On that note, I know a lot about you but that's beside the point. The point is that you have been well protected here because no one can find you, except your little girlfriend. Now, you can stay protected and handle a little business for us and you'll be ok, you'll get more detail when you handle more business, you are special Mr. Jones and we need you. Now, take care of Reck's crew and everything will be ok. Jesse and T-Dog know that we have met, and they'll fill you in on everything else" explained Murphy who now has Rico in a state of shock with the revelations. "By the way, don't say shit to anyone from this point on, you are only authorized to speak to Jesse and T-Dog, and you will all map out how to get Reck's crew" warned Murphy as he escorted Rico through a different side of the jail to get to his cell. When Rico got back to his cell, the entire jail was in lockdown because of what transpired in the cafeteria. Before Murphy walked away Rico asked him "so who got taken out?" "One of Reck's enemies, Psycho, an Aryan Nation member who had been muscling in on Reck's drug trade and a person that he had a physical altercation with; it was perfect" said Murphy as he closed Rico's cell door and locked him in. Rico was amazed by the information that he had just received regarding the plan. It seemed like he had a lot of help, but he had to stay focused and be ruthless. But was this guy really who he said he was? It would take a lot of energy to know who Rico was without doing some research. The only thing that Rico was concerned about was if Murphy was truly a man of his word and would let him operate and secure him with the money and clemency of his charges. Hopefully, because to Rico, it was worth the shot; He had always loved to be in charge of things and this would be his opportunity to do so, even if this guy was lying about what he could do for him, Rico would soon be able to control the jail and maybe start making hooch, or selling drugs. Hopefully not, but life was so funny at times that Rico didn't too much worry about what could happen; he tried to worry about what would happen and how it would manifest into him getting richer. But even with all of this he was infatuated with Jordan and couldn't wait to write her a letter and see her again. With so much on his mind, he gets his pen and paper out and began writing a letter to Jordan and put behind him the stress of his jailhouse politics.

"So, you sure that's taken care of? We don't have time for second guesses" said Gaden into the phone talking to "Brandon Schultz" and his accomplice. "Yes, it's a done deal, and we took out the trash" said "Brandon." "Well, you need to get on the jet and head for Maine" said Gaden who was telling the guy to meet them in Miami. "You got it boss; one more thing" said "Brandon." "What is it" said Gaden knowing that they were going to ask for something. "Those guys took all of the papers. Just thought I should let you know" said "Brandon." "Don't worry about that, I got that covered you just make sure to meet me asap I am en route there now myself" said Gaden. Gaden always was one to stay one step ahead of everyone. He had gotten word that the cops were headed over to see Harden, but he knew that Harden would fold like a bad hand in poker. He had anticipated this long ago and had set up the decoy in order to lure the cops to the cabin. But he didn't account for Harden, who he had figured, too stupid to know anything. But by the time the decoy could get back to Harden the cops had already been there. So, he hid waiting for the perfect time to strike. Once he had it, he wasted Harden and got rid of his body. Though Harden had surrendered documents that could harm their cause, Gaden made sure Harden was dead before anything else had gotten told to the cops. Justin

Stone and Frank Houston were with Gaden as they were leaving Turkey after conducting some business. Stone looked over and asked him "Everything okay out there?" "Fine, except the cops have some documents that Harden turned over to them" said Gaden who was in a deep thought. "Don't worry; everything connected to us is gone right? I mean they won't be able to find anything useful" said a confident Stone. "That's true, but what about Gresham? You think they will release some things to save their own asses? In my opinion they will" said Gaden who now worried about his operation being exposed. "Don't worry about that, everything that we made never even showed up in the system, and what are they going to do, give descriptions? There are hundreds of millions of people in this country, good luck trying to find us" said Stone. "We still have to be prepared for the worst. You don't operate the way we do and don't stay one step ahead of your adversaries" said Gaden. "You're the one with all of the secrets of war, I'm just the good talker" said Stone with a big smile on his face. "Stone, sometimes you talk too fucking much" said Gaden unappeased by Stone's humor. "Well whatever you two decide to do, we have to make sure that we protect our interests. I mean, how else can we really be successful" said Houston. "Yes Frank, you're right, but remember, there is no 'I' in team" said Gaden, who had really started noticing Frank's selfishness come to light more and more. As the jet got closer to Miami, Gaden began to realize just how dangerous this situation could become. Perhaps it was time to contemplate that permanent move to Australia; or maybe some other place where he could reign supreme, like Ethiopia. The operation wasn't how it used to be. More snakes in the grass than that could be counted, and he began to not trust the members of his corporation, or "Organization" as he liked to call it. Luckily, the Australian Militia that he had just done business with had bought nearly $100 million in weapons and the Turkish government had just hired some of his men to protect them from incoming troops, some even American. Gaden had become an international figure of respect, but no one knew him. So many thoughts, so much work, so little time thought Gaden as they flew over the Atlantic Ocean. "Frank, call Murphy and see how things are going that way, we might need those guys sooner than anticipated" said Gaden

Rico had been sleeping for about an hour when T-Dog walked into the cell and woke him. "So, Murphy told you a few things, huh?" "Yeah, he said something about money, freedom, and traveling the world or something" said Rico who was still a little groggy from just waking up. "Well it's true, you'll see soon enough, but Jesse out setting up the meeting between us and Reck's crew. We'll get those dudes on our side, I'm sure of it" said T-Dog. "Ok good, so what do we do until then? I'm trying to get a grip over how everything is going down" said Rico. "Don't worry about that, it's a win-win for us, too bad they can't say the same, it's either they want to live, or they don't. Rico, you'll be surprised over how much is truly going on around here. But, just chill out and enjoy the ride, it's been confirmed, you are the #1 draft pick this year buddy" said T-Dog speaking cryptically. "What are you…" before Rico could finish his sentence, Murphy opened the cell door and got both Rico and T-Dog out. "You guys ready? Its show time" said Murphy who himself was excited about everything. Murphy opened a door and they all walked down the same mysterious hallway that he had brought Rico back from the visiting room.

Next, they walked downstairs into a deep, dark, narrow tunnel and went into a room that looked like it had been a laundry room, some centuries ago. When they entered the room, Jesse was there with The Sorcerer, Lysol, and Rocky. CO's Motley and Brasham were also in attendance. "Well, gentlemen, I'm glad that everyone could be here" said Jesse playing the arbitrator of the situation. Rocky was frowned up and said, "Fuck all of that, what did you punks do with Reck?" "Well sir" said Murphy "I hate to tell you this, but that motherfucker is dead." Lysol rose up and said "Dead? Stop playing this meeting was called to make peace, now if Reck is dead, how can there ever be peace?" "Easy" said Rico "we wipe the slate clean and start fresh." "Who the fuck are you? Do you know who I am, I will break your fucking face chump" barked Rocky walking close to Rico. All the sudden, Brasham pulled out his knife stick and whacked Rocky upside the head. "AHHHHHHHHHHH!!!!!!!!!!!!!!!!!!" yelled Rocky as Motley got prepared for anyone else's quick moves. "You sons of bitches, you turned on us, and now you tell me that y'all killed our friend and think that we're supposed to be cool? Fuck that; Motley take me back to my cell" said The Sorcerer. Murphy got face-to-face with The Sorcerer and said "I see you motherfuckers just ain't learned how to handle business have you? None of you will be happy until you're all dead. We only want to give you the opportunity of a lifetime, but if you want to play hard then we will. Just remember, Reck is dead. Without him, you have no power; not to mention that Motley and Brasham works for us now. Ask yourselves a real serious question; do you really want to die in prison?" The Sorcerer, now the unofficial leader of the group, looked around and realized that with no Reck or Motley and Brasham, his crew had now become powerless. "Alright, what the fuck do y'all want? Ain't nothing for free around here" said Sorcerer. "Easy, you guys still operate the way that you do, and kick us 25% of your profits. Plus, if we get into some situations, we will need all your miraculous services" said Rico, as he extended his hand out The Sorcerer, then Lysol, but Rocky wouldn't shake his hand. "This shit ain't right y'all, they killed Reck and now we gone sit here and make a deal with them? That's fucked up" said Rocky. "Rocky, shake his hand man, it's over man, Reck is dead, don't you see that we ain't gone walk out of here unless we cut this deal? Don't be stupid" said The Sorcerer. "Fuck that..." Rocky charged Murphy but was instantly pummeled and repeatedly beaten by Motley, Brasham, and T-Dog. "Alright, he's had enough, Rocky get up and shake their fucking hands!" shouted Lysol. "That's enough" shouted Murphy. Rocky got up bloody and beaten, which prompted Murphy to order him to segregation until his wounds healed. Rico stood back, watched the entire thing, and asked the Sorcerer again "so do we have a deal?" "Yes" said The Sorcerer. Jesse looked at Sorcerer and said, "if you have any problems go to Rico or me and we will get you situated." "Alright we're taking these guys back" said Motley as he and Brasham escorted The Sorcerer and Lysol back to their new assigned cell blocks, while Murphy took Rocky to segregation; this left Rico, T-Dog, and Jesse alone in the room. "What the fuck is going on? I mean it seems that you two are very privileged and are always right in the middle of this whole thing. I know it's a bigger picture here, so let's hear it" said Rico. Jesse looked at T-Dog and then began the story that Rico had been looking to here. "Okay, well, you're right, we are privileged. Me and T aren't inmates, we got here after a call was put into us to scope you out" said Jesse. "Yeah, once you came back from court, an order was put in so I and Jesse came here to scope you out and we must say we're very impressed with your instincts, brains, and courage" said T-Dog. Rico, now shocked, asked "so if you guys aren't doing time, who are you?" "We're recruiters, someone said that you were perfect to roll with us, so we checked you out and got everything going" said T-Dog. "So why me? I mean, any Joe Schmoe probably could have fit in better than me" said Rico. "That's where you're wrong. We know you went to Stanford; we know that you've got a 160 IQ, and we know that you and your roommate picked off $250,000 of bribe money going to the Fed" said Jesse. "Bribe money? Is that what this is all about? And how..." said Rico as he was cut off by T-Dog. "Look, don't worry about it, we're not here to hurt you, we're here to help you. We both took a liking to you and we plan to make sure that you are a well-respected, rich man before this is all said and done." Rico was almost satisfied by what he was hearing, but had one more bone to pick, "so is this why you guys opted to kill Reck? Who was he to you?" "Reck was a disloyal informant who tried to shut down everything that we had going. We didn't try to use you as a pawn, but the fact that you were willing to go the distance to protect your life and manhood, shows us that you are overly prepared for what lies ahead of us" said Jesse. "Look, just know this, the cops can't find you because you don't exist. You won't be charged for anything, and when you leave here, you're going to be filthy rich. What more could you ask for? Relax and don't worry. Whatever you do, don't talk to no one, you got it? There is a lot at risk now, and you can't afford to; no correction, we can't afford to fuck anything up" said T-Dog as Murphy returned to the room. "Okay, it's all set, just got off the phone with the Boss. I told him about how everything was going here, and he said he'll probably need us sooner than he thought. We have to leave in the morning" said Murphy. "What? That's going to fuck everything up, we had something going here" said T-Dog. "Look T, you can always come back for your little boyfriend, but we have to go in the morning" said Murphy while T-Dog frowned up. "Can I finish now? Here is the plan; I will schedule a double, meaning I would come in at 6:30. At that time, T, you and Rico will come down and help me serve trays around the jail. From there, I will sneak both of you into the laundry room which will have guard outfits there. Jesse, there will be one for you in the supply closet, under the trap door which you will use to escape and access the van. Now, the keys will be in the pocket on the shirt of the uniform and it will be the unmarked black van. You will not have to sign it out because I have taken the liberty of erasing its existence in the system. You will pull to the very bottom of the parking garage and from there, we will jump in and you, along with Rico and T will hide on the floor while I pass security checkpoints. I have already logged in the system that a van will be taken out at 8:02 a.m. for repair, I didn't specify, but these idiots won't notice. Questions…" "Yeah, I got one" said Rico "who the hell are you guys, the CIA?" Murphy found it entertaining but still answered "Just know one thing Jones, we don't fuck up. If you fuck up, you get fucked up; got it?"

Chapter 12

"This is great work guys" said an excited Captain Nicholson "a lot of the guys from Washington and a few other places have made it in so I'm flying out in the morning." "Well Cap, it's going to be a sad occasion to see you go" said Shapiro sarcastically "but we have a lot of work to do people; Jankowski, I want to go down and meet this Harden myself." Jankowski looked over and said, "We'll get a truck and head on over, I'll give him a heads up." "No" said Shapiro "we'll just head over; the element of surprise is an amazing feat. Plus, he doesn't close for like what, another hour? We'll get over within 20 minutes he'll still be there." "Alright well lets rock and roll" said Jankowski just as Nicholson was walking over to Shapiro, "Jack, I just wanted to tell you to make sure that you keep an eye on these young guys. With so much corruption and temptations that are floating around, how can we expect them to stay loyal? You make sure that they are focused and not worrying too much about things that won't help the case." "You got it Cap" said Shapiro as he Jankowski and Cooper began to head back to Harden's warehouse. "Is McNamara not making the trip?" Shapiro asked as they headed to the SUV. "No boss, it doesn't look like he is, said something about a briefing that he wanted to hear amongst the Washington agents, see what their objectives were" said Jankowski. "Well that little bugger sounds like he is a leader" said Cooper as she hung tight because Lee wanted her to be the mole for the Billings PD.

Cooper drove them all to the warehouse, but upon approaching the facility, Shapiro began to get a strange feeling that boiled within his stomach. It got even worse as they got closer and saw that all the lights were off as if he had closed. "I don't know boss, looks like he left early" said Jankowski which prompted Cooper to say "yeah, I don't know sir it looks like he closed for the day." "That would make sense but what doesn't make sense is a man who has always been known to not only stay open, but to stay late at times, is closed early" said Shapiro as he examined the store more and more. "Maybe he's in the back doing his records, or straightening up, we did make quite a mess earlier" said Jankowski. "Yeah possibly, let's go back there" said Shapiro prompting Cooper to pull to the back. Upon arrival to the back of the store, Shapiro instantly noticed tire tracks, but Harden's car was still back there. Along the shipping docks, there was a trailer sitting in one of the docks. "Anyone know what is going on with that trailer?" Shapiro asked. "That is a delivery that is going to Wyoming I believe. The driver left it here because Harden had to wait for another shipment to come in to complete the order. Since it would take a day or two, the driver left it and kept going" said Jankowski. "But that is weird why would anyone leave a full shipment and keep going? And this happened before you guys got here?" Shapiro asked with a stern look on his face. "Yeah, that's what Harden told us, and it's even documented in his records" said Cooper. "Okay, well maybe Harden isn't who we think he is; sure, he acted dumb when you guys came around, but he has to know more. I can't take this suspense anymore; I am about to go and get him" said a determined Shapiro. Shapiro stepped out of the car and began mercilessly beating the door. "Harden! This is Agent Jack Shapiro, FBI.

Open up, I have some questions for you" said Shapiro as he beat the door. "I'll go and check the front" said Cooper as she jumped back in the SUV and headed to the front. Jankowski got out and joined Shapiro in trying to get into the back door. After about 10 minutes, Cooper pulled the SUV back around and got out as Shapiro and Jankowski desperately tried to break the door open to no avail. "Well guys, I didn't find Harden, but I broke a window to get in the store. When I did that, I found this video in the surveillance camera, I think you better see this" said Cooper. They all jumped in the SUV and headed back to the window that Cooper broke to get in and played the video. Cooper rewound it so they could all see Harden be brutally murdered and carried out by two heavily covered assailants in all black. They also saw the vehicle they pulled off in, but in a surprising twist, the vehicle had no license plates. "Isn't this great, how the hell do we explain this to Cap" said Shapiro. "You're worried about Captain Nicholson, but now Lt. Lee is going to dive headfirst into this. This case is turning more and more into a free for all" said Cooper. "Yeah, a free kill for all in which the most important keys to our investigation are all dying or escaping" said Jankowski. "Based on what's going on, we know one thing for sure. These guys have intelligence in what we are doing. Because of that, we either have a mole or these guys are psychics. Either way, we got to find the source, either that or we'll never solve this case" said Shapiro. "Yeah, well, I think that's what they are counting on" said Cooper.

Rico woke up at 3:30 a.m. and looked up at the ceiling in his cold cell. He wondered to himself, "What the hell am I doing? And who the hell are these people?" He just couldn't quite wrap his mind around the idea of some secret society that could walk in jail and walk right back out as if nothing had happened. And how were they able to change his identity? And how did they know that he and Brandon were the ones that took that bribe money? And speaking of bribe money, who were they bribing and why? So many questions that Rico didn't have the answer to and probably never. The only thing that he knew that these people promised to make him a rich man and that's all Rico ever wanted; to be a rich man with no strings attached. But wasn't he attaching strings? That's just the thing, Rico didn't see it as attaching strings, he saw it as venturing into a business deal that could prove to be very lucrative. Sure, there were risks, but high risks yielded high rewards. In this state, Rico didn't want to have done more time than he should, and he was glad to have the chance to embark on something undone by many. So, he swallowed his fears and remembered that when he was rich and successful, he would have so much to offer Jordan because all he wanted to do was make her happy. The girl had surpassed her duties as a girlfriend and Rico planned to return the favor tenfold. "You ready ain't ya?" asked T-Dog. "Yeah, but I'm still kind of nervous. How do I know y'all aren't trying to kill me?" asked Rico. "Simple, we're not liars. If we want you, we want you and will teach you the way things are supposed to be, the right way. If we wanted to kill you, then you and I wouldn't be having this conversation right now" said T-Dog bold and brazen. "Point taken" said Rico who continued to look at the ceiling.

A few hours later, Murphy opened the cell door and smiled at both. "You guys get the honor of helping me today." In role, T-Dog played an irritated inmate upset at having to get up earlier than usual, "come on man, I'm not even woke."

"Well, you woke now, so get the fuck up and come on before I throw your ass in the hole!" yelled Murphy as T-Dog and Rico both cleared the cell. They began to serve the trays to all the other inmates; some questioned why they got to help, especially since this was other inmates' job. "Hey, I'm running this shift today so shut the fuck up" said Murphy. Within an hour, they had finished serving the cellblocks they were required to and got part one of the plans situated; with Murphy sneaking them into the laundry room where two uniforms waited for them. They swiftly changed, walked out of the laundry room, and headed down the back entrance where inmates were transferred to their cells. Along the way they noticed a short, hotshot CO with black hair who was next in line for promotion for lieutenant. "Hey! I don't know you guys, and I know everyone!" T-Dog braced himself to stab the CO until he changed the tone in his voice. "Bahahaha, you guys must have just come in with the new class. I'm CO Beckowitz, soon to be Lt. Beckowitz. You guys know where everything is right? Rico responded quickly, "yes, we do buddy, but if we need anything, we will certainly look you up." "Well, alright, you know what they say; life is about who you know and who you blow. Well neither one of you guys will be blowing me, but you know me. I will look for you two when my promotion becomes official. I will definitely need a team; Jackson and Franklin" said Beckowitz as he read the names on their name tags attached to their uniforms. "Yes sir" said T-Dog as the he and Rico continued walking toward the garage to meet Murphy. "That was a close call," said Rico. "Yeah, for him" responded T-Dog showing Rico the blade that he was carrying.

They finally met Murphy in the hallway, and they were advised that they were being watched. "There is this snooping fuck named Beckowitz walking around. He thinks that I transferred in, but I did spread the word that I'd be showing the two new guys around" said Murphy. "Good, because we saw him, and he assumed that we were with some new class. Thought we were going to have shank him" said T-Dog. "Don't worry; it should be smooth sailing from here" said Murphy as they all headed down the corridor into a section that would lead them into a staging area until Jesse would bring the van around. After waiting and pretending to be talking to the two new "CO's" Murphy heard the van and double checked to make sure that it was Jesse. When he saw that it was, he motioned for Rico and T-Dog to follow him. As they were walking out into the garage, Beckowitz reappeared and began to question what was going on. "Where do you think you're going? These guys got some other things to learn other than how to put gas in the vans!" said Beckowitz which was throwing off the time. "Hey, don't worry, you can have them back as soon as I'm done" said Murphy who was very irritated. "What gives you the right to teach the new guys anything, I am next in line for that lieutenant position. I think these guys can go with me and you can go and do what you need to do" said Beckowitz. "Yeah, sure thing, I mean you are a man of a very high position here at the MCC, aren't you?" asked Murphy sarcastically because before Beckowitz could respond he was bashed upside the head and knocked unconscious by Jesse. Quickly, Murphy jumped in the van while Rico, T-Dog, and Jesse carried Beckowitz and threw him in the back. Rico, T-Dog and Jesse all lay on the floor while Murphy drove through the checkpoint, "Damn that shit was close, this little fucker just couldn't mind his own business, now could he? Well, too bad for him" said Murphy. "Murph, this dude is a big shot up there. Sooner or later, they will notice that he is gone" said T-Dog. "Yeah, well, that's why we are who we are. Now we'll get rid of this trash and head to our destination" said Jesse. Rico, who was shocked by all of this, now realized that he might have signed on for something that he wasn't ready for. Unfortunately, there would be no turning back now.

Gaden, Frank Houston, and Justin Stone all sit in a penthouse suite overlooking Miami Beach. "So how do we address these guys?" asked Stone regarding the hitmen. "We pay them Stone, I think that is pretty obvious" said Gaden who was, as usual, in a state of deep thought. "I think that we pay them about $15,000 apiece and call it a day" said Houston. "Frank, I think that you have completely gone insane" said Gaden "you can't pay these men a measly $15,000 and expect them to continue to be loyal. Besides, I've been underpaying them the whole time they've worked for me. I'm going to pay them $50,000 a piece especially for the big risks that they have taken." "$50,000? I am completely with you no matter what, but that is a nice chunk wouldn't say?" inquired Stone who himself was shocked to see Gaden pay these men this amount of money. "Look, the shit is hot right now, these guys killed police officers and directly killed a witness in an ongoing investigation. This isn't the usual hit; this was a big one. Honestly, I still think that I am underpaying them for their risks" said Gaden. "Alright well that makes sense" said Stone. "No way, I don't care how much of a risk..." Houston was saying before the phone rang. Gaden walked over to answer, "yes...yes...let them up" he looked over to Stone and said, "they're here." "Frank, I have carried you, to the point that you have become like a spoiled child. But this time you're going to earn your respect. You're going out on the next mission; you will head the team and you will do it right" said Gaden who had become disappointed with Houston lately. "Whatever, I don't care about running the team, it establishes me as the true underboss" said Houston as he looked over at Stone with a grin. Within moments the two hitmen knocked on the door and Houston locked and loaded while opening the door. After frisking the both, he allowed them to walk in. "Jack and Duke, how are you two gents doing today, have a seat" said Gaden, "Frank, get these two fine gentlemen a drink. What will it be?" asked Gaden. "Scotch" said Jack who was the imitation Brandon Schultz. "Cognac" said Duke who was his accomplice a very toned and defined black man who stood about 6'0. Houston walked over and handed the men their drink and Stone joined them with a briefcase to open discussions about finances. "Alright, gents, we've been up for a while negotiating what we were going to pay you" said Stone. "Look, I am going to speak honest" said Duke, "we have been getting shafted, but we've dealt with it because we call ourselves trying to earn respect. But this time is different; we took a lot of risks for you guys. We have put our lives and freedom on the line and now we want what is owed to us." "Gentlemen, we understand your concerns. Therefore I, being the facilitator, have decided to triple your normal pay. Does $50,000 sound fair?" asked Gaden. "Hell yeah..." Jack began to comment but was cut off by Duke. "$50,000 aye? Well, that sounds wonderful, but what does this mean? Does this mean that we get no more work from you?" "On the contrary, you guys have actually earned a promotion. "We got a team coming in from Chicago and we want you guys to link up with them to deliver some goods to North Korea. Frank here will lead the team and if all goes well you two, along with the Chicago team, will become my top guns. How does it sound?" asked Gaden. "Now we're talking, Duke, I know that you like the way this sounds. Plus, no more grunt work" said Jack. "Alright, so when do we leave?" asked Duke. "The Chicago team should be here by tomorrow and you guys will leave immediately. Now remember this is North Korea we're talking about here; you can't just fly there without getting shot down by American troops stationed in South Korea. There will be an awkward route you will take, but we will work all of that out once the rest of the team get here" said Gaden. "Now that all of the details have been worked out, are you guys ready to get paid?" asked Stone as he opened his briefcase. "Yes, but what? You guys paying us in checks?" asked Jack. "No, I'm just recording it. Plus, I'm writing down where you can find the money. It's going to be two duffel bags in two lockers at the Greyhound station. Be careful, because people might be curious as to why two guys are both carrying two duffel bags. So, watch your surroundings and here you go" said Stone who handed them two small keys that would fit in the lockers and directions on how to get there. "Check back in tomorrow at another location that will be told to you. Don't worry about how we will find you, we always do" said Gaden who was always careful not to inform anyone of his intentions. "Alright boss, we'll be ready whenever you are" said Duke as he and Jack were leaving the suite with Frank letting them out. "You better hope these guys in Chicago are as good as you say they are" said Houston. "Well Frank, whoever they are, they will be more capable than those incompetent slackers that you brought in" said Gaden giving Frank a dirty look and motioning Stone to come with him. "You stay here and watch everything, me and Justin have some business to attend to" said Gaden as he and Stone walked out of the door. Just as Gaden had tired of Houston, Houston felt the feelings were mutual. But he had some plans that would undermine the entire operation and it lied with the CIA.

Chapter 13

Murphy pulled the van into an abandoned warehouse while Jesse and T-Dog

held down Berkowitz, Rico tied him up. "You fucks will never get away with this; I

am a lieutenant of the Bureau of Prisons. You are all dead men, you hear me!" yelled

Berkowitz. "It doesn't matter about any of that, you want to know why? Because I am

about to kill you" said Murphy as he was pulling out his 9mm with a silencer. "Look,

I know who you are okay. Your name isn't Calvin Murphy, its Fred Bauer. You aren't

a CO you're a member of an arms dealing organization that has ties in with almost

every government agency and have intelligence on almost everything going on in

the world" said Berkowitz who seemed to know too much to be a CO. "Who the fuck

are you?" asked T-Dog as he too pulled out a 9mm. "I am a CIA operative keeping

an eye on you guys, my name is Agent Doug Grimm" said the man that was believed

to be CO Berkowitz, "I wouldn't have come 50 ft. of you guys if it was my choice, but

the powers that be made me spy on you. Once I saw you guys leaving, I knew that I

had to follow you; by any means necessary." "So, you mean to tell me that you

almost got your head blown off to gather information for the CIA? I should really kill

you now" said Bauer/Murphy. "That won't be possible Bauer, he works for me" said

a tall, white man with salt and pepper hair entering the warehouse flanked by two

men in black suits and sunglasses. "Well, if it isn't the real deal, Agent Conley" said

Bauer. "That's Cmdr. Conley to you and he is one of my men Bauer" said Conley

motioning over to Grimm "let's go, your work here is done. Untie him" "Conley,

what the hell are you doing following us, everything is on the up and up; plus, you

know what is going on" said Jesse. "Well, you're right about one thing, I do know what is going on, but everything isn't on the up and up. The Montana initiative was an utter failure with no purpose. Tell Gaden I said I want him to contact me immediately; we have some things to iron out. The FBI wants answers and I have a feeling that we are being watched, my operation in particular" said Conley who had a very displeased look on his face, "other than that, you men are free to go; for now." "Well, I will let him know, but in the meantime, we have work to do" said Bauer as they all prepared to change into suits and change vehicles into a black BMW 745. "Bauer remember one thing, Gaden doesn't control you; you could always make decisions on your own behalf" said Conley as he turned to walk with his men. "Hey, I am fully competent and understand my position in this whole ordeal" said Bauer as they all started changing. "Okay, this is all tripped out. You guys are plugged with the CIA? I was only joking back at the MCC, but this operation is more serious than I thought. I am all in, but where are we going?" asked Rico as they were getting finished putting on the suits. "Yes, this is a very serious initiative and I am sorry that you had to get a bulk of this information from Conley. Don't worry about him, he just likes running a smooth operation. We aren't CIA agents; we are only an organization that happens to have the CIA as one of our biggest resources. As far as anything else, we'll talk about it on the plane. By the way, we're heading to Miami, we got to see the boss" said Bauer as they all got into the 745. "Don't worry Rico, I told you that you would go far with this and you will. Just make sure that you pay close attention. Anything you see can, and probably will, help you along the way" said T-Dog. "So, if you're Fred Bauer, who the hell are you two?" asked Rico looking at Jesse and T-Dog. "I'm Terry Jennings and that's

Marcus Bradshaw" said T-Dog pointing to Jesse, "hope you remember that because it will be the last time you hear it. The only people that have tabs on us is the CIA, because they're the CIA. Is there anything else? You're probably wondering how we're getting to Miami? You just watch, because we certainly aren't driving that far." "Well, I am not worried and if we're about to head out, I am just sitting back waiting for the show to begin. I will tell you guys this much; I can't wait to meet the boss, sounds like he is a dude that's well connected" said Rico. "Oh, don't you worry, the boss is going to be proud to meet you as well, now enjoy the ride" said Bauer as he turned up the music and headed down a busy city street.

"I can't believe that Cap left on us, knowing that this case is at a dead end" said Jankowski. "Well I think that is probably why he left in the first place. I mean, why would he want his name tied into this? 'Leave it to Shapiro so he can have his career reassigned to Timbuktu" said Shapiro. "Well fellas, I think that you are all looking at this case ass backwards" said Lt. Lee who was now being more hands on with everything. "Lee, this is not the time for your cowboy bravado, okay? We have some serious problems going on here and I do not believe that we are going to close this case. I am an investigator, got that? This is what I do, I have been with the Bureau for 15 years and my whole livelihood has been investigations," belted Shapiro. "Well" said Lt. Lee "if your whole livelihood has been investigations, then you would realize that one of your people is giving up information, I swear you can't trust you Federal guys..." "Lee, that is enough, this is not getting us anywhere, we have to get McNamara in here, he has to track phone calls, and any spotting of a black van. We also checked every single rental car agency, and all police reports in the state for stolen black vans. Cooper, I want you to go look at that tape, get an exact make and model of the van and it will narrow down what we are looking for. Jankowski, I want you to start going through those records and finding the nearest Gresham office, no calls, we will be just showing up. In the meantime, I am getting on the phone with Captain Nicholson to secure some finances and I will meet with the agents from Washington to see if they have gathered anything. People, we don't have much time, we must get some intel about what is going on" ordered Shapiro who have now not only come out of his slump but commanded his team to prove that he was worthy of running this operation. "What about the mole theory, Agent" said Lt. Lee with a smirk on his face. "Lee, have you ever taken time to think that your men could be the mole? Since you want to be involved, come with me and meet the agents from Washington, it's the only way we can get some more manpower and get everyone caught up. You are Lt. Major of the Billings PD, right?" asked Shapiro. "Well of course I am" answered Lt. Lee. "Well, then you oversee all the local authorities not only for the Billings, but you are responsible for the Sheriff's men as well, that Deputy Sheriff kid is a PR stunt, he can't run this task. Now I ask you Lee, can I depend on you, or do I have to tell the Bureau that you are incapable?" asked Shapiro. "You bet your ass you can depend on me Shapiro, and another thing, we're in this together, so I will work with you guys and command my people, but don't you ever threaten me with the FBI ever again. 'Round these parts, those are fighting words, Agent Shapiro," said Lt. Lee.

"Alright men, meeting adjourned," said Assistant Director David Rogers. Rogers was the perennial lawman; father was the Director of the Philadelphia FBI office. He joined the Marines at 18, earned numerous medals and left at age 25 to work for the CIA. After 5 years working for the CIA, he decided that he didn't want to work to keep the public uninformed and began his rise to power in the FBI. Now, at age 40, he is the 2nd in command of the entire FBI. Shapiro may have been lead agent on this case, but even Capt. Nicholson would have to take a back seat to this person. "Director, could I have a word with you please?" asked Shapiro, as he locked eyes with the Rogers' blue eyes. "Sure thing, hey let's relax it a little, huh? Why don't you call me David, now how can I help you?" said Rogers. "Well, I am Agent Jack Shapiro, lead agent of this case. This is Lt. Major Jed Lee of the Billings Police Department. My Captain has returned to San Francisco and now I oversee the case. Just wanted to touch bases about strategy and any intel that you guys might have" said Shapiro. "Well, Jack" said Rogers "I believe that we are both alike, natural-born leaders. Your subordinate, Agent McNamara, came in and gave us a briefing on some of the information that you San Fran guys have gathered. He also gave us some details in relevance to the explosion, I'm sorry to hear about the Sheriff, Lt. Lee." "Well, if the Sheriff were alive, he would want us to get to the bottom of this whole thing" said Lee. "So, Shapiro, let me get this straight, all of this is tied in with an on-going investigation that involves a $250,000 deposit that was stolen from the Fed of San Francisco, correct?" asked Rogers. "Yes, it all started with that, all of the sudden there were chains of events that started once Agent McNamara was able to access the IP address, which gave us the location of the interceptor" said Shapiro. "Then, one of the suspects, some college student, was seen several times purchasing chemical compounds that could be used to create explosives, after that the Big Bang" said Lee. "Well, gents, I have spent 15 years in

investigations. I have investigated some of the most top-secret crimes ever

committed and I have investigated some of the stupidest ones. This is a combination

of both. On surface, it seems like the jerks that pulled off the interception of the

funds got nervous. They split, the white guy ran to the country where he wouldn't be

obviously spotted, but he got nervous, probably the result of smoking too much

meth. Anyhow, he constructed some high-power explosives and when the cops

came, Boom!" said Rogers. Shapiro took in Rogers' theory for a moment before he

began his rebuttal. "That's what we were thinking, but there was no way to prove

that this was a case that simple, me and my partner went out to the warehouse that

supplied these chemicals. He said he normally sold only to people in the demolition

and construction industry but had an encounter with a guy with a badge as a

certified scientist working for some government agency. Once this was discovered,

we gathered evidence about this guy's background, and he turned out to be some

idiot who had come into an inheritance when some men came to him and

propositioned him with an idea of what he should do with the money. He bit, and

now that company sold their stake to Gresham and has disappeared into thin air.

Not only that, that guy is missing. My partner and I went back to ask him a few more

questions and when we got there, he was gone. But according to the security

camera on the scene, he was shot to death, rolled in a rug, and thrown in a black van

with no license plate" said Shapiro who looked overwhelmed with all of the

information he had shared. "It sounds to me like there is a real situation going on

here, and these guys are pros. And let me guess, the accomplice of the shooter was the other kid" assumed Rogers. "Well that hasn't been determined; the other figure was covered in black from head to toe. We have some people checking on stolen black vans. We've also got people trying to get in touch with some people from Gresham to get some information about this acquisition," said Shapiro. "Sounds like you guys got it all together so let's go and see what everyone is up to. By the way, that kid McNamara, sharp as a tack. I'm not going to lie to you Shapiro, we would use him in Washington. You know collaborating with the SEC to catch security frauds and insider trading. Ever since Enron, those things are career makers" joked Rogers as he, Lee, and Shapiro all headed back to the main office where the other agents and officers worked.

Miami looked calm and serene with all the bright skies, beaches, and beautiful women. Rico couldn't believe that this same day, he had waken up in a prison cell facing serious charges for hacking bank accounts. Today, he was a normal guy walking down Miami Beach scoping all the beautiful Cuban and Haitian women. After he was briefed on what was transpiring, they headed to the Palwaukee Airport outside of Chicago and jumped a private jet to an even smaller airport outside of Miami, where another black BMW awaited them. Now they were walking to a hotel on the beach to finally meet the maestro of this entire operation. Rico had become curious as to who this man really was. A man with this much power and these many connections had the ability to access things unknown to the average man. Rico came to realize that this is all he ever wanted was to be a man of respect and power and that meeting the boss of this organization could unlock his dreams in a way he never imagined. He just continued to be patient even though it seemed that time slowed down once they walked through the front door of the hotel and no one even noticed that they were there. They calmly walked through the hotel and stepped onto the elevator. Another indicator of the power of this man he was going to meet. He had the penthouse suite at the top of the building, truly securing Rico's every fear, but giving him the motivation to carry on with no hesitation.

Once the elevator opened, all Rico could see was a humongous window that led to a balcony where he could see three men sitting and talking. As they got closer Rico was prompted to stop for a moment while Bauer went to announce his arrival to Gaden. Once Bauer told him what was going on, he motioned for Rico to step onto the balcony. Once on the balcony, Rico's eyes almost fell out of his head. "Stone, what the hell is going on?" asked Rico as he stood in complete amazement and disbelief. "Hi Rico, we've been waiting for you" said Stone with an arrogant smirk on his face. "You are my lawyer, is that how you get so many people off?" asked Rico who still couldn't believe what was going on. "No Rico, for the rest of those guys, I actually have to go to court, but you're special" said Stone with a smirk on his face. During this exchange, Gaden watched calmly, quietly to perhaps get a feel of Rico. Before long, he interrupted their conversation and said, "so now that we know that something is a little awkward about this situation, should we begin to worry that a lot of people are going to hear about this? I mean you must understand something Rico, this is a secret society. Right now, we look like businessmen and that's how I like it." Rico turned his full attention to Gaden and looked at him. He noticed a man cool, calm, and collect even under a situation that is uncertain. He finds himself just staring at Gaden and Gaden just staring at him. "I don't believe we have met yet" said Rico, "Rico Jones, computer extraordinaire looking to make some money." "Gaden, director of this operation" said Gaden as he looked at Rico. "Now, if you are done bickering with this ingrate, we can get down to business," said Gaden in a stern and serious tone. "Sure, but this man is my lawyer he is the best in Chicago and to see him..." said Rico before being cut off by Gaden who now seemed irritated. "Chicago? Justin Stone is the best in the world. He has gotten off many men in many cities in many countries. Did you know that he speaks Spanish, French, Russian, German, Arabic, and Chinese? Did you know that he has put his stamp in law and, you have been carefully screened Mr. Jones? Understand that you wouldn't be here if we weren't sure about who you were. You would also still be in a fucking 8'6 waiting for your three hots and a cot." Frank Houston came out and caught wind of the conversation. "Say Boss, we need to get moving. It's almost time." "Great, we should...." said Stone as he was cut off by Houston. "Stone, you got a client to see up in New York. Tony DeLuna of one of the five families has been busted for racketeering and murder they need you pronto. The family has a private jet and limo ready for you." "DeLuna? What the hell has he done now? Did they say it had to be me?" asked Stone. "Yeah, they need your expertise and they need your connections and you know exactly why" said Houston. "Yes Stone, they need you to get money to places so make sure you get there in the next few hours. The organization needs you to do your job" said Gaden in a very calm and serious tone. "Alright, I'm out of here, Bauer can I get you to drive me?" asked Stone. "Sure, but before I go, I have to tell you that Conley and his men intercepted this mission. He said he wants to speak with you as soon as possible" said Bauer. "Conley? I haven't heard from that prick in over a year since.... Did he leave any way for me to find him?" said Gaden in deep thought. "No, but I would assume that you find him the way that you always do or did or whatever" said Bauer in utter confusion and haste as he motioned Stone to follow him. "Frank, I think that we need to get in touch with him, don't know what he wants, but it must be important. Get Jennings or Bradshaw to set up a meeting, he'll know them.

"Mr. Jones come with me we need to talk, and I am tired of sitting in this same spot. You never know who is watching" said Gaden. "Sounds like a plan to me because I am still lost" said Rico. Rico, Houston, and Gaden walked out of the penthouse down a hall to the elevator. Rico was still in shock because he was a free man in Miami in a penthouse suite trying to figure out how this whole ordeal transpired. As they walked out of the elevator, Frank motioned to a Cuban man who stood by the door in an all-black suit and sunglasses. The man led them to a limousine in front of the hotel and they entered the limo one by one. Rico thought to himself how surreal this whole thing seemed, but he was more nervous as to what would be said to him. Gaden and Houston both said nothing for the first 3 minutes of the ride. Rico began to get nervous and started randomly thinking that this could be a setup for his murder. Maybe Brandon had gotten to someone and ordered his murder...While Rico was amid his conspiracy theory, Gaden finally spoke. "I hope that you heard everything that Stone said, because that's the last time you will hear those words. I run an operation of a great magnitude. Most of my men came with me from New York, handpicked and screened to ensure loyalty and quality service. This operation is tight, and we ask for full confidentiality. Therefore, you were sprung from prison; your identity has been wiped clear of the system. Thanks to my connections in the CIA and FBI, I know that there is a manhunt for you and your accomplice, Brandon Schultz. Schultz is wanted in connection of a bombing of a cabin in Montana. There were police officers Rico, lots of them and he is now public enemy #1" said Gaden. Rico let the information sink in but remember that Brandon could have no way possibly could have done this, prompting him to inquire about the situation. "Brandon? A mass murderer? I just do not see it; I spent a lot of time around him and the only thing he ever wanted to do was drink Jager Bombs and play Call of Duty. He was a fucking geek, I think I was the one who helped him lose his virginity, so why would I believe that a guy like this can turn into a mass murderer?" Houston looked at Gaden and in his mind, wanted to expose the truth, but decided that it would be better if Gaden did it. "Who gives a fuck rather you know if Schultz did it or not, what matters is that he is wanted. Now, there is a manhunt for you my friend. There are federal agents constantly watching your mother's house. Don't worry she hasn't been there in days, we set her up nicely on Lake Shore Drive far away from your crummy neighborhood. I need to trust you, but of course I covered myself, if you for any reason fall out of grace, your identity will be redeemed, and you will be apprehended immediately. Not only that, we will not protect you so you will be charged with escape. Now, we don't have to let it go down like that so just roll with us. Besides we're the ones that got you out of that hell hole and into a life of luxury. You will amass a fortune with us Rico, and you will also be able to move into power positions abroad. I ask you for your loyalty and it's not a request, per se, it is your only survival. So, what is your decision, Mr. Jones?" asked Gaden as he stared at Rico as if he was trying to read his mind. "Well, Mr. Gaden, I must say that you leave me with no other choice, I am not going back to jail, and I damn sure want to amass a fortune, so where do I sign up?" asked a joking, but serious Rico. "You sign no names; you just meet your operation team and you guys get busy. Mr. Jones, what I like about you is that you are not only a genius, but a leader and orchestrator as well. For that reason, we need your programming skills to create a virus that we can track in a foreign government's security system. Once we have bypassed the system, the team will go in, take some things and you guys will leave. Sounds simple right?" asked Gaden. "Yes, but why are we taking things and how much are they worth?" asked Rico with a naive look on his face. Gaden immediately laughed and looked over at Houston who also chuckled. "Rico, you really have no idea. They aren't worth anything, it is information that certainly isn't in the system" said Houston. "I see, well who will be going in with me anyway?" asked Rico yet again with a naïve look on his face. "You won't be going in, you're going to man the command post and guide the men because we are also going to plant cameras in the facility and tracking devices on the men" said Gaden in a more serious tone. "So this, in a sense, is an espionage mission; Black Ops almost" inquired Rico. "No, all of that shit is government. We are an independent organization, but when the Black Ops departments of our friends at the CIA get too scared to do shit.... you get the idea," said Houston, even though Gaden looked displeased with him for disclosing that information. "So, when do I meet the rest of this 'team' you speak of?" asked Rico. "Actually, right now" said Gaden.

The limo pulls up to a hangar off the port of Miami. It proceeds to go inside the completely dark hangar and the doors immediately close, indicating that they were not alone. Suddenly, lights come on and three men appear. They all exit and Gaden begins to introduce everyone "Jennings, Jack, Duke, this is Rico Jones your technology specialist." "Oh, so what we aren't smart enough to handle computers?" asked Duke. Gaden was quickly upset and walked into Duke's personal space and stared at him in the face. "Who do you think you are? You want to question me, but I just made you a rich man? I think that you need to get your priorities straight and worry about doing your own job, you got me?" asked Gaden in a very angry stance ready to pounce on Duke if he were to make any moves. Duke flinched up, though he wasn't a small man, but he was no match for Gaden on any level. "Sorry about that Boss, just let the money go to my head that's all" said Duke. "Hey Rico, you ready to make some big boy moves?" asked Jennings to loosen the tension in the air. "Oh yeah, let's do it I'm ready anything with computers have never phased me" said Rico. "Good because we need you to work quickly and efficiently. You won't have much time, and if you fail, that means that your team dies" said Gaden putting even more pressure on Rico than he was already facing. "Frank, I know you know what is needed from this point. I will let you brief the team and you guys can get out of here through the tunnel" said Gaden as he headed back to limo. In true Gaden fashion, as quick and fierce as his presence came off was as quickly, he was gone. "We will take that tunnel to the hangar next door. That hangar will have a private jet, fully supplied with all necessary items; clothes, food, alcohol, comfortable space for rest, and flight attendants willing to do anything sexually that we desire. It will be a fun flight, but make no mistake, we have a job to do and it is imperative that this gets done properly. As the boss has said, any mistake cannot only cost us our lives, but many people will die. Rico, I will brief you on the jet because I have some layouts of the building as well as some information you will need to access the system," said Houston who asserted himself as the leader of the mission.

Chapter 14

"We found it!" exclaimed Jankowski running through the Billings Police Department like a mad man. "Found what?" asked Shapiro as he tried to calm down an excited Jankowski. "The van, we found the van!" yelled Jankowski as he went to grab his jacket. "Wait, where?" asked Shapiro before Cooper answer blurted it out. "On the Beartooth Highway, but it's weird, these two guys are gone, and they just completely abandoned this van." "Wait a minute here guys" stepped in Rogers. "This could be what these crooks want, think about it, the Beartooth Highway is something that everyone in the area would take or know somebody that would have to take it. They wanted us to find this thing. We're going to need some Bomb Squad guys to have a look at this thing before any more officers lose their lives" said Rogers with a voice of concern. "Don't worry Director, we're going to take care of this and gather all evidence that we can, let's move out guys" said Lee. "Shapiro, I want you and McNamara to stay here and look over some of the documents that our IT people found" said Rogers. "Okay, Jankowski you got this?" asked Shapiro. "Sure, thing boss, I'll keep an eye on everything and make sure this thing is done properly," said Jankowski as he walked out with Lt. Lee and the rest of the brigade. "Alright, well, I was just showing Dir. Rogers here these codes that I picked up as a correspondence between Rico Jones and his girlfriend. Apparently, this, guy was doing some time on a wire fraud and was awaiting trial. The problem is, he just disappeared into thin air" said McNamara. "Yeah, me and Jankowski discovered that about a week ago while we were still in the San Francisco area searching for Mr. Schultz" said Shapiro. "Really? Because I could have sworn that was an important factor, I mean, people just don't disappear into thin air every day," said Rogers who was not pleased with the fact that his major case was compromised by a blunder. "Well, Jones was never implicated in the bombing. Also, Harden never spotted the 'scientist' with anyone else. Finally, we never got a clear look at the accomplice in the murder of Harden. These factors led us to believe that it wasn't as important to track Rico Jones, especially since we didn't have the intel or manpower as to where he may or may not had been" said Shapiro. "Well, Jack that would make a lot of sense, but Jones was in a Federal Correctional Center. Did it not dawn on you to possibly check to see if he had bonded out or had been sentenced and sent away to another prison? I mean think about this, we have two former roommates; one has turned into a bomb-making maniac and the other has been arrested for a federal crime. Did you even take the time to figure out why he was in there?" grilled Rogers who continued on without allowing Shapiro a chance to defend himself. "What about his mother? Who, for your information, moved out of her house a few days ago? Are you kidding me? Shapiro, I respect your work, but this was a blunder on your end" said Rogers, insulting Shapiro for his work, even though he had brought his team from a simple investigation to an all-out manhunt. "Well, since we are talking about Jones' mother, did you know that you can check your system and find that Rico Jones' information has completely disappeared? Not even a picture. Did you know that the school's computers were wiped out as well? We couldn't get into his mother's house due to a lack of a warrant, but here is an unethical measure performed just to get a leg up in the investigation" said Shapiro as he handed Rogers a picture of Rico at his high school graduation. "But how did you..." said Rogers as he was cut off. "I know your type, big shot out of Washington coming up here barking out orders and thinking he's smarter than everyone else. Let me tell you something Rogers, I have been working this case for nearly 6 weeks and still have gotten no closer to the perps as I'd like, but if you would like to take this picture and have McNamara scan it and send it over to the home office then you go right ahead. Hell, you can even have the credit, but I don't give damn who you are, if you ever disrespect my credentials again…" said Shapiro, cutting himself off because he realized that he was talking to a superior and knew that he must hold his composure. "Well, Jack, I had no idea that you had compiled all of this information. McNamara why didn't you tell me?" asked Rogers. "Well, I'm new and you're the Deputy Director of the Bureau, I didn't want to step on anyone's toes" said McNamara with a bashful look on his face.

Once the explosion soothed between Shapiro and Rogers, they were finally able to help each other out with the information that they both had. Rico's mother had moved, true. Rico also had contact with Jordan, the only thing close to a girlfriend that he could possibly have. It was time to act on these bits of information and see what happened. Because we need someone from this team to get direct information regarding this case, I want you to choose someone from your team to link up with the Chicago branch and meet up with this girlfriend and get some intel" said Rogers. "Why don't I go, I'll leave Jankowski in charge of the men here and I'll go and see what is going on" replied Shapiro. "Come on Jack, I need you here with me to continue to help orchestrate this whole thing. Plus, two of you need to go, I don't want any agent traveling alone" said Rogers. "Well, in that case, why don't McNamara and I go? It will help him to get some field experience," replied Shapiro.

Just then, Jankowski, Lee, and the rest of the brigade had gotten back from investigating the van. "Hey guys, we got some good news," said Cooper as she strutted in and braced herself to explain what she had found "we were able to recover a fingerprint from the van, but even better, this" she said as she flipped up a business card. "Dir. Rogers, I would like to see you have your men obtain a match in the database for this fingerprint," said Shapiro as he walked over, grabbed the business card from Cooper and read it. "People, I don't believe that we have to look any further for a contact at Gresham. Apparently, one of the killers had a direct contact with a vice-president of the company based out of, all places, Chicago" said Shapiro who immediately looked back over at Rogers. "Sir, I'd like to say that Agent Jankowski and I would like to make that trip along with McNamara in order to conduct the interviews and collaborate with the Chicago branch in order to proceed in our investigations." "Well, if that is who you would like Agent Shapiro, I have no problem granting that to you, considering the magnitude of the information that has just been received" said Rogers. "Alright, what is going on here?" asked Jankowski in a state of utter confusion. "I'll tell you all about on the way to the airport" said Shapiro who motioned for McNamara and Jankowski to gather their things.

Upon entering the flight, Rico was amazed to find that Houston did not lie about the excitement that waited upon the private jet. The flight attendants were exotic dancers paid to service them on their flight to Korea. Jack and Duke both were busy being entertained by two of the Korean beauties while Houston, Rico, and Jennings discussed how they were going to execute the plan. "So, if you look in each corner of the building, it is easy to tell that we need to plant cameras in each one. It works to our advantage that there are exactly five areas and we have a spare camera" said Houston. "But what if we didn't plant the fifth one in this corner? What if we planted in the back of one of the men's equipment and gave them cover? In addition, we have the schematics right here. We don't need to plant cameras in every section of the building, just along the path that they will take to get to the area that they need to get to" said Rico strategizing the most efficient way to successfully complete the task. "Well both of you guys have a point but, I will say that Rico's plan makes the most sense as far as the cameras and Frank, yours make the most sense in order to infiltrate," said Jennings looking to find a cool medium to the plan that the men were putting together. "Well, as far as infiltration, are we all in agreement with the stealth move; we have the uniforms and the IDs to get in, we just have to be swift" said Houston who seemed worried about this plan all the sudden. "Don't worry, I'm on board with that, I just now need an idea of who this company is so I can hack into their system" said Rico. "That won't be a problem, I have the IP address to the last person who accessed the system" said Houston. "If you can gather that, then what use do I have?" asked Rico. "I'm not exactly an expert; we have an insider who passed this information on to me. Don't worry Rico, we brought you in for a reason and you won't be overshadowed," said Houston. "I don't mean to come off as an asshole, but I just want to make sure that we are all on the same page" said Rico. "Listen, we have phase 1 complete, we can work on phase 2 or..." said Jennings as they all looked over at the remaining Korean "flight attendants." "Well, I'd say that our briefing is done, let's have some fun gents" said Houston as the men moved over to the lounge area to pick and choose a woman to have fun with. This was not so bad thought Rico as he headed to a corner with one of the women. However, even

though he was amid prospective sex with an unknown beautiful woman, Rico could

not shake off the fact that he missed Jordan. This is when he realized sex and love

were two different things though they intertwined often.

"Excellent!" exclaimed Gaden, as he found out that the plans were in motion

to pull off the heist of corporate bonds and certificates of deposit in offshore

accounts. North Korea was a warzone for the typical American, but not Gaden. No

one, except for Stone, knew the value of these seemingly worthless pieces of papers

he sought. But what if his operatives knew that these papers would give him access

to over $250,000,000. "Greed is good" Gaden said to Bradshaw as they drove out of

Miami. Gaden was a mastermind of appearing and disappearing. Bradshaw was

able to get a hold of Conley and set up a meeting up in New York at Gaden's office.

Instead of going back to the same airport they arrived at in Miami, the limo was now

going to drive up to Palm Beach and he would jump on a completely different private

jet to New York. Life was good, big money on the table. With this kind of

advantage, Gaden could operate an entire country. However, that was not his plan,

yet. He planned to see how good Rico was with his computer skills. If this mission

passed, he knew that he could count on Rico to unravel the most sinister plan of them

all; overriding the CIA and finally being able to act completely independent without

"big brother" watching over him. Gaden hated the idea of having to answer to

Conley, a racist Irish prick with gray hair and a German mustache. Conley,

however, was the one that saved Gaden from a world of small-time crime. Conley

once was a Black Ops agent working in Cuba, when he discovered that Gaden had sold some Cuban refugees some AK-47s. Instead of killing him, he conspired with Gaden to not only sell to these enemies of the U.S., but to others which includes North Korea, Libya, and even Iraq when Saddam Hussein was in power. Still, he had grown tired of taking orders. Gaden was a man of unlimited power, yet he was the CIA's whore. Enough was enough, but, one more meeting with Conley and he could plan out his mission to perfection. He himself was amazed at the confidence he had in Rico Jones, but he had no other choice. Gaden aspired of being the first Black man out of the United States to be taken seriously. Not Barack Obama, but the complete opposite, Gaden didn't want to change the world; he wanted to own it. Everything was riding on the success of this mission in North Korea and of course the acquisition of the dictator's accounts. With that kind of money, the sky was the limit and Gaden had every intention of trying to get there.

Chapter 15

Where did he go? For some reason she couldn't shake off Rico even though he seemed to have disappeared in thin air. She believed that Rico had not only bonded out and didn't tell her, but she believed that he had run off. But why couldn't he tell her? She cried upon discovering that he had no longer resided in the Metropolitan Correctional Center even though she had just gone to visit him a week earlier. While she was caught in her thoughts she walked to the washroom and looked in the mirror. Jordan was a beautiful girl with dreams, though she didn't leave town for college she resided on the dorms at Chicago State University. She maintained a high GPA and was making good to get more scholarships to help pay for her school. That's why she couldn't understand how Rico could just leave, was she ugly? fat? Neither one was the case as her beauty resembled that of Dorothy Dandridge, but for a man to just pack up and leave without saying anything made her wonder what she did wrong. In the process of having a nervous breakdown, she heard a loud bang at her door. She assumed it was her roommate but to her surprise, it was two White men flashing badges at her. "Can I help you gentlemen?" asked Jordan who was in complete shock.

"Excuse me ma'am, I am Agent Jack Shapiro, and this is Agent Cody Jankowski of the Federal Bureau of Investigation. We are looking for Jordan Riley do you know where we can find her?" asked Shapiro. "Sure, that's me, is it about Rico? Is he okay?" asked a now concerned Jordan. "Ma'am we understand that you were in a relationship with Rico Jones" said Shapiro as he and Jankowski put their badges away. "Maybe" said a nervous Jordan, she never had to deal with law enforcement in anyway and she certainly didn't want to incriminate Rico in anyway. "Ma'am rest assure that you aren't in any trouble, we just want to know if you know where he is, there is a possibility that he is in some trouble" said Jankowski. "Officers, I am not sure what you want with him, but he was in jail and now he isn't, and I don't know where he is," said Jordan. "Ma'am, so what you are saying is that you corresponded with Mr. Jones while he was incarcerated?" asked Shapiro. "Yes, and he seemed nervous about his case, but I haven't heard from him in a few days, that's when I went to visit him" said Jordan. "So, you visited him a few days ago and he was there under his real name? I mean we are trying to rule out all possibilities," said Jankowski. "Yes, he was there as Rico Jones, I signed for him and it was the name attached to his inmate number. But the weird thing is that even with his inmate number, he is still out of the system, which leads me to believe that he bonded and just didn't want to tell me" said Jordan who was now becoming upset again. "Well ma'am we're sorry for the disconnection between you and Mr. Jones but is there any way that you could relinquish that inmate number?" asked Shapiro. "Sure, I have it on a letter he sent me, I'll give that to you" said Jordan as she walked into the dorm room. "Well what do you think? She seems to be on the up and up" said Jankowski. "Yeah, she does and she's cooperating, we won't rule her out, but we won't grill her. Let's just get this information and see what we can get from there," said Shapiro. "Okay, guys, I believe that this is it," said Jordan returning with a letter in her hand. On the letter, Rico Jones is written at the top with an inmate number that should be able to trace. "Thank you, ma'am, and if you have concerns or if you hear from him, here is my card" said Shapiro as he handed Jordan a card to contact him. "Thank you, I'm glad that someone is looking for him one way or the other. If you see him tell him that I hate him," said Jordan as she closed the door. "Whoa, hell hath no fury like a woman scorn huh boss?" said Jankowski giving Shapiro a nudge in the arm. "See, that's, your problem. You are focused on the part of the case that does not matter. Her anger could be sincere, but it could be a way of throwing us off. Let's just stay focused on what's necessary," said Shapiro.

Upon arriving at the Metropolitan Correctional Center in downtown Chicago, both Shapiro and Jankowski were amazed at the skyline and the entire infrastructure that Chicago displayed. "This is amazing, I mean for one city to house all of these buildings and this much commerce" said Jankowski who had never been off the West Coast with San Francisco being the biggest city he had seen. "This is nothing compared to Manhattan" said Shapiro who had been born in New York City. As they drove through the traffic, they reach the facility and pull into the garage where they are met by two correctional officers and two federal agents of the Chicago branch. "Hello, gentlemen, Agent Marcus Brown and this is my partner Agent Steve Graham" said Brown. Graham was a tall White man with brown hair and blue eyes who resembled an NBA player more than an FBI agent. "Well, I appreciate you all taking the time to brief us on this problem," said Shapiro. "This is definitely a problem for me, see, I arrested and interrogated Jones. I remember it like yesterday, honestly, I roughed him up a little bit before his hotshot lawyer came and saved the day" said Brown. "Lawyer? So, Jones had a private attorney?" asked Jankowski. "Yes, some asshole who makes his living corrupting the system. His name is Justin Stone, and I believe that he knows something about this. I mean for a person to just disappear out of the system is unheard of here. This place prides itself on having a low escape rate, but this has to be an inside job," said Graham. "So, what would make you assume something like that Agent Graham?" asked Shapiro just as the warden of the facility walked into the garage. "Hello gentlemen, it is a pleasure to meet you. I am the warden of this facility Gregory Mitchell, if you would like to follow me, I can show you to our records department" said Mitchell who seemed quite anxious to get the FBI out of there as quickly as possible. "Sir, if you don't mind, we would like to ask you a few questions about this incident," said Shapiro. Mitchell was a short, pudgy man who was in his 50s and seemed to be a candidate for a stroke. "Sure thing, what do you want to ask" said Mitchell. "Well, how often do you count the prisoners?" asked Shapiro. "Once in the morning, once in the afternoon, and once at night after lights out" said Mitchell. "I see, can you explain to me how is it that no one noticed that Mr. Jones with this inmate number was nowhere to be found?" asked Shapiro now stepping closer to Mitchell. "Well sir, my assumption is that some officers were a part of this. We have suspended two officers who worked the cellblock that day and we are currently conducting more investigations. We have also warned the suspended officers that they could be brought up on criminal and civil charges," said Mitchell who felt a little intimidated by Shapiro's ice-cold stare. "That is the first bits of information that you can turn over, along with records of counts, guard activity, and equipment that may have been signed in and out during the time that we believe Rico Jones was incarcerated," demanded Shapiro. "Sure, just follow me to the records department and they can get you everything that you need" said Mitchell.

"Here it is, our state-of-the-art records department that houses all of the records of everything that occurs around here," said Mitchell. "Yeah state of the art my ass, tell your people to get some disks prepared for the date that Jones was booked. If his girlfriend is telling the truth, then the last time she saw him was about the 12th, so get us info to about the 16th. We will have McNamara review them all while we go and see Mr. Stone" said Shapiro looking right at Jankowski. "Next, I want to come back with some of the Chicago office's men and conduct interviews with the inmates on that cell block between those times," said Shapiro. "My officers actually conducted interviews and we will gladly turn over the transcripts," said Mitchell. "Well, we will take them and still conduct our own interviews. In addition, if any of the men on the cellblock were released, we need that information as well. We will also need a list of every officer, administrator, nurse, or whoever worked that day. If your theory is that this was an inside job, I think I want to get to know the inside of this place a little better," said Shapiro who was acting more like a commander than ever. "Agent Brown, I ask that you get your men in here to help carry every piece of this evidence over to your offices, Agent Jankowski and I are going over to Stone's office and see if he knows anything" said Shapiro. "Alright Shapiro, we will take care of this and hopefully this McNamara kid is as good as you say. Let's go guys, get all of this stuff out of here!" yelled Brown to his men. "Don't worry about McNamara, this is one of the smartest kids I ever met, it surprises me that he wants to work with us" said Shapiro as they walked out of the records office and started heading towards the garage. "I think I heard of this Stone guy, but the weird thing is that he has offices in Chicago, New York, Miami, Washington D.C. and Los Angeles; seems kind of weird that a criminal defense attorney needs that large of a network" said Jankowski. "Let's just hope he isn't too far," said Shapiro as they waited on an elevator.

Chapter 16

After a long flight, due to the numerous different passages that must be taken get to North Korea without detection, they arrive in a small airport outside of Pyongyang. Due to the tensions between the U.S. and North Korea, Rico was nervous but was told how to approach the situation. "We will wear turbans, and if questioned by anyone, let me do all of the talking as I am fluent in Arabic. As for Jack, we will say that he is a Swede who we are closing a deal with. But because of our connections, we shouldn't encounter anyone" said Jennings. The jet pulls up and outside, there is a limo and Korean man in a black suit awaiting their arrival. "This guy Ono is a jerk by the way, but he knows that we all are here to handle business" Jin Ono was a powerful man in the North Korean military who had given the intel of the project for a 30% cut of the earnings. As they step into the limo Houston notices that Ono is in the limo. "Ono, what the hell are you doing here?" asked Houston. In his Korean accent, Ono answers "Well, Mr. Houston, I see that you and your team have made it and look, you partake in affirmative action." "Hey, who the hell…" said Jack right before he was cut off by Houston. "Jack, shut up, and Ono you joke but you know that we get things done right" said Houston. "Of course, you do, if you didn't, I would be bringing you to Pyongyang to kill you," said Ono who began to laugh at his own attempt at a joke. "I just hope that you are giving us correct information, we can't afford to fuck this up" said Jennings. "Well, you see I can't either so if I allow you guys to fuck up then I fuck myself. I love to fuck but I don't get fucked" said Ono who now had taken the smile off his face. The men enter the limo and they head into Pyongyang in disguise as Arabic nationals helping a

Swedish businessman close a deal with the national bank of North Korea. The limo ride is calm, and Ono begins to smile as he knows that this will be a payday for himself. "I estimate that these bonds are worth around $250 million." "That is U.S. dollars, right? The money over here can't be worth too much" said Duke who began laughing, but no one else in the limo shared his sense of humor. "Duke, it's always U.S. dollars, remember that" said Houston. "So exactly where are we going?" asked Rico who now noticed that buildings were now turning into forest and forest caused the night to darken. "The war room" said Houston. "What the hell is that?" asked Rico. "Oh, it is a room where our dreams will come true tonight gentlemen" said Ono. The further into the forest they drove, Rico noticed a small shack that could easily go undetected in the night. The limo approaches and Ono notify the driver to pull to the "side." Once the limo pulls to the side of the shack, it stops and Ono motions for everyone to get out. "I don't know what the hell this is, but I will say that it is very well hidden" said Jennings. "Just wait, you will be amazed by this" said Houston who had been to the famous war room before himself. The men enter the shack and notice that it looks on the inside as it does on the outside, until Ono presses an old light switch and a secret door emerges. "Well I'll be..." said Jack who was amazed by what he was seeing. The path came with a long flight of stairs that went into the ground and the men began to venture down the stairs. Upon entering the so-called "war room" they notice the armed militia that are in uniforms with M-16 rifles; they also notice a command post, equipped with surveillance footage, radar to track planes flying, computers to monitor legit operations such as stocks, and computers to monitor illegal activities like tracking of shipments that included guns and heroin. "Holy shit, this is the most amazing thing that I have ever seen" said Rico whose eyes were wide. "Oh yes, Mr. Jones, I have heard that you are an expert in accessing information. You will very much be needed, and you can call this your office" said Ono as he motioned him over to a computer that was custom designed for hacking. "Alright, well I better get to work, where is this IP address so I can begin decoding the information?" asked Rico as he jumped right in. "Ambitious, I like it, so what will you gentlemen need?" said Ono motioning over to Houston. "Well, I am going to stay here and monitor surveillance as well as guide you through the place. Rico will access the company's accounts and move the money over to Ono's account, so we can get him out of the way" said Houston who cut his eyes over to Ono as he felt that 30% of over $250 million worth of bonds was unreasonable. "Rico will also assist me in all other technical aspects, if you guys get into some trouble, Ono has already notified his militia on the inside of the place to provide aid and assistance. But guys, we don't want to fail, we want to do this as smooth as possible so everyone can stay safe and we can ease out of here with no incident" said Houston as he turned it over to Ono. "Ok guys let's do it; the limo will take you the site at which point you will be escorted inside" said Ono. "Mr. Jones, once you have created the virus and accessed the system, let us know right away. We will install the cameras between now and then." "Good luck Rico, we are counting on you, let's go guys" said Jennings as he, Jack, Duke, and Ono bypass the guards and head back to the ground level. "Dude, this shit is trippy man" said a shocked Rico as he began creating the virus. "You have no clue. So, once you create that virus and access their programming, I got a proposition for you" said

Houston. "Oh yeah? And what might that be Frank?" asked Rico. "Well, here is some info about another North Korean company with a few millions in escrow. If time allows you, access their account and transfer the money to this account, I will give you half of it" said Houston. "Now Frank, why do I get the feeling that this is an independent venture that you stumbled across" said Rico with a big smile on his face. "Because it is and if you can do it, you can't tell anybody, got it?" said Houston. "For half of an undisclosed number of millions of dollars, my tongue wouldn't work if I was tied up and Halle Berry danced naked in front of me" said Rico who began to chuckle and so did Houston. "HEY!! You guys get to work, Mr. Ono pay you lots of money" said a guard who obviously had no clue about what was going on. Rico and Frank looked at each other, smiled, and continued to work on their respective projects.

"So, I see that you silly bastards haven't had enough of pissing off the government" said Conley, who greeted Gaden and Bradshaw with his disdain. "Conley, you worry too much you know there is always a method to my madness" said Gaden with a smirk on his face. "Oh really, well I want to know what the hell you guys were thinking in Montana, cops lost their lives Gaden" said Conley. "I didn't know that those cops were going to close in on our guy that quick, the house was set to explode before they got there. Our guys were already gone when that place detonated so please Conley, understand that was those cops' fault for chasing behind a lead that was going nowhere" said Gaden. "Have you gone insane? What's next? You and your little militia is going to bomb the Pentagon?" said Conley who now seemed concerned about Gaden's tactics. "Conley, I am going to tell you like this; I have been nothing but loyal to you since we met all of those years ago. I have been the biggest gate keeper of a secret that could land all of us at Guantanamo Bay for the rest of our lives. A commander in the CIA you are, but you and I both are war criminals. With, Montana... that's collateral damage, my team has always been flawless in our operations, but there is more to the story than just the dead cops, now isn't Conley?" said Gaden in an arrogant tone. "Why matter of fact Gaden, there is, you guys got big problems. I got a report from the FBI that has put Brandon Schultz as public enemy #1. Now you think you covered your ass on all aspects of that problem, but you forgot about your recruit, Rico Jones" said Conley. "What about Mr. Jones, he is nowhere to be found and I certainly will keep it that way" said Gaden. "Well, that sounds all fine and dandy, but you forgot about his girlfriend who turned over a letter that identifies that Jones was in the Federal Prison in Chicago. Now the entire facility is under investigation, so I hope that you paid for the records to be destroyed" said Conley. "Oh Conley, I did one even better, Mr. Jones doesn't even exist in the Social Security database anymore. When he and the team get back from their mission, I will get him a new identity" said Gaden who seemed to have all grounds covered. "Well good work there, but what about this mission, is this kid really that good? What if he fails?" asked Conley. "Well, if he does fail, then he dies. Then we can really say that Rico Jones doesn't exist" said Gaden. "Well for his sake, I hope he doesn't fail. Stone is meeting with DeLuna supposedly there is a very wealthy group of investors in Sicily that wants to buy weapons for security. These guys have acres of poppy that they use for heroin so they are going to need as many weapons as we can get them. And Gaden, for the record, don't ever use any fucking explosives again. This isn't Brooklyn, America actually cares about those innocent people" said Conley walking out of the door. "Innocent people die everywhere Conley" said Gaden who had now gotten upset because he knew what Conley had meant by that statement. Gaden came from the Bed-Stuy area of Brooklyn, a predominately Black area where drugs and murder were part of everyday life. But since White cops in Montana had died, now it made for a bad and scary situation. This is when Gaden began to wonder what he was really doing in this lifestyle. Was it self-fulfilling, because he wasn't doing anything to change the world or make it a better place? He was a merchant of death and promoter of evil. Gaden pondered this for about another minute and turned to Bradshaw. "We got to meet with Stone, I want to see what this DeLuna guy is talking about" said Gaden. "Definitely, this is more money..." said Bradshaw before he noticed a re-emerging Conley. "I forgot to mention that the Feds are on to your little dummy corporation that put Harden in business, hope you disposed of all of the documents and completely destroyed the company" said Conley. "Of course, we sold all our products to Gresham along with trucks, and we sold our buildings to investment groups who turned them into malls and grocery stores. Furthermore, we contracted a phony CEO and board of directors to completely throw them off our trail" said Gaden. "Well, that's a start, but everything has to be airtight from this point on. No more shenanigans that can damage this operation, of course if I was to shut it down you would be alright, wouldn't you? You've made millions" said Conley. "And so have you Conley" said Bradshaw. "Hey, what I have done over the years doesn't matter, I truly believe that if we shut down now..." said Conley before being cut off by Gaden. "You wait a damn minute Conley, me and my crew travel the world doing your dirty work and this is the thanks we get? I say that it's time for you to evaluate your priorities." "My priorities? Don't worry Gaden, you can bet that my priorities are straight pal, what you and your team need to do is clean-up after you fuck up. As far as the operation, understand that at any time I can and will shut this thing down when it gets too close. I have a career and a reputation to worry about, more than you can say. You may be the quarterback, the captain of the team but I am the owner, general manager, and coach. I think that you are the one with their priorities out of whack" said Conley as he walked towards the door. "You're right Conley, I understand" said Gaden to please Conley for the moment. Truthfully, Gaden had plotted the North Korea move without authorization from Conley. The millions that he was stealing from them, would be enough set-up money to go completely rogue, at which point he would flee the U.S. but continue to operate.

"Alright, I'm in" said Rico as he created a virus that got inside of the company's system and gave him all the necessary information needed to gain access. "Good, here is Ono's information, how much are you calculating in the company's accounts?" asked Houston. "Well, it looks like around $90 million" said Rico. "$90 million? The rest of it must be tied to those bonds, if you find anything else move that as well" said Houston. "Good deal" said Rico who was now deadlocked on his task. As Rico was working on his project and Frank monitoring the situation, he notices that Jack is careless with the way he is moving through the facility. He places one of the cameras, but it is crooked giving off an awkward angle. He tries to radio Jack, but to no avail. He investigates the screen and see that Duke and Jack are having a conference of some sorts, while Jennings is putting his camera in its proper corner. "I don't know what the hell those two are up to, but I told Gaden that I didn't trust them" said Houston.

Meanwhile, Ono is in the limo sipping champagne when he receives a strange phone call. "Hello Jin, I am glad to see that you are a snake and a coward of a man" said the man on the other end. "What are you talking about, we are in business" said Ono. "No, I am in business, you have just cancelled yourself out, two of your friends gave up your ulterior motives, as a matter of fact I have paid all of your guards and now your guys are going to die. As for the two men that turned you in, they will live like Gods" said the mysterious man before hanging up the phone. At this point Ono, knows what he must do, one of the men on the inside were going to die and the other two were in on the set-up. All he could do is get the limo back to the war room and rescue Frank and Rico before it was too late. He and Gaden had done a lot of business together and telling him that everything failed would put Ono's life in danger. Plus, he was going to need to leave with them, as he double-crossed one of the most powerful men in North Korea. "Driver get out of here now" yelled Ono. On command the driver pulled off and headed back towards the war room.

"Holy shit" yelled Houston. "What's the matter with you?" asked Rico. "Jack and Duke double-crossed us; they're working with the militia. I'm calling Ono" said Houston. "What about Jennings?" asked Rico. "He is still in there, those snake motherfuckers. We got to get the hell over there and see what's going on with these guys" said Houston. "No time" yelled Ono as he came sprinting into the room. "What do you mean there isn't time, I have to save my comrade" said Houston but not before Rico motioned to both to watch the horror that was taking place on the screen. "Oh shit, this is bad" said Houston. "They aren't going to kill him; they're going to kidnap him for ransom" said Ono. "It could be worse, maybe they will torture him until they give up information about the Organization. Gaden, you, and even me" said Rico. "All of the men have been bought out, the CEO of the company gathered intel and now all of the guards on the inside work for him. We don't stand a chance" said Ono. "Ono, we have to do something, we can't leave Jennings in there, if I could just get my hands on one of them damn traders" said Houston. "Where did these guys come from anyway? Gaden seems to have a keen sense of character when it comes to people" said Rico. "Gaden didn't pick these guys, Stone did, claiming they were stand up guys that he had previously represented. Hey, you don't think Stone..." said Rico before getting cut off by Houston. "That son of a bitch, Stone set all of this up, that low-life cocksuckin' motherfucker." "Guys, the CEO is a very important man here in North Korea, double-crossing him is like double-crossing God" said Ono looking nervous as he continued to speak. "I must come back with you to America. If I don't, I won't live past tonight." "Nobody is going back to America until we get Jennings, how hard is that to understand" said Houston. "Frank, there is no way that we will be able to get him out unless we get more guys, is there any way you can contact anyone else?" asked Rico who was trying to improvise on a way to correct the situation. "We got a team of al-Qaeda friends who stay about 100 miles away. The only problem is they live in the woods and typically don't like visitors. "In this situation, I think we might have to..." said Houston before being cut off by a call from the radio. "Frank, this is Duke, unfortunately we had some problems. Had Jennings cooperated he would still be alive now." "So, you are telling me that you and that fucking Backstreet Boy reject killed Jennings?" asked Houston. "No, we ordered the guards to shoot him with all of the fury in the world" said Duke. "What do you want Duke?" asked Houston. "It's simple we want what Gaden has, we want all of his secret connections to the CIA and FBI, we want knowledge of his operation, and we will take $100 million or else" said Duke. "Well, Duke, I will tell you like this, you will get nothing that you asked for, but you will get a bullet in your head very soon and you can count on that" said Houston. "Oh Frank, such a tough guy, you won't be so tough when we go public with all of this, nor will you be so tough when Gaden falls right into our trap" said Duke. "Well, I hope these guys are ready for war, the last person that killed an Organization member ended up beat, fucked in the ass with machine guns, repeatedly shot, and thrown from 30,000 feet in the air so I hope you guys have it all planned out, but then again you two are too stupid to plot anything like this so I hope you guys are ready to get fucked" said Frank as he shut down the radio. "Alright Ono get us the hell out of here, all of the money is in place, but we have to get out of here. "The limo is outside let's get..." said Ono before shots began to be fired. "Fuck, where are the guns?" yelled Houston. "Over there" pointed Ono to an artillery closet that was slightly open. Four armed men attempted to storm the war room but were shot by Ono's men. Rico, Houston, and Ono all hid in the artillery closet until they didn't hear shots. Houston stepped out first to see one of Ono's men dead and all four of the assailants scattered from the entrance and all over the passage from the ground level. "I think we got them all" said one of Ono's men. "That's good, but let's carefully get out of here" said Houston.

Slowly they all crept up the passage, stepping over dead bodies and they reach the top to be greeted by Jack, Duke, and the CEO. "Well Jin, nice job you managed to kill all of my hitmen, but I have two of the best right here. Thanks to these two men, I am going to be able to go into the 'war room' and steal all of your evil little secrets" said the CEO. "I don't think so" said Rico as the ground shook and the sounds of an explosion went off. "Noooooo!!!!!!!!!! What have you done?" yelled the CEO who took off running towards the explosion. Jack and Duke looked nervous about what was to happen. They raised their guns, but Rico and Houston raised theirs as well. "You know just for being some coward ass traitors it is going to feel good to blow your heads off" said Houston. "Oh, I see that you didn't know about my self-destruction mechanism, well to watch you men die will be a great feeling" said Ono. The sound of gunfire erupts into the dark forest, as Rico and Houston fatally shoot Jack and Duke. Jack is shot 7 times in the chest by Houston with perfect precision. Duke is shot in the arm, shoulder, leg, stomach, chest, and finally throat as he choked on his own blood while begging for his life. "Damn Rico, you really aren't a killer" said Houston as he chuckled at Rico's poor shooting. "What do you men want?" asked the CEO as he came back close to the group. "We would love to have Jennings back, but that can't happen now can it? You dumb fuck, now we will have to kill you like we just did these two stupid fucks" said Houston. "Or, the CEO can buy his life" said Ono rubbing his hands together. "Buy his life? He bought his way to hell, I'm not letting him live" said Houston. "Well, let's take him to Gaden,

the ultimate judge, jury, and executioner; let him decide" said Ono. "Okay, that can

work, Ono tell your men to take this garbage out. Let's take this piece of shit to the

boss" said Houston who now pointed his gun to the CEO's temple and brutally hit

him with the butt of the gun "get in the fucking car bitch." The CEO obliged and the

men all climbed inside of the limo and headed back to a Pyongyang airfield. "Put a

bag over his fucking head so no one can see that its him, we got some military

uniforms; put them on. Ono tell security at the airfield that we got $1 million for them

to hear no evil and see no evil" said Houston. "You got it Frank" as Ono immediately

put in the call. Frank Houston was a clear genius lieutenant of a squad of soldiers

hired to execute dangerous missions beyond one's belief. While Gaden

masterminded everything, Frank was certainly the expert of execution of sinister

plans.

Chapter 17

"Where the fuck is Stone?" asked Shapiro, speaking to Dan Taylor, an associate attorney at Justin Stone's Chicago law firm. Taylor had been giving Shapiro the run-around about exactly where Stone could be located. "Listen guys, according to his log, he had a big case up at his New York office. If you guys watched the news you would know about that huge indictment that came down on the DeLuna crime family. Tony DeLuna has been indicted under the RICO act" said Taylor who cracked under pressure. "Well, Mr. Taylor, do you care to explain why your boss has offices in five major markets along with ties to international firms?" asked Jankowski. "Listen, I work out of this office, Justin Stone has been really good to me and pays me a lot of money to handle his low-profile cases. I don't ask why he operates the way he does, but he has visions of being the biggest criminal defense attorney in the world" said Taylor. "Ok, well for now that's all of the questions that I have for you at the moment, but I want all of the locations of all of Stone's offices" said Shapiro to Taylor. "Not a problem, but why do you guys have such an interest in Mr. Stone?" asked Taylor. "Well, it's none of your business, but since you have been cooperative, I will just say that Mr. Stone represented a client that mysteriously disappeared" said Shapiro. "Oh, you must mean..." said Taylor before he realized that he was about to reveal information that could damage Stone. "Mr. Taylor, do you realize that lying to federal agents can lead to a charge for perjury?" asked Jankowski before adding, "you just told us that you don't know anything. Now you were about to reveal information involving this case. Save yourself now, because Stone wouldn't do 5 years for you." "5 years? Hey man, I got into law because I wanted to stay out of jail, not go in" said a concerned Taylor. "Well, it seems that you know something about this. If you would like to have a confidential conversation with us, that is fine. Trust me Mr. Taylor, Stone won't know that we talked and it will be beneficial to your own well-being, as well as assistance in helping federal agents nab a fugitive" said Shapiro to Taylor who seemed to be ready to help the agents get on track for this case. "Gentlemen, I don't know much, except that Stone was on the phone going on and on with someone and he told him that he was going to love this kid Rico Jones. The next thing I know I heard that Jones had disappeared, and the FBI was investigating the MCC. Other than that, I have no clue about what is going on. I swear..." said Taylor who didn't want to pass this information but reluctantly did so because he didn't want to be involved in anything that Stone may or may not be involved in. "Well, thank you for that information Mr. Taylor, by any chance did you happen to hear this guy's name?" asked Jankowski. "No, but he might be a business partner of Stone's" said Taylor. "Business partner?" asked Shapiro. "Yeah, Stone has several investments on the stock market also in real estate and I remember him being a major player in a deal with some chemical company... Gresham, I think" said Taylor. "Really? Because Gresham was loosely tied to some illegal chemical sales in Montana, and when we were beginning to get close, the owner of the warehouse was murdered... In cold blood" said Jankowski. "Well, that would have been nice to know before I started talking to you guys..." said Taylor who now had become scared for his life. "No worries, Mr. Taylor, we will not allow that same thing to happen to you. But I will say that it is greatly appreciated that you were willing to work with us. If there are any issues just call" said Shapiro as he handed Taylor a card with his contact information. "Thank you, gentlemen, and I will stay in touch" said Taylor. Shapiro and Jankowski walked out of the office and there was a form of relief. On one hand, they had gathered information on the whereabouts of Stone and pinpointed him as one of the men involved with the company that was sold to Gresham. The only issue is finding concrete evidence that Stone was the guy who had coerced Harden to go into business. "I don't know about you, but I think Stone's new name is going to be Glass" said Shapiro who had made a poor attempt at a joke. "And why do you say that?" asked Jankowski. "Because once we get him, he is going to break" said Shapiro who picked up the phone to call Washington to allow he and Jankowski to travel to New York.

"Stone, you lowlife scum-sucking piece of shit. What the fuck happened to my millions that I have paid you for this shit?" asked Tony DeLuna, head of the DeLuna crime family, the biggest and evilest of all of New York's five families. "I paid you millions to get the Feds off my ass, and what happens? Me and my whole crew gets pinched on some racketeering beef. And to find out its all under the RICO? You got some explaining to do…" DeLuna continued with his dissatisfaction of Stone's work. Tony DeLuna was a short, fat, Sicilian man with a tanned skin complexion and oily, slicked-back black hair. He looked something like Danny DeVito, but not as short. He had risen to power by murdering numerous marks, including two off-duty New York detectives. He had beaten the case through some jury and witness tampering and because he didn't rat, he earned a high-ranking in the family. Upon the death of the Don, he had moved to underboss. He and that boss never saw eye-to-eye and at a New Year's Eve party, DeLuna and two of his henchmen walked right in, unmasked and killed him. No one said anything... And when he went in front of the Commission, they demanded an explanation. The wrong explanation could have had him murdered. However, after some clever maneuvering, he walked away from the Commission with not only his life, but control of the family in which he renamed in his own namesake. "You are going to get me off of this fucking beef... Dead or alive!" said DeLuna with his cold blue eyes. Stone sat in a chair and took his chastising in silence; he had gotten sloppy with delivering bribes. Once upon a time ago, Stone never mixed business with pleasure. He delivered the bribes in a firm no-nonsense manner and demanded that they oblige by their agreement or face severe consequences. Now, he had gotten so comfortable with all his connections that he delivered thousands of dollars in bribes over a coke buffet with alcohol and strippers in a public place. "Tony, I want to assure you that the money that you gave me was delivered. The Department of Justice is working this one though, and they got some renegade DA from Georgia assigned as the special prosecutor. Don't worry, we'll have to take care of it through the jury. They have sequestered them, but I've got insiders who will give us all the information we need. At that point, my organization will handle it from there" said Stone. "What fucking organization are you talking about?" asked DeLuna. "It's a network, we get things done, don't worry. You don't think that you beat 2 murder beefs, a previous racketeering case, and a weapons charge without a network of people doing everything that needed to be done to beat those cases do you?" asked Stone before continuing "this thing is bigger than me, you, or anyone in your organization. This is the government going after organized crime. And before you start pointing fingers at me, take care of your own guys. What the fuck are you guys thinking? You and all your captains drive Porsches, Ferraris, and Aston Martins. What guy in the construction business drives that shit? You guys parade around the city, mostly Manhattan, in your tailor-made Armani suits and wear diamond pinky rings. Oh yeah, you guys have been under heavy surveillance. What about the rats? This shows poor judgment, you made the guy because he was Italian and could kill a guy, but what about the rest of him? Why didn't you really test the guy, put him under some pressure and see how he comes out. You can point fingers at me all you want, but at the end of the day, your family was doomed when you took over as boss" said a pissed off Stone. "Fuck you Stone, you ain't no fucking tough guy" yelled DeLuna as he lifted Stone out of his seat and pressed him against the wall. "Who the fuck gives you the authority to tell me how I run my family. Yes, that's why membership has increased because I take care of my guys. But make no mistakes, the toughest wise guy can become a rat when he is looking at spending the rest of his life in prison." "That is correct Mr. DeLuna, but I am certain that by releasing Mr. Stone and calming down, all can be resolved" said Gaden walking in the room lighting up a cigar flanked by Bradshaw with his weapon drawn. "Hey, you fucking moolie, put that gun down now!" yelled one of DeLuna's henchmen drawing his own gun. "Hey fuck you wop" yelled Bradshaw as he raised his gun higher. "Hey, Vinny, put the gun down. I'm sure this gentleman here can get his uh, friend to do the same" said DeLuna as he stared Gaden down. The tall, well-dressed Italian man named Vinny puts his weapon down and so does Bradshaw once Gaden looks at him and nods his head.

"Well Stone, let me guess this guy is either a fucking cop or a kingpin. Hey between you and me I have made millions from heroin, maybe we can do some business" said DeLuna assuming that Gaden as a well-dressed Black man must have some ties to the drug underworld. Gaden laughs at this statement and looks at Stone. "Let's just say that me and Justin here has some deals in the work, but as much as I would love to venture with you in the heroin business, I have not been involved in that business in over 10 years." "Fair enough, so what the hell are you doing here during my time? My attorney and I are having a very serious conversation" said DeLuna. "Well, obviously, I can help you or I wouldn't be here Don DeLuna. Now you want to know about that DA covering this case. His name is Everett McKinley, a DA with dreams of becoming a Supreme Court justice. He will be arriving in New York one week from today and will be highly protected at The W" said Gaden with a smirk on his face. "Huh? Where the hell did you get all this information? And how do I know that I can trust you?" asked DeLuna. "Tony I told you that my people get things done" said a now cocky Stone. "Well, no one, and I do mean no one would give this information without expecting a fee of some sort" said DeLuna. "How about a favor, I would say that I am well set from the standpoint of money. Let's say that you guys get to Mr. McKinley and all the sudden you get some unknown DA to move the trial along and you get the opportunity to buy him off. That would save all of you. So, I would think that it would be necessary to do something for me. That something would be this: A hit on an undisclosed lawman who has become a problem to me and my operation. Do we have a deal?" asked Gaden. "Hey, I'm lookin at takin out a DA, specially brought in for my case. I don't believe that taking out some police officer would be much of a problem" said an ecstatic DeLuna. "Good, well why don't you come back tomorrow, and you will have all of the information necessary to get to Mr. McKinley" said Gaden. "Sure thing, but who are you? Some private eye or something?" asked DeLuna. "Let's just say I am your Guardian Angel" said Gaden hesitant to reveal his identity. "But if you really need a name on me, why don't you just call me Mr. Black." "Okay, Black, I will be back tomorrow. And Stone, you be sure to have my information. Let's go boys" said DeLuna as he and his cohorts left the office.

Waiting for DeLuna and company to clear the office, Stone began to speak. "Man, you guys saved my ass" said Stone. "Fuck that, why don't you explain to me why Conley is busting my balls about Montana and all of my other moves right now?" asked Gaden who wasn't too happy. "Well, considering that many cops including a county sheriff lost their lives, I would say that you are lucky that all he did was bust your balls" said Stone walking over to his desk, pulling out a bottle of scotch and pouring himself a drink. "I suppose you are right well fuck it he won't be a problem for too much longer anyway. Have you heard from Frank?" asked Gaden as he took a seat. "No, and I am starting to get worried. I mean usually Frank would find a way to get in touch. I don't know man, this seems to be one of the most dangerous missions to send these guys on, especially Rico, I mean the kid's first mission and you send him into a war zone" said Stone. "What do you care? It's a win-win for us. If they are all killed, then there is no trace. If they survive, we are hundreds of millions of dollars richer. Sure, it was risky, but I trust Frank to lead the team to do what is right" said Gaden as he reached for the scotch bottle and a glass and poured himself a drink. "Well I just hope you are right about this, not to say that your high-risk high-reward stunts haven't worked in the past, but don't you think that it is time to look into other ventures?" said Stone, who not only poured himself another drink, but now stood up and looked out of the window of his Manhattan office. The office had a magnificent view of the New York skyline as well as the Statue of Liberty. It was blocks away from the site of the 9/11 attacks, but thinking of those attacks reminded Stone that power, no matter how strong, can be brought down when a stronger force blindside it. "Is someone getting scared? Aren't you the guy who decided to get involved in the weapon industry? Who decided that real estate wasn't enough side money to make with a six-figure salary? I don't want to hear anything about other ventures. What the fuck do you think I am doing here? My guys are putting their lives on the line to move us into world power. Don't worry about other ventures. Worry about getting DeLuna situated, worry about putting us in play with some of these billionaires in the oil and technology industry. Hell, a sit down with Warren Buffet would be nice. You are our squeaky, clean genius of law and investment, let me worry about the overall direction of the team because we will eventually be legitimate and when its time, your job and my job will intertwine and we will take over the world" said Gaden who really had Stone's attention and reminded him that Gaden's international dealings no matter how dangerous was the reason that they were able to hobnob with the high society. "Nice speech, if I didn't know you, I'd think that you were trying to run for mayor" said Stone who always put a humorous spin on serious situations. "Stone, I would kick your ass for being a jerk, but I don't have time, I have to get to my office and sort some things out" said Gaden as he finished his drink, adjusted his suit jacket, and walked out of the door with Bradshaw flanking him.

Stone stared at them as they headed to the elevator and then closed his door. His true intentions were now needed to take shape, at one point he trusted Gaden because he was working as power broker for Conley who was with the CIA. However, Gaden had gone completely rogue from Conley. The only reason Stone hadn't reported the North Korea mission to Conley was because he was playing chess with this situation. Gaden was a loose cannon, a wild card. As cunning and intelligent as he was, he still possessed a temper and a prowess for violence that could scare the most dangerous serial killers. So instead of starting a war head up, he decided to try and outsmart him which was very difficult. Gaden was not only a criminal mastermind, the man was a certified genius with an IQ that was at least 20 points higher than his own. But Stone knew that his next move was crucial because he could easily find himself embroiled in this sinister plan with Gaden forever, or he could give himself an out. He had an ace in the hole, but he had to play it the right way. As he pondered his next move, he decided to call Taylor in Chicago.

"Dan how is everything?" asked Stone. "Everything is going good, no major issues at all" said Taylor. "Did our friends come by?" asked Stone who now seemed to be making his next move on the chess board. "Yes" said Taylor. "Did you tell them what I told you?" asked Stone. "Yes Justin, look can I get the hell out of here?" asked Taylor. "Yeah, go ahead. And Dan, good job" said Stone as he hung up the phone. Stone had planted the seeds, if he gave the feds a little help to gather information, he could double-cross Gaden and get his ticket out of this craziness that he gotten into, he had planned on giving up the whole operation, but first he needed to bring Conley over. However, that could be difficult since Gaden had made Conley millions, but if Conley didn't want to get crossed himself, he could easily give Gaden to the sharks. But first he needed to find out if everything had went as planned in North Korea. Jack and Duke were two very ineffective idiots and for $100,000 he knew that they would throw their lives away; he had been prepared for all angles. If Jack and Duke somehow prevailed, the operation would be dead, and Conley would shut everything down and cash out. However, this was likely not going to happen. So, when they failed, they would be killed and wouldn't be able to tell exactly what happened. He and Gaden would take the money that they came back with and move forward with Stone still working his angle with the feds eventually leading them to Conley.

Chapter 18

"I haven't been to New York in over 10 years," said Shapiro, as he and Jankowski landed at JFK airport in Queens. "Well, at least you have been here before. Tell me, how is it that an investigation that started as a wire fraud took us from San Francisco to Montana to Chicago and now to New York?" asked Jankowski who was beginning to get to wit's end with the length of the investigation. "Well, I'd say that we are shoe-ins for promotions. Look Cody, I know that this is one of the hardest things that you have probably done in your life, but hey kid it's the grind of the Bureau. I know you're tough, other than that I would have recommended you fly back to the office with the Captain. So, let's just get to the bottom of this case and then we can go back home as heroes" said Shapiro who Jankowski was looking at with true admiration. Jack Shapiro had really made an impression on Jankowski as he had gotten winded by the whole situation. "Well Jack, let's just make this our focus. Crack the case and get back home" said Jankowski as he now found his sense of purpose and got ready to dive into the Big Apple.

"Wild times fellas, Im just trippin' on all of this money" said Rico, who couldn't believe the dangerous caper that he had pulled off. Unfortunately for him, it was done in solitude. Secretly, Rico missed Jordan and couldn't help but to think about her. The adventure, the money, or the services from foreign concubines couldn't satisfy his thirst. "Rico, you were brilliant, I never doubted that you were good, but to know that you could access all of that money and move it to where we need it to be? That is just outstanding. Kudos" said Houston as he raised his champagne glass and toasted with Rico. "Fellas, this is the start of a new adventure. We lost a soldier in the line of duty. But that's okay Jennings will be loved and honored in true Organization fashion. But as for us Rico, straight to the top" "Well, I hope it is for me as well I put a lot on the line in this situation" said Ono in his heavy Korean accent. "Don't worry about nothing Ono. We're going take care of you, first thing first, we must get you a citizenship and some fake credentials from South Korea. Then we can use you to set up some new business ventures for us" said Houston. "So where is the CEO?" asked Rico. "Oh, I got him tied up in the bedroom" said Houston who began laughing at that thought. "So, what are we going to do about Stone? I know you just want to take him out on sight. But I think we need to ask him what his intentions were" said Rico. "Fuck that, I'll handle Stone, the boss needs to know if he can't trust this guy. I mean don't get me wrong Stone has been a solid member and has helped us branch out into bigger and better things. But, if he is trying to double-cross the boss, then we will have some issues" said Houston, a loyalist to the cause. "I'll tell you this much, if the boss says he wants him offed, it's a done deal." Frank Houston couldn't stand to think of Stone double-crossing Gaden. He had been with Gaden since the beginning when he got the crazy idea to start selling weapons. Houston had proven his loyalty to the Organization by being the one who did all the "dirty" work. Before he was the operations commander, he was a simple street thug who had spent 2 years in the Marines before being dishonorably discharged for disobeying a direct order in combat; that order was to murder a 12 year old militia member in Bosnia who had already given up intel, the way Houston saw it, there was no need to kill a child who had given all of the information necessary to catch their

perps. However, his commanding officer didn't see it that way. As a street thug,
Houston had a chip on his shoulder because he saw that in America, so long he put
his life on the line he would be loved. But because he was Black, there was no true
opportunity so life must be taken into your own hands. When he came home, Gaden
was the biggest drug dealer and was dying to get into the weapons industry. So, he
decided to be the one to take the risks and let Gaden handle the masterminding.
Houston learned combat tactics and strategy in the Marines, so he never worried
about his life. He just needed Gaden's connections to keep him out of legal troubles.
Once Justin Stone became a member that was the last of his concerns; but had Stone
really tried to cross them? Or was he just a naïve recruiter who trusted some idiots
with some major tasks? One thing that was for sure, he was going to get to the
bottom and find out what Stone was up to.

"This is it, the Gresham Corporation" said Jankowski, who felt a heavy weight
lift off his shoulder. "Well, let's get to it" said Shapiro as he was walking in the door
to greet the receptionist. "Hi, I am Special Agent Jack Shapiro, and this is Agent
Cody Jankowski of the Federal Bureau of Investigation" said Shapiro to the
unsuspecting receptionist. Gresham had a beautiful lobby that emulated many of
the fancy Manhattan banks; high ceilings, contemporary colors, artwork, and
elegant marble floors. "How may I assist you?" asked the receptionist, a 40-
something blonde woman sitting behind her desk drinking a cup of coffee. "Yes, it
is to my understanding the CEO of this company operates out of this building at the
top floor. We were hoping to have a chance to discuss some things with him" said
Shapiro. "Well, I am sure that Mr. Martel would cooperate with you by all means,

but he is not in at the moment" said the receptionist. David Martel was one of the most rich and successful men in New York City. His father was a researcher who made brilliant discoveries in the use of explosives and the compounds needed to create them. He went on to make millions by patenting his ideas and not selling them until he squeezed the life out of the industry. He earned more millions in selling his patents at which point his son began to implement mergers, acquisitions, and changed the name from Martel Innovations to simply Gresham; named after his biggest acquisition, which he paid a cool $250 million. "Do you know when he will be back by chance?" asked Shapiro who hoped to gain some information from that question. "Actually, he won't be back until next week sometime. He is out of town conducting business" said the receptionist. "If you don't mind us asking, where is he currently?" asked Jankowski who upset Shapiro with that question. "Well, I am not at liberty to disclose that information sir" said the receptionist who cut her eyes at Jankowski. "Ma'am pardon my partner's shrewdness, but we are working on a case that the Gresham corporation may become the centerpiece of, now it would be nice to talk to someone who could be close to this situation. Is there another officer of the company that I may be able to speak with? Perhaps a CFO, a COO, even a vice president" said Shapiro who was now desperate to gather information. "I believe that Ricky Herrera is available, he is the Junior V.P. of operations" said the receptionist who immediately picked up the phone to phone Mr. Herrera. While she called, Shapiro began to feel overwhelmed, he didn't know if it was the wear and tear of so much traveling without adequate rest or was his mind tired of trying to connect the dots of the case. Whatever it was, he surely didn't believe that he would quit after coming this far. It was as if he had to obtain what he was looking for, an answer for the string of issues that had arisen as he was investigating this case. Was it a trap? Were the perps trying to lead him to them? Or was he simply paranoid because he couldn't fathom how they could do all the things they were doing. "Yeah it's been a wild ride" said Shapiro as he looked at Jankowski, who just gave him a nod of agreement. "Ok, I will send them right up" said the receptionist to whoever was on the other end of the phone. "Alright gentlemen, Mr. Herrera will see you on 20th floor, room 2007. Walk over there to elevators, go up, and when you come off, turn right and you can't miss it" said the receptionist who was actually very helpful. "Thank you, ma'am," said Shapiro as he and Jankowski headed to the elevators. "Jack, I believe we are getting closer to the end of this thing" said Jankowski. "Well, if this guy knows just a little bit of information, then it will help this case get closed. I mean look once we put it altogether and secure some indictments, we can just let the courts handle it from there. But we are gathering solid stuff" said Shapiro who optimistically took a step into the elevator once the door opened. Jankowski followed and they both headed up to the 20th floor.

Chapter 19

After walking through the massive traffic of the Manhattan streets, Gaden and
Bradshaw found their way back to his office. Walking past the front desk, Gaden
noticed a very familiar face and knew instantly that something wasn't right. "Well, if
it isn't Mr. GQ himself" said David Martel, CEO of Gresham. "David, what a pleasant
surprise; what brings you to my headquarters?" asked Gaden who was still in shock
of seeing Martel. "We need to talk" said Martel who instantly began walking
towards the elevators, more than likely, trying to avoid exposure to the public.
"Well alrighty then" said Gaden as he looked at Bradshaw and shrugged his
shoulders. Gaden already knew that there was an issue, he hadn't seen Martel in 2
years and yet here he was in his office and needing to have a "talk." Gaden and
Martel had masterminded a huge acquisition to ensure that they would both make a
huge sum of money and stay untouched. Gresham bought all the chemical plants
and warehouses from Stone and Gaden who had illegally constructed them. They
were gold mines but couldn't be used by either of them because they didn't have
the permits or clearance to build or operate them. So, after getting everything
together, they used Harden to operate their major distribution point in Montana and
pitched it to Martel. Upon hearing how they had so masterfully put all these
operations together but couldn't legally open them for business, Martel dove in.
How could he not? The labor-intensive construction and expensive overhead of
funding construction were done. So, he paid $75 Million dollars for the rights of the
entire operation and went on to make hundreds of millions closer to the billions from

all that they had put together. Harden being murdered and the on-going investigation had really begun to worry Martel.

Upon going to the top floor of the building, they all exit the elevator to see Amber working hard; she was giving herself a manicure while on company time. "Oh my Mr. Gaden, I was on my lunch break" said Amber who instantly came up with a lie to rationalize why she would be doing a leisure activity at work. "It's fine Amber, I have an urgent meeting right now so just continue with your ugh... lunch break. Brief me on all that has been going on when I finish" said Gaden as he followed Martel, who now had walked into his office. "Yes sir" said Amber who watched as they closed the doors in relief, she had never been a slacker, but with Gaden spending so much time out of the office as of late, she had gotten quite lax in his absence.

"So, what's going on Gaden?" asked Martel who was so panicked that he couldn't have a seat. "David, please, relax" said Gaden who walked towards his mini bar, which looked significantly low, "guess Amber has been getting antsy" thought Gaden to himself. "Would you like a drink?" asked Gaden. "No, but I will tell you what I would like, an explanation" said Martel, a short White man with brown eyes, brown hair, and bald spot; possibly from years of stressing over being rich and successful, and even though he was, he still stressed on going broke. "An explanation you say? Well, I would need to know what I am explaining" said Gaden who helped himself to a simple bottle of water and went behind his desk. "An explanation for Montana and Harden. How is it that a shit load of cops ends up dying and Harden takes bullets to the chest for some shit that he didn't even know about. Hey, I thought you guys were businessmen like me. Now I see that you are nothing more than gangsters who muscled their way to success" said Martel who still hadn't sat down and was still pacing back and forth. "I don't know what I am going to do, but I will tell you this much, I'm not going down for this bullshit you got me? Did you know that Feds are at my office right now talking to Herrera?" asked Martel who was really uptight about everything. "Really" asked Gaden who surprisingly didn't know. Gaden had prided himself in being in sync about what the Feds were doing regarding his capers. However, this time he was left in the dark. "Yeah really, but luckily, I always worried that this would come back, so I had a contractor install a silent alarm that my receptionist can push so I can jump in my escape chamber, that I also had specially designed. The escape chamber is a one-way elevator, that takes me directly to the car garage and I can leave in the escape car; the car has phony registration, plates, and tinted windows" said Martel who was relieved just based off his own genius. "I see, so what did they want to know?" asked Gaden who had to readjust his focus to the point at hand. "Hell, if I know, I'm waiting on Herrera to give me a call" said Martel. "Well, how do you know that you can trust him?" asked Gaden who had become quite concerned. "Simple, he only knows what I told him" said Martel. "I see, and what did you tell him?" asked Gaden. "Just that there was a deal that I was involved in that could at some point in life generate attention from the Feds" said Martel. "Well, had you told him nothing, then we wouldn't be worried about him double-crossing you" said Gaden who looked upset that Martel would even reveal that much information. "What's done is done. But I will say that Herrera is the perfect guy for this type of questioning" said Martel. "And what gives you that type of confidence?" asked Gaden. "Well, Ricky is very... dare I say, naïve. This guy just wants to move up in the company and he is willing to do anything and everything to do so" said Martel. Gaden thought for a minute, what if Martel was working with the Feds to give him up? Also, what would happen if Conley got wind of the Gresham deal getting turned upside down; that this could be breaking point of their success leading to disaster. "I hope you know what you are doing David. Let's be honest, we are all up shit's creek if this thing blows up in our face, but if you say your man is as good you think he is, then there should be no issues and we can strategize on keeping them off of the case" said Gaden who now confidentially waited with Martel on that phone call.

"Gentlemen, how can I help you?" asked Ricky Herrera, a very well-dressed Cuban man with a very trendy spiked hair style; reminiscent to the Jersey Shore cast. "Well, we can start with a warehouse in Montana. How is it that as soon as we question Harden, he ends up shot and disposed of? Hell, the bastards even left the surveillance video at the scene so we could see how it all went down" said Jankowski who got straight to the point with Herrera. "Listen I assure you that I don't know anything about that. This is all I know; Mr. Martel flew out there to talk with some businessmen who were the actual owners of the warehouse. After some negotiations, he had bought the warehouse to use as a distribution point to some of his Western operation" said Herrera. "Ok, that makes sense, but what about the man who purchased chemicals from Harden and used those chemicals to murder several police officers?" asked Shapiro. "If I were to take a guess, I would assume that this man was some serial killer with a vendetta against local authorities. I watched coverage of it on the news network, but I never heard them say that the perp had been apprehended" said Herrera who now sat behind his desk with a calm presence. "Well he hasn't, there was an APB out on the suspect, but he has disappeared without a trace. Furthermore, after watching the surveillance video, I believe that the guy was a doppelganger; he dressed himself up to look like the suspect" said Shapiro who had a feeling that Herrera was going to play dumb, but actually had the information necessary to open this case up against Martel. "I see, well why don't you tell us about Justin Stone" said Jankowski. Herrera looked shocked; he didn't expect the agents to know about a correlation of any form between Gresham and Justin Stone. "I am not sure of the exact details, but Stone was part of the deal with the Montana warehouse in some shape form or fashion" said Herrera who was now unsure about his choice of words regarding Stone. "Interesting and you are sure that is all you know? I would hate to think that you would withhold information from federal agents investigating. Remember this Mr. Herrera; this is a case in which officers of the law were savagely murdered for doing their job. Not to mention that a $250,000 wire fraud has led us down this road. Don't get yourself in too deep" said Shapiro who was hoping to intimidate Herrera. "Well, if I knew more, I'd tell more" said Herrera who was beginning to get nervous but was fighting for it to not show. "Alright Mr. Herrera, here is my card give me a call if you get any more information about Mr. Stone or even the whereabouts of your boss. If all of this turns out to be true, realize that you would be working with a man who has committed federal crimes on many levels. I don't think I would want to protect someone who puts me in the line of fire, especially if I didn't want to really be there. Have a nice day" said Shapiro as he and Jankowski began to walk back toward the elevator. "Wait" said Herrera who had a moment of clarity. He pulls out a pen and pad and began to jot down some information, he then hands Shapiro the note and says "Have a great day" before closing the door to his office. "Whoa, that guy is good" said Jankowski as he and Shapiro walks to the elevator. The note lets them know that he does have more information, but it might not be wise to speak about it in the office as Martel may have the place bugged. He agrees to meet them in the Bronx near Yankee Stadium at 9 p.m. to discuss in detail what else he knows. He writes that he will arrive in a limousine and will be parked on East 155th Street not too far from the expressway. "What do you think this guy is going to tell us?" asked Jankowski who had a big smile on his face. "I don't know but I can guarantee you this much, this guy knows where Martel is, and he as scared as shit" said Shapiro which spawned laughter from Jankowski.

Ricky Herrera now found himself in a real jam. He was ordered by Martel to report that the agents had left and that he was now in the clear. Unfortunately, he now saw that there were some serious issues going on that could blow up in all their faces. The most important thing to do was to get him out of the situation as fast as possible. So, he had some time to think if he would meet the agents in the Bronx or would he stay with Martel. One thing for certain he had to call Martel and let him think that he was still with him 100%. How could he not? David Martel had given him the opportunity of a lifetime. Herrera was born in Havana; poor with no hopes for the future. His mother snuck him into the country on a banana boat in the middle of the night and they did what they had to do to make it from Florida up to New York. Living in one of the worst sections of the Bronx, all young Ricky could do was accept the mistreatment from his classmates because of his raggedy clothing; but he was smart. He made straight A's through high school earning a scholarship to Fordham University. That scholarship opened a window with Gresham, starting as an intern and now Vice President of Operations. David Martel had heard about the young man's aspirations and gave him the opportunity to grow. If getting involved with Martel could lead him to being implemented in a criminal investigation, then Herrera had to draw the line of his loyalty. Unlike Martel, Herrera didn't have millions to fall back on if anything was to ever happen. While he did make a six-figure salary, him being arrested and losing his job would be the end of life as he knew it.

"Hey, great news; those fuckers are gone" said Herrera who snapped into character quick. "Great news Ricky, I assure that you told them what I told you to tell them" said Martel who had gotten relieved at the fact that Herrera had gotten them off his trail; so, he thought. "Of course, nothing more and nothing less but what do we do now?" asked Herrera just trying to get a feel of the situation. "What the fuck do you mean we? I got it from here Ricky, you don't have to worry about getting too involved in this situation just make sure you handle your end of the job. Now let's keep our eyes on the prize; I need you to go down to Jersey and check on the Eastern distribution center. Make sure everything is going good, gather a few reports and turn it in when you get back" said Martel who wanted to keep Herrera as far away from this mess as possible. "Sure boss" said Herrera who promptly hung up the phone. "I love that guy" said Martel with a big smile on his face, "he always just gets the job done. I'd say he is a shoo-in for President of the company. "Well while you are rejoicing, let's focus on what we have going on here" said Gaden who had been anxiously waiting on that phone call with Martel. "Sure, what's going on?" asked Martel. "I think that it's time for you to get out of dodge for a while. I didn't know that the Feds were looking into this shit" said Gaden who now was ready to reveal his discomfort to Martel. "Oh, come on man, I think that you are overreacting. Ricky said we're good and I know that I can trust him so we're good" said a confident Martel. "Listen to me David, you will leave town for at least 2 weeks. You like and trust Ricky, right? Well he can run the operations, your VP of finance can run the money, and your President can do everything else" said Gaden, who seemed to be hell bent on getting Martel out of the picture. "And what would happen if I didn't leave?" asked Martel who was getting irritated with Gaden's demands. "Let's just say that the unspeakable will happen" said Gaden with a cold stare. "Let me remind you of something Mr. Gaden, I made you. If it wasn't for me, you and that idiot Stone would have gotten booked for racketeering years ago. Not to mention that I know things. Oh yeah, I know about you and Conley's secret dealings. Millions in weapons supplied to the Cubans, Iranians, and the al-Qaeda. I know about your militia operations in Egypt, Turkey, and currently, North Korea. I don't think you want to fuck with me" said Martel who looked at Gaden unphased. Gaden was shocked at how much Martel knew. At this point, murdering him was the only option simply because Conley had revealed information to him unnecessarily. However, why did Conley tell Martel about all of this? Gaden sensed a double-cross on the horizon and was deadlocked on his next move. Killing Martel would relieve one issue but what about Conley? In war, just like chess, it is necessary to avoid capturing a pawn for the overall goal of winning. So, in this case, as much as it killed him to do, he would spare Martel until he could sort somethings out. "You know what David? You are right, I am overreacting. It's just the stress of my operation, along with these damn Feds sniffing around" said Gaden who verbally apologized but mentally still intended on murdering Martel. "Its fine, I'm sorry for saying what I said man. We have made hundreds of millions of dollars together; we need to find a way to avoid these kinds of spats" said Martel who extended his hand to Gaden as a sign of good faith and friendship. "Listen, I am going to get out of here I got some investments to go and see about in Long Island. Why don't we catch up tomorrow and see exactly where we're going to go with all of this?" said Martel. "Sure thing, money is always a good way to relieve stress" said Gaden with a slight laugh. "You got that right" said Martel who was walking out of the door.

Gaden followed him out to the elevator and waited for him to get on before turning back to Amber. "Now on to you, why would you be at work giving yourself a fucking manicure Amber? Do you know what that makes me look like?" asked Gaden. "No Mr. Gaden, what?" asked Amber who was getting nervous. "It makes me look weak, in my office" demanded Gaden. Amber followed him into the office and closed the door. "Mr. Gaden, please don't fire me, I need this job. I have told you before that I would do anything to work for a man of your caliber. Please just let show you how much I mean that" said Amber who began to walk closer to Gaden. "Oh really, and how do you plan to do that?" asked Gaden who kind of had an idea of what Amber was up to. As she walked closer, she kissed him and pushed him down in his chair. Within 60 seconds she began unbuckling his belt and proceeded to have oral sex with him. Gaden couldn't believe it was happening but after so many stressful events in such little time, some relief was in order. Amber was quite good, better than several prostitutes he had in the past. Minutes later, Gaden released and Amber stands up and smiles at him. "Well, my dear, I'd say that a write up will not be necessary. Here is a room key to the W room 812, tonight at 10, be there" said Gaden who began to fix himself up. "Oh, I would be honored, I'm glad I can be of service to you" said Amber who walked out slow and sexy so Gaden could be happy with the decision he had made. Now it was time to decide what he would do next, one thing for certain, he had to get in touch with Frank to see was going on with the operation.

"It's the Boss" said Houston who could now get signal as they crossed the Atlantic. "What's going on?" asked Houston who promptly answered the cell phone. "You tell me Frank, it's nearly been a couple of days, how are things?" asked Gaden. "Well, things got crazy, we need you to meet us at the airfield asap" said Houston. "I'm in New York, you will have to land in Jersey" said Gaden. "Ok, that'll work, you actually told me at the right time we're not too far off course" said Houston "Frank, don't tell me too much at this time as I would like to see for myself, but is this a good crazy or a bad crazy?" asked Gaden who would have liked to have some kind of comfort about the situation. "Well, Boss, I would tell you that it's not too bad, but then I would be lying. Nothing we can't handle, but it is definitely a bad crazy" said Houston. "Alright, I'll get everything set up and meet you guys out there, how long?" asked Gaden. "Give us about 2 hours and we'll be there" said Houston.

"Over and out" said Gaden. Houston had a serious dilemma and so did Gaden.

What to do with a man that Ono dubbed as "the most powerful man in North Korea?"

Furthermore, what if Gaden is pissed about the way that he handled things, and what

if bringing Ono back was a bad idea? These things worried Houston to a certain

degree, but for the most part he just wanted to get to Jersey as quick as possible just

to see how things would play out.

Chapter 20

Rico had his own thoughts running wild. What would he do about his mother, Jordan, Brandon, everything? What had he really gotten himself involved in? In one trip, he had gained access to a lot of money but was all this necessary? Maybe had he just stood up and took responsibility for his actions than none of this madness would be going on. However, did Gaden really leave him a choice? They had his mother, they knew where Jordan was, and somehow, they had used Brandon in a conspiracy. He began to wonder about his choices and if he could start over at some point in time. All he could do was really sit back and wait to see how all these situations played out. Maybe if he could get in contact with Stone, he could find a way out of all this madness.

McNamara sat in his hotel room tracking several devices that Rico had been known to use. For him, this was a deeper case than most could ever understand. He had an interest in Rico that the rest of the bureau could never know about. But if he knew his own true intentions and knew what evidence he was looking for, then he knew all would be ok if he stayed focus. The thing was where was Rico? He knew that he had somehow gotten involved in something that would cause him to disappear without a trace. Suddenly his phone rang, and it was Director Rogers. "Hello sir how is the case moving from where you sit?" asked McNamara who quickly snapped back into action. "Good, we've got an ID on that fingerprint from the van, but still haven't found Harden" said Rogers. "Alright, I will get right to work on locating that person. Could you send that information to me?" asked McNamara who was now interested in this mystery person. "No problem, hey McNamara would you be interested in meeting a few agents and going to interview this person? It is imperative that I get back to Washington so I'm going to leave my team here to continue to work with the Montana initiative and I am going to get back to bureau" said Rogers. "Sure thing, where am I going to meet with these agents if you don't mind me asking" said McNamara. "You're going to love this, right there in Chicago. The person's last known address was in Chicago. I think that whoever is involved in all of this has been trying to throw us off their trail. This guy is nearly identical to Brandon Schultz and with a few alterations to his appearance, could easily pass for him" said Rogers. "Wow, that is amazing" said McNamara who knew, better than anyone, that Brandon Schultz wasn't their actual perpetrator. "His name is John Richer and has a rap sheet as long as my arm. Here is something more interesting; in his last case he was represented by Justin Stone. Now here is a guy that was not only an idiot, but a career criminal with no known work experience. I am trying to figure out how he could even afford Stone's services. I don't know exactly how or why, but Stone knows something it is important to not only find Richer, but Stone as well" said Rogers. "Well, sir, I will begin investigating his whereabouts and send you information as I gather it" said McNamara. "Alright, well since Shapiro has been anointed lead agent, you can report to him, but since I am personally giving you this assignment, I would like to stay in the know about everything that is going on. Good luck McNamara" said Rogers who promptly hung up the phone. The second in command of the FBI had just given McNamara an objective and that made him smile, not only has his intelligence and hard work paid off but he is as close to the case as he wanted to be. What the director had done was played right into McNamara's hand.

Upon getting the information, McNamara immediately got Agent Brown on the phone. He knew that while he could go vigilante and do it alone, it was safe to have an experienced agent go along with him. "Agent Brown, this is Agent McNamara, the director has just sent over some information regarding the investigation in Montana. There was a fingerprint left behind in the van that took the warehouse owner away and the person of interest's last known address was there in Chicago" said McNamara. "Well, come on down I'm at the office. Oh, and you're going to love this, one of the suspended guards finally came clean about the Rico Jones situation. Apparently, he was paid $100,000 to look the other way while some guys infiltrated the facility, posed as inmates, and sprung Jones. The thing is Jones had no clue that it was going to happen, so this could be kidnapping. Just come down and we'll figure out what's going on with that, as well as your lead" said Brown who had done an excellent job with continuing the Chicago investigation with the departure of Shapiro and Jankowski. "Alright, on my way down" said McNamara as he hung up the phone. This was now beginning to puzzle McNamara, who would want to spring Rico without his knowledge? Rico had an unbelievably high IQ, could the thugs that he was running schemes for had sprung him? Or was it a higher power who learned of his whereabouts and sprung him to participate in some secret operation? Whatever it was, he was going to get to bottom of it.

"So, is everything moving how we planned?" asked Stone to a man that he had picked up his cell phone and called. "Yes, but Justin, I need you to be sure that you know what the hell you're talking bout" said the mysterious man. "Of course, look I will get all of the information you need to bust up this assassination attempt. Everett McKinley's life is in danger and as a practicing attorney, I feel the need to protect the life Mr. McKinley" said Stone who had so much conviction in his voice. "Alright Stone, but I might need you to wear a wire and get all of this information recorded" said the mystery man. "Alright, sir, no problem, I am just scared for my life and in having this information I feel safer working with you guys than those guys" said Stone. "Well, when will this meeting be?" asked the mystery man. "First thing in the morning, the guys are going to make the arrangement before court" said Stone. "Well, it sounds like Mr. DeLuna's bail needs to be revoked on some random reason. You will have to make that happen Stone" said the man. "Yes sir, I thank you for taking the time to listen to this Dir. Rogers, I assure you that you will be pleased with the results" said Stone, revealing that Deputy Director David Rogers was the man on the other line. "Stone, once you complete these objectives, I will need you to promptly report to Washington where you may need to be placed into protective custody. "Not a problem sir, by the way, where would I be able to get this wire?" asked Stone. "Oh yes, well I have a few field agents out of San Francisco working a case" said Rogers. "Wow sir, what brings them all the way to New York?" asked Stone. "Well, they are searching for some stockbroker who bilked a few affluent people out of millions, one being of the York family, owners of the San Francisco 49ers" said Rogers, who had knowingly lied to Stone because he had fell right into their trap. "Alright sir, well you tell your guys to give me a ring so we can set up a time to meet" said Stone. "Will do" said Rogers as both men hung up the phone. Rogers couldn't believe this. Justin Stone was a person of interest in the wire fraud/explosion/Gresham case. Had he not known that the feds were looking for him? Either way, Rogers looked at it as an opportunity to not only uncover this case but this assassination plot on Everett McKinley. What Rogers didn't know, was that they were both connected.

Upon hearing that everything was beginning to fall into place, Stone broke out a gram of cocaine and made 3 lines. After he separated the lines, he rolled up a $100 bill and began snorting the cocaine line by line. When he completed the third line, he slouched back in his chair and began to space out. Most of his spacing was due to the cocaine rushing up his brain and flowing through his blood. But there was a part where he didn't know what he was doing. He had committed to betraying Gaden before this assassination came into fruition so he could still save himself. He began to think why should he be loyal to Gaden and Conley? Neither of them could be trusted, plus they both held an advantage over him; they both had armies of soldiers trained to kill at the drop of a dime. If they ever felt that they couldn't trust Stone, he could easily disappear. By aligning himself with the FBI, he could not only get that army of killers, but he could also come out as the last man standing and retain his worldwide successful law firm.

Chapter 21

"Alright we're landing right now" said Houston motioning to his crew that it was time to get everything ready. As they landed Rico and Ono grabbed the CEO and headed to the exit. "Make sure that sack doesn't come off his head. The last thing we need is some nosey motherfucker seeing this dude's face" said Houston as he made sure that the CEO's identity remained concealed. "Mr. Houston, I can make you a very rich man" said the CEO. "Shut the fuck up" said Houston as he punched him in the stomach. "Frank don't rough him up too much, he could actually be a valuable asset" said Rico. "You're right, the government might have some use for this piece of shit" said Houston. "Prepare for landing" said the pilot as the jet hit the pavement and began to slow down. Looking on the airfield Houston immediately noticed a limo sitting far off and knew automatically that it was Gaden. Gaden always would meet them at the airfield because it usually took a few phone calls and payoffs for one of their jets to land without any questions being asked, plus he wanted to be sure that the jet came back in one piece and wanted an immediate briefing of the mission. "Is that Gaden?" asked Rico. "Oh yeah, the Boss usually always beats us to the scene" said Houston. "Cool, I just hope he doesn't blow a gasket when he finds out about all of this" said Rico. "You and me both" said Houston who was staring at the limo and thinking to himself about how he could make any of this make sense to Gaden.

In Chicago, McNamara walks into the FBI field office downtown to meet with Agent Brown. He is still puzzled on this scheme to spring Rico, but what really surprised him was how Brown secured the confession. Upon entering he is questioned of his identity; he promptly shows his FBI ID and can walk into the back of the building. A routine normal looking facility and was more formal than the other makeshift headquarters he had been at in Montana. "Hi, I'm looking for Agent Marcus Brown" said McNamara to an agent who was probably of high rank. "Sure, keep down to the end of the hall and turn left. His office will be to your right, room 104" said the agent. "Thank you" said McNamara as he continued to walk. One thing he noticed about this office was the silence as if they had soundproof rooms in all offices. Either that, or they just did all the dirty work upstairs. "Agent McNamara, good to see you" said Agent Brown who was in the middle of writing report. "The information that you gave me on the phone was riveting, but how did you get the guy to confess?" asked McNamara. "Oh, I have my ways..." said Agent Brown who began to chuckle. He motioned McNamara to follow him and they walked out of the office. They walk down the hall and Agent Brown opens a door to the right and reveals that it is an interrogation room. "This is Officer Martin, one of the dumbasses that was on duty when they walked out of the facility jumped into one of the vans and high-tailed it" said Brown. "Look man, I'm sorry, but I just don't want to go to jail ok? I got a newborn baby at home. I swear I will give all of the money back" said Officer Martin, a frail Black man who had a drug addiction. He had been reprimanded once for testing positive for cocaine on a random drug test. "You junky motherfucker, do you realize that you have put people's lives in danger? You disgust me. Don't worry you won't go to jail, but you better sign this agreement right now or we're going to fry your ass" said Brown. He slid Martin the paper and a pen, and after staring at the ceiling for a few moments, he signed the deal. "Good job, but here is what I want to know, what interest did these guys have in Rico?" asked McNamara. "Sir, honestly I don't know they just said that they had to break him out it was an order" said Martin. "An order from who?" asked McNamara. "That I don't know, but they always referred to him as 'The Boss'" said Martin. "So, what you are telling me, is that there is some higher power calling this play? Interesting" said McNamara who now seemed intrigued at the idea of someone having enough power to order someone to be broken out of prison, federal prison at that. "Sir I swear that's all I know, I can tell you that there was a guard in on it too, yeah his name was Murphy he pretended to be a guard, but he was one of them too" said Martin. "Really? Now how is it that none of the other CO's seemed to recognize that this guy wasn't real?" asked McNamara. "Well, his story was that he transferred from another state, so he actually had papers and everything that said he was a CO for the Bureau of Prisons. But the day they got Jones out of there he left with them and was never seen again" said Martin. "So, this guy didn't play his card until the job was done, so now we must go down to the facility, gather some surveillance, and try to find out who this guy really was" said McNamara. "Nice work kid, I'm starting to see why the director likes you so much" said Agent Brown. "Just sit tight somebody will be in shortly to follow up with you Martin" said Brown as he and McNamara headed out. "So, what do you think is the deal with the Richer guy?" asked McNamara. "I get the feeling he was just another hired idiot, the x-factor here is Justin Stone. We have to find that guy" said Brown as they walked out to the garage and got in one of the Bureau's Chevy Tahoes.

As the jet landed, Gaden stood there eyeing the jet anticipating what waited. "Hello, gentlemen" said Gaden looking at Rico and Ono. "Ono, I am surprised to see you here… I was not made aware of any visitors. Where is Jennings and Frank?" asked Gaden. "Well, Gaden, that's what we need to talk about" said Rico with no hesitation, "but first, it might be wise for you to pull your limo up closer. We got a package that we need to get in there really fast." "Well, why don't you bring the package out, I would love to see it" said Gaden with a sadistic look on his face. "Frank" called out Rico, "the Boss says bring the package out." In a matter of seconds Houston exposed the "package" to be a man in a suit with a sack over his head. "You sure you don't want to get the car?" asked Houston. "I'll be right back, keep that up there" said Gaden walking fast and motioning the limo driver to pull closer. "Alright you motherfuckers, what is this shit?" asked Gaden who was now infuriated. "Well, we get there to pull the job off and low and behold your boys Jack and Duke double-crossed us when they got inside and got Jennings killed" said Houston. "Are you kidding me? One of my best soldiers is dead because two pee-ons decided to get big-headed? So, what happened to those fucks?" asked Gaden. "That's the best part they were tempted by this asshole" said Houston as grabbed the CEO's neck and squeezed, "and showed up at Ono's war room, they had no clue that it self-destructed killing their manpower and me and Rico here took the honors of killing Jack and Duke. But we wanted to deliver this genius straight to you" said Houston shoving the CEO in the limo as it approached. "Great work, but you mean to tell me that those two-bit idiots had the balls to double-cross us? That makes me wonder what Stone was thinking bringing these guys in" said Gaden. "I don't know what's going on with Stone, but I will tell you what Boss, you know it's nothing for me to find him a hole in the woods" said Houston. "No, let me find out what possessed him to recruit some flakes into my organization and if it comes down to it, I want the joy of killing him my damn self" said Gaden as they all entered the limo.

As Agent Brown approached the rundown neighborhood in Chicago's Logan Square area, he began to wonder if Richer was really from this area or was it some phony address that Stone put on his file. Only time would tell as he turned right off Milwaukee Ave. onto Central Park Ave. and hooked a quick left on Wrightwood Ave. "This is it" said McNamara who looked around the neighborhood to see if could develop any kind of idea who this Richer guy was. He and Agent Brown approached the home, which looked old and decrepit, and attempted to ring the doorbell to no avail. "I don't think this thing works" said Agent Brown who immediately began banging on the door saying, "Federal Agents we are looking for John Richer." After a few knocks the door opens and an older White man with gray hair appeared. He and McNamara immediately show their badges to establish identification. "Good day sir, I am Agent Brown, and this is Agent McNamara of the Federal Bureau of Investigation. We were here to ask a few questions about a man by the name of John Richer." "Alice" said the man who looked irritated as opposed to concerned, "some agents are here asking about Johnny." "So, you know Mr. Richer?" asked McNamara. "Sure, he's my son. A good-for-nothin' lowlife, but my son nonetheless" said the man. "Well sir, if you don't mind, I'd like to ask a few questions about some of your son's activities of the last few weeks or so" said Agent Brown. "Well, hell, I don't know what the boy has been up to. Last time I heard from him was about a couple of months ago when he mysteriously made bail and got off on some credit card scams, he was running. He said he was ok and that he was going to make everything right. Hell, I didn't know what he was talking about; I thought he was loaded when he called. But the next thing I know, you guys show up" said the man who had no problem exposing that his son had gone down a path in life that made him a career criminal. "So, he not only made bail, but got off on the case? If you don't mind me asking, where was he running these credit card scams?" asked McNamara. "I don't know, hell, he was probably down there in Humboldt Park with some of those damn Puerto Ricans he loved hanging out with, but I am sure that it was some deep shit this time, I mean you guys are the Feds right? Sounds like Johnny got a hell of a fight on his hands this time. What did he do jump bail?" asked the man. "Well, sir, it's not that simple. He was cleared on the case, but now he is a person of interest in a murder in Montana and for the bombing of a cabin that killed several decorated police officers, including a county sheriff" said Agent Brown. "Well, he really is in some deep shit, now isn't he? You know? I told that dumb ass boy years ago to get his act together, but he kept chasing that damn fast money now he is knee deep in shit and can't escape. Oh, don't you boys worry, if I see him, I'm going to turn him in. I'm too old for this shit, worked hard all my damn life to give my kids everything I never had, but then there is always that one rotten apple. Got a card?" asked the man who was very bitter at his idea of the American Dream being thrown flushed down the drain. "Sure sir, and yes please if you encounter him just give me a call and we can end all of this madness, I am sure you would love to enjoy your retirement" said McNamara. "You're damn right, Donald Richer" said the man extending his hand to Brown and McNamara. "You have a good day sir" said Brown. As the two agents left the house, they began to converse about the possibilities of what they just heard. "I think he knows more" said Brown the more experienced, non-trusting agent who believed that he was always right. "Yeah, but what if he doesn't know more?" asked McNamara who began to wonder about the integrity of a man who fathered a son who would take part in a heinous crime as what happened up in Montana. "Well, whatever the case is, I'm going to try and get more information on what this guy is" said Brown. "That's all fine and dandy but let's focus on what we do know... He was locked up, made bail, had Stone representing him, and was part of this Montana thing but he is nowhere to be found. Let's put out an APB on him so if he is doing anything anywhere, he will be picked up and we can go from there. The x-factor in this equation is Stone. If we find him then we will be ok. Shapiro and Jankowski have already been to his office here in town. But maybe they can visit his office up in New York and locate him. He knows too much because he wouldn't be hiding if he didn't" said McNamara. "Damnit kid, you're really on your way up the ladder. You're right, hell with Richer he was just a pawn in a bigger game than what we're all focusing on. What if Stone knew something about the Rico Jones thing too? I mean hell, he was his lawyer even though Jones actually had the money to pay him" said Agent Brown. "See now things are starting to really open up Brown. I'm going to head back to the hotel and get in touch with Shapiro and see if I got any hits on my traces. I will link back up with you so we can review" said McNamara as they both got in the Tahoe and headed back downtown. "Excellent idea, it sounds like Stone is the guy we really need to bust this case open" said

Brown who was overly excited as he started the vehicle and headed back towards Milwaukee Ave.

Chapter 22

The limo began to head back into the city and Gaden was lost. "What the hell am I supposed to do from here?" thought Gaden to himself as he contemplated where he would take the man. He began to get frustrated and snatched the sack off the head the CEO and was surprised to know exactly who he was. "Son-Li Kim, well while I am surprised to see that you would have the balls to attempt a stunt of this magnitude, it doesn't surprise me that you could have the brain power to mastermind this caper" said Gaden. Ono, in complete surprise, looked at Kim and Gaden, then asked, "You two know each other?" "Sure, Son-Li was one of our intelligence officers stationed in Asia. This fucker is Korean but was born right here in New York. He was recruited so we could have an Asian connection to all our contacts in Korea, China, the Philippines, Thailand, and Japan. The Asian culture doesn't feel comfortable unless there was an intermediary. Then all the sudden he disappeared about a year ago, which is when we brought you in Ono" explained Gaden. "Yes, these are true" said Kim, "but explain this to me Gaden, you are an arms dealer, when the hell did you get into stealing government funds?" "Oh Kim, over the last year we have been venturing into many different things. You chickened out and ran off. Now they call you the CEO over in North Korea? Who did you kill and how the fuck did you get a gang of Koreans to work for you?" asked Gaden. "It wasn't hard, money talks, especially in North Korea. A man appears with millions to give the President and all his men and an army of his own, it wasn't hard to be put in position. And with North Korea being communist, they just simply turned over control of businesses and several government operations to me" said

Kim. "Well, Kim, is that why you had Jennings killed? Because he could expose who you were?" asked Gaden. "This is exactly why. I figured that I get rid of him word wouldn't get back to you or Conley. But I supposed my plan failed. Gaden you will certainly kill me, but before you do, I have intel for you about your good friends Conley and Justin Stone" said Kim. "Oh really, this should be good, and what information might that be?" asked Gaden. "Conley is getting scared; he believes that you and the Godfather are loose cannons who don't have the operation's best interest at heart. He has gotten Stone to see things his way and they are currently working on a plan to not only sabotage the operation, but to take you down" said Kim. "Well, it doesn't surprise me that Conley is getting scared, the Godfather has always made him nervous, but I always felt that his ultimate goal was to use me as a tool to not only kill the Godfather, but to carry out his bullshit then have me killed as well" said Gaden who now looked to go into deep thought. "Ok, I am lost" said Ono, "who is the Godfather and what role does he play in all of this?" "He is the true mastermind of the Organization; he stays hidden and only communicates with me. No one, and I do mean no one, not even Frank knows who he is" said Gaden. "It's true, I have been down from the beginning and have never seen the guy" said Houston. "Conley plans to do things that's against my best interest like send me to Turkey to deal with al-Qaeda operatives who are inexperienced and only want to cause destruction... His plan would have been golden if he didn't forget one detail, that I am always one step ahead" said Gaden. "Let me ask you something Kim, if all of this is true why did we have to capture you to get this information? If you were really a friend of the Organization, then you would have contacted Gaden from the beginning. How are we to believe that you aren't working for Conley?" asked Rico. "Well, if I was working for Conley, I would have known you were coming" said Kim. "That's where you're wrong Kim, this mission was not sanctioned by Conley my team gathered the intel and went in under the Godfather's orders, not Conley's" said Gaden. "Even if I did work for Conley, he would abandon me now you guys know better than anyone that if you're captured Conley has a CIA mentality, he will not come save you and you are on your own" said Kim. "This is true, I think the Montana thing might really have him scared, I haven't talked to my mole in the FBI, but I will soon enough... So, Frank what should we do with Mr. Kim here? I mean not only did he double-cross us, but he had Jennings killed. Hell, for all we know, he might be working for Stone. What if Stone and Conley are working separately on double-crossing us?" asked Gaden. "That's true Boss, I mean we really don't have any use for Kim unless he was to help us set up Conley and take out Stone... But I don't believe that he has the balls to take part in anything like that" said Houston. "I had the balls to take over an entire country and reveal this information with the risk of still being killed, how could I not?" asked Kim. "All of that sounds good but once again instead of dealing with the music when you saw Jennings you had him killed therefore we must avenge his death" said Gaden, "However there is one way you can save your own life" said Gaden. "If you don't work for Conley or Stone or whatever, I want you to call Stone and put him on speaker and see what he thinks about your friends Jack and Duke and their double-cross. We will change the number of a phone and the number that will show up will be a North Korea number... you will tell him that Rico Jones and Frank Houston are dead and that you are plotting on taking me out, upon telling him this I want to know his reaction and see how he responds so I will know how to deal with him" said Gaden. "No problem, when do you want to do this?" asked Kim. "Now" said Gaden very sternly. Gaden needed to know for certain that Stone was trying to double-cross him and wanted to see if he and Conley were in cahoots.

"Jack, you're never going to believe this, Richer had to be working for Stone, me and Brown went down and talked to his father and he told us that Richer had mysteriously made bail and got off on a case for some credit card frauds" said McNamara, who had promptly gotten back to his hotel room and contacted Shapiro. "That's great McNamara, some lowlife mysteriously makes bail, beats his case, and have Justin Stone representing him? Just doesn't sound right" said Shapiro. "Tell him what we're doing Jack" said Jankowski who was very excited with their next mission up in New York. "I'm getting to it" said Shapiro to Jankowski who promptly redirected his attention back to the phone, "we've got Stone." "Wait, what? how the hell did you guys do that?" said McNamara. "Well, apparently he hasn't been hiding he's been here in New York hard at work on the Tony DeLuna case. Rogers called us from Washington and said that Stone was about to bust open an assassination plot against Everett McKinley, a high-profile Federal DA from Georgia who is currently campaigning to be Attorney General. They are bringing him in because they know that DeLuna has enough money to make this case go away. Well, according to Stone, DeLuna and a mob of other guys have got the drop on McKinley and plan on having him killed before the trial can get underway. Cody and I have the honor of wiring Stone up before this big meeting that all of these guys are going to have in the morning" said Shapiro. "Wow, talk about an open and shut case" said McNamara who began to laugh, "I guess the guy here didn't let Stone know that he was wanted for questioning" said McNamara. "You know what? I didn't think about that. What do you think is really going on here Josh?" asked Shapiro who was now taken aback a little. "I think that Stone is scared out of his mind for some of the things that he is involved in a now wants to rollover on all of his cohorts" said McNamara. "Yeah, he must feel the pressure and he knows that the heat is closing in on him, better to work for us then against us. Well, keep us posted on any new information you get, we are supposed to be meeting Ricky Herrera, one of Martel's lieutenants at Gresham to see if we can connect the dots on Stone and this deal Gresham made out in Montana" said Shapiro. "Alright, hey Jack, I bet after all of this good investigating you're doing you will be a shoo-in for a promotion, maybe a post right in Washington" said an optimistic McNamara. "Josh, after all of this I think all of us will be doing some major moving up with the bureau" said Shapiro who then hung up the phone. He never took the time to think that this case could open more opportunity for his career. Sure, it was draining and tedious, but he knew that only good things could come from so much dedication. "That kid is a hell of a motivator, isn't he? Maybe one day he'll be director" said Jankowski who finally got a chance to relax as he and Shapiro were back at their hotel room putting pieces of the case together and waiting for their meeting with Herrera later that night. "Why do you think Stone would get himself wrapped up with crime lords? Here is a guy who obviously was a law genius created methods in trial to bring up reasonable doubt and got several high profile criminals off, hell he probably could have gotten DeLuna off just with his litigating skills" said Shapiro who couldn't understand how a man of Justin Stone's caliber with intelligence and a legendary career as a criminal defense attorney be so ignorant to the decisions that he made. "I'll tell you why" said Jankowski standing up to express himself, "Because he is a greedy, lying, conniving snake whose only interest was in money. Hell, you see him on the news talking about how he wants to give everyone a fair chance of decent legal representation. He got that one drug kingpin off, uh what was his name again? Terrence Jackson, they called him Cutthroat. This guy ran cocaine from San Diego and spread it from there to LA, Kansas City, Chicago, Philadelphia, New York, and who knows where else. The agents on the case did a great job with surveillance, even sending a guy undercover. He got so deep that the prosecutor was sure that Jackson was going down for at least 50 years, hell the guy was worth $100 million. But all the sudden the undercover agent comes up dead, the jury acquitted him, and even after a retrial he was acquitted again. Stone is a hell of a lawyer, but I think he paid some people off in that case. Which is just my point, Stone is a lowlife just like the rest of them he just has money, a law degree, and is a licensed attorney. If it wasn't for those things, he would be another pee-on." "Wow didn't know you felt so strong Cody, it sounds more personal than anything" said Shapiro. "Look, Jack, we're out here on the grind busting up the bad guys while Stone is living in a life of luxury helping the bad guys out and when it gets too hot, what does he do? Just rat them out, it's not fair that some of us work our ass of and some of us just has the best things passed on to them" said a frustrated Jankowski. "Rest assured that we're going to bring these assholes to justice. No one is above the law" said Shapiro patting Jankowski on the back to help calm down his spell of anger. "Look, just wake me up when it's time to go meet this Herrera guy" said Jankowski who finally settled down to take a nap. Shapiro began to contemplate his next move; Herrera could open some doors on Martel who would in turn open some doors on Stone. It would be nice to not only shut down an assassination plot, but to put Stone out of commission. He was dirty, he was the one who set up the deal out in Montana; he was the one who hired someone to unleash an explosion at that cabinet; he was the one who corrupted Martel having him sell Gresham out for profit; finally, he was the one that got this kid Rico Jones on the lam, where were all of them? What was Stone really involved in that has him doing all of this? It was fascinating, but at the same time all Shapiro wanted to do was just get him in custody so they could ask some questions and get some honest answers. Stone was a criminal defense attorney, so without some charges, he wouldn't say anything.

After planting a chip in the cell phone and having Rico verify that the number would appear as a North Korea call, Gaden handed Kim the phone to put the call into place. Kim looked nervous almost as if he didn't want to make the call. However, with the thought of his life on the line it could have been anxiety as to ensuring that the call went right. "It's ringing" said Kim. Gaden calmly nodded his head and motioned to everyone else in the vehicle to keep quiet during the call to be sure that Stone wouldn't get the idea that he was being set up.

Stone was in the middle overlooking the DeLuna case. He felt that if he was doing business the way he had always been then it was a no-brainer in to how to beat the case. The first was to view all the video surveillance that was in question. Though he hadn't seen any of them yet, Stone could imagine that Tony DeLuna was calm and reasonable as to how he was conducting business. DeLuna was never big on talking over the phone only saying things like "let's meet at the place" or "why don't you come over and talk to me." He never would have been dumb enough to say what he wanted or needed done in his office or his restaurant or anywhere that he felt the Feds could bug him up. Only an informant could gather that intel by wearing a wire. But now Stone was faced with the issue, who was the snitch? This would only be an issue if he hadn't given himself an out from DeLuna and this whole assassination plot. This was not Stone's idea, and that is probably what ate him up the most. "How could Gaden contract a hit without my knowledge?" is what Stone thought to himself. McKinley, though ambitious and looking to fight him tooth and nail, was an innocent bystander. Stone had grown tired of Gaden's rebellion to the plan. The plan was all about money that was it. But once power began to come into play, Stone realized that he would always have more power than him simply because he was a legitimate practicing attorney. He had connections and access to things that Gaden could never get without him. Sure, Gaden had the army, but Stone had the legitimacy that Gaden wanted so bad which what made them a perfect team. An assassination plot was not on Stone's shortlist of things to do to be made. Hell, Stone was already a made man for all the hard work that he had provided for the legal system. Sure, he worked for the bad guys, but the bad guys had plenty of money; blood money, but what does it matter? The money didn't know where it came from. Stone's conscious began to weigh on him heavy. He began to want to withdraw from

Dir. Rogers and get back on course so he could re-legitimize himself with The Organization. The only problem was, where would he want to be after that? At this rate, could they continue to trust Conley? He was the real problem because he had the CIA connections, and with a CIA army, Conley could really hamper things. Maybe he was stabbing the wrong party in the back. Gaden had always proved his undying loyalty to him and for him to turn his back on him now was the biggest mistake he could make. Luckily, he hadn't crossed anyone now, sure he told Dir. Rogers that he would unfold an assassination plot, but who were the real murderers? Not the ones who were going to pull the trigger, but the mastermind who set it all up. While Stone pondered all this his cell phone rang with a strange, obviously foreign, phone number appearing on the screen.

"Hello Justin" said Kim. "Kim... Son-Li Kim, is that you?" asked Stone. "Why yes, it is old friend how are you?" asked Kim. "Fuck you, that's how I am... What the fuck happened to you when we needed you? You were our tech savvy guy. That's how it was, our set up was perfect, I was the legit front man, Gaden the brain and the muscle, and you were the geek. You couldn't get any better than that" said Stone who began to ramble on and on about loyalty. "Whoa, whoa, what is wrong old friend? I thought that you would be happy to hear from me" said Kim. "Happy? You abandoned us in the middle of some major heat coming down and Conley jumping all down our fucking necks" said Stone, "and the worst part is that you don't feel any remorse for running off like the coward that you are. Here is my question, where the hell are you?" asked Stone. "Well some wires got crossed and I ended up here in North Korea. The government gives me full room to operate and I have an army under my belt" said Kim who winked at Gaden, knowing that if Stone was trying to set a trap, this would be his opportunity. "Really? Well I'm sure that your guys can't hold a match to the muscle right in the organization, but I believe our guys will still kick your ass" said Stone. "Oh Justin, how you have not learned that it doesn't matter the skill level of the muscle that you have at your disposal, you don't have an army. Armies are prepared with their own weapons and their own tactics. The government here in North Korea has given me the most honored high title without any political experience" said Kim. "Oh really? And how is that?" asked Stone who was diligently listening. "Well when you come over from with $50 million in cash, a lot of things can go your way" said Kim. "Sounds like you have the right idea... The only problem is, where the hell did you get $50 million?" asked Stone. "Well, over the time I worked with you all, I skimmed a little here and a little there. Not to mention my own payouts from working with you. If you noticed I never spent a penny" said Kim who was smiling because he knew that he had Stone's attention. "Ok, I can see that... But let's cut the crap, why are you calling me after all of this time?" asked Stone. "Well Justin, I have a very lucrative offer for you. How would you like to get out of the law business and come over here and help me run things? I mean you were truly the genius and I need a man with brains to help me run this operation. The only thing you can't tell Gaden or Conley, you would have to come alone and abandon the organization like I did. But there is a catch" said Kim. "A catch? And what might that be Kim?" asked Stone who was focused on what was going on with this conversation. "Well, I would need you to give Conley up to Interpol the only people who could stop him. And for Gaden... let's say you just have him killed altogether. He is a loose cannon and really have nothing to lose" said Kim looking at Gaden who had a furious look in his eyes but kept quiet. "Interpol? Really? Do you think they are strong enough to put Conley to sleep? This guy was a decorated Marine vet and has been with the CIA for 25 years. He is a fucking Commander for peep sake do you think that Interpol would believe me over him? How about this, me killing off Gaden" said Stone who began laughing sadistically at the idea, "look Kim, it sounds like you have a nice thing going on there but it's not going to happen. I stepped into this mess that I am in with these guys because I trust them. Sure, Conley is a dickhead who is the dirtiest player in the game, but we have been doing business for 10 years and if he turns on me, he turns on himself. Don't forget I am an attorney I have plenty of audio and video of Conley's wrongdoings if shit ever goes wrong. And Gaden? Are you out of your fucking mind? How do you kill a guy who not only surrounds himself with killers but is a known assassin and maniac himself? Who am I going to hire? The same guy that killed O.J. Simpson's wife?" said Stone who began laughing even harder.

Kim stared at the phone as Stone was laughing. He looked at Gaden, Houston, Rico, and then Ono as if he knew his fate. Frank Houston had his .50 caliber Desert Eagle drawn the whole time. Rico looked at him but didn't seem threatening and Ono had a look of pity on his face. Gaden coldly stared at Kim as if saying if you don't get information, you will die. At this point Kim could only pull out his one and only trump card and see if it worked. "Justin, I am glad that you think that this is a laughing matter, but I actually came to help you" said Kim. "Well if this is your idea of help, I don't want any part of it" said Stone. "What if I was to tell you that Conley has been listening on the other line the whole time and is now sending agents to

your office to kill you? You talk like a really bad-ass but there is no help for you now

you are going to die Justin" said Kim. "Wait, one minute you tell me that you want

me to go to Interpol on Conley then the next you're telling me that he is on the other

line? Oh, you really fucked up Kim and this is how I know that you're lying. If Conley

has been listening and knows about the evidence, I would already be dead. Second,

if Conley was really on the line then why suggest that I report him to Interpol? Was

he testing my loyalty? Either way it doesn't matter, but I do know this something

isn't right and there is someone on the other end of that phone besides you. The

only problem is who? Can't be Gaden he's right here in New York, so maybe it's

just you trying to lure me into the country so you can kill me. Now Kim, here is what

you don't know, we're currently wrapping a mission right there in your territory and

I am sure you had to know it was going down. Not only that I am starting to believe

that those guys, especially that Rico Jones kid put you up to this. I liked the kid, but I

don't think that he was tried and true and it dawns on me now... Where is he? Tell

that kid that we are the reason that he is making big moves. If he betrays us, he can

stay right there in North Korea with you. He's going to be miserable though, you

guys can only use the internet 2 hours a day right" said Stone who began to

sadistically laugh once again. Rico looked in amazement. What does this do for his

case and everything else he had run from? "Tell Jones he's toast here, I will be sure

to notify the MCC that I have his whereabouts. Come on Kim, you know you don't

want bloodshed all over your country. Interpol is some mean motherfuckers and

won't have a problem putting your brains on the wall to get him back here. You're not that tough though are you Kim?" asked Stone who had lit a cigarette and looked very messy with his hair frizzed over his head and tie hanging off his collar. "Stone, you don't know what you're saying" said Kim who was really getting nervous. "Don't worry about it when Gaden finds out he's going to finger fuck the both of you with a pool stick like he did the Iranians who tried to pay for guns with counterfeit dollars" said Stone, who reminisced on a bad weapon deal with an Iranian terror group that had ended in 4 deaths and Gaden torturing the men for hours. "I don't know a Rico Jones or what the hell you are talking about are you high on cocaine Justin?" asked Kim who was really getting backed into a corner. "No, Kim, I just know that you are a lying coward and for you to call me means that someone put you up to it? Was it Frank?" asked Stone who seriously wanted to go. Gaden had heard enough, Stone was obviously high and drunk, and Kim had gotten way off course with the conversation he motioned for Kim to hang up the phone immediately. Upon that motion, Kim quickly told Stone that he had to go and hung up the phone.

"We've got a problem" said Gaden, once he was sure that Kim had hung up the phone. "Stone has been keeping surveillance of all of us. I never thought that he would be so fucking paranoid." "See Boss, I told you we can't trust that motherfucker; he is going to be the one to put us all down. We got to bring him up on some charges for violating Organization code. We move in secrecy. But how much secrecy is there when he has footage of all of us doing and saying God knows what" said Houston. "We have to throw him off our trail, he can't know what we are going to do next. With this whole DeLuna deal tomorrow I'm going to no show. There is no way in hell that I am going to let him capture audio of me setting up

Conley or assisting in killing McKinley. They will both die, but on my terms. You are right Frank; we move in secrecy and secretly we're going to weed Stone out" said Gaden. "What about me? I mean this guy is the one who masterminded the entire plot to spring me from jail" said Rico. "Rico, your case is different. I can't promise that Stone won't dime you out, but I can promise that you will get paid for your time. Frank, I want you to get the Ford Taurus out of the garage in Harlem and drive him to Chicago. Obey the speed limit and don't do anything stupid. Take him to his mother's hideout on Lake Shore Dr. When you get there, ditch the car and fly back immediately, we got a lot of shit to figure out" said Gaden. "This shit is amazing, exciting, but crazy" said Rico who had now realized the error of his ways, always searching for the easy way out, but he got a hard lesson. The easy way out is the easy way into some things that's harder to escape then what one was avoiding. "No problem Boss, but damn right away? Can I get some rest first?" asked Frank. "Sure, it will be better for you guys to leave at night anyway. Just hurry up and do what you need to do and get the fuck out of here, I expect you back by tomorrow night. Rico, Frank will have your money for you" said Gaden. The limo was stuck in the heavy traffic leaving out of New Jersey heading back into the city.

Chapter 23

Back in Chicago, McNamara decided that it would be a good time to visit Rico's mother along with his girlfriend, Jordan. First stop was to his mother's house, which unfortunately was still vacated. After all this time she still hadn't returned home which made McNamara believe that she knew everything that was going on. But instead of just accepting that theory, McNamara decided to ask the locals what was going on. He proceeded to go to a neighbor's house whose windows could reveal a good view of someone coming or going to the house. He proceeds up the stairs only to see a young Black man sitting in the corner of the porch in a plastic lawn chair. Typically, it would be protocol for McNamara to reach for his weapon, but he instead speaks to the man and takes a chance on him not being a perpetrator. "How are you sir" said McNamara to the young man who was indulging in a cigar filled with marijuana. "Who the fuck are you?" asked the dark-skinned Black man who wore a black Chicago White Sox fitted baseball cap, black jeans, black Nikes, and an all-black hoodie. "Agent McNamara, Federal Bureau of Investigation." "Holy shit" said the man who immediately stood up and changed his attitude, "how can I help you?" "Well, I just wanted to ask about a woman who used to stay next door here. According to city records, she actually is still listed as the owner" said McNamara who really had the man's attention now. "That's Ms. Jones, she had a son named Rico, but then he went to jail. One day I guess a boyfriend, or somebody pulled up in a limo and took her with him. She had several bags with her and there were like 2 bodyguards with the guy. I guess he was like a pro-ball player or something" said the guy, who was obviously clueless as to the grand scheme that was being put in motion. "A black limo?" asked McNamara. "Yeah, but that's all I know" said the man. "So, what would you say about Ms. Jones? Do you think that she was a decent neighbor?" asked McNamara. "Yeah, one of the nicest neighbors one could ever think of. Her son Rico was a genius back in the day even had got a scholarship to some big school out of state, but a little while ago the Feds came and hauled him off to jail while everybody sat out here and watched. I couldn't believe it, Rico really seemed like he had a good head on his shoulders, but I guess you never know who people truly are" said the man. "Cool, well does anyone else stay here at the house with you?" asked McNamara. "Yeah, my grandmother, I look after her. She was pretty close with Ms. Jones too" said the man as he motioned to get up and go in the house. McNamara waited because it might have meant that he was going to check to see if his grandmother was up to talking with him. As he waited, he felt that he was getting things done more rapidly just working the case by himself. But he couldn't help but to wonder why? Why weren't the Chicago agents monitoring this case? Were they on payroll with these guys? Only time could tell as he dug deeper into the case.

"She said come on in" said the man as he motioned for McNamara to come into the house. As McNamara walked in with the man flanking him, he could see a house that was really a home. Pictures of family members perhaps her children as the pictures seemed to be older and the styles of hair on the woman and children in the picture seemed to be of another era. He also saw beautiful furniture and artwork of Christian symbolism and scriptures on the walls. By the time he and the man had reached the kitchen where the woman was located McNamara knew that he was about to talk to a woman who was full of wisdom and would speak the truth about Ms. Jones and her whereabouts, if she knew.

"Hello, sir" said the woman, "can I get you something to drink." "No ma'am but thank you. First, I would like to ask about your neighbor, Ms. Jones. She is the mother of Rico Jones who is a centerpiece of an ongoing investigation that involves wire fraud and a prison escape" said McNamara in a very matter-of-fact manner. "Well, I am Ms. Sherman and Rita Jones has been my neighbor for 10 years. One day I went over to see her, and she wasn't there. I had been talking to her about how her son Rico was holding up in the jail and all she would say is that Rico was in a better place" said Ms. Sherman. "Well, ma'am, did she ever elaborate on what that better place was?" asked McNamara. "No, she just said that he was in a better place and the case would be resolved in a matter of months. I found it strange that she always put me on hold to get on the other line with somebody. One time she thought that she had clicked over, and she said a name... I can't remember that name, but I let her know that she wasn't talking to that person" said Ms. Sherman. "What was her reaction when she realized that she wasn't talking to that person?" asked McNamara. "Nothing too much, I think that she said 'oh, I'm sorry' and clicked over" said Ms. Sherman, who now looked as if she was in deep thought. "BAUER!!!" that was the name that she called!! I want to say that her exact words were 'Hello, Mr. Bauer'" said Ms. Sherman who seemed very pleased to remember the information that was necessary to help answer McNamara's question. "Are you sure ma'am?" asked McNamara who wanted to be sure that he was getting the most accurate information. "Yes, I am... I had never heard of her dating a man by the name of

Bauer or having anyone she had to talk to for any reason by the name of Bauer" said Ms. Sherman. "Ms. Sherman, that is good, that means that whoever this guy is must be plugged into the cover-up of what's going on. Ms. Jones' disappearance, Rico's recent troubles, and answers to every other question in this case. Thank you, Ms. Sherman, but I must be leaving. Before I go, is there anything else suspicious that you can remember?" asked McNamara who suddenly felt optimistic about catching a lead in the case. "No, just that when she left in the limo, that lawyer was with her. The one who used to have those cheesy commercials and now he is a big shot..." said Ms. Sherman right before McNamara jumped in an finished her sentence for her. "...Justin Stone ma'am, he has been a person of interest in all of this, so it doesn't surprise me to hear you say that." "He surely looked nervous looking all around moving 100 miles an hour, I couldn't figure out if he was high on drugs or what, but he was walking around yelling at these big bodyguards that were with him. It took them about 10 minutes to leave and Rita ain't been back since" said Ms. Sherman who noticed that McNamara was very much ready to go, so she got up and walked him to the door. "Ms. Sherman thank you for your help, the Bureau will now be able to go further into this investigation due to your observations" said McNamara. Ms. Sherman didn't say anything just smiled and waved at him as he left to go get into the Tahoe. McNamara was amazed, sure Bauer was a typical name, but he would just run it in Stone's case files to see if a name comes up and if several come up, there would be work cut out for him. In the meantime, he figured that he might as well go and visit the Riley home and see if Jordan would reveal some more information that he can connect. One piece at a time is what he thought to himself, so he wasn't too concerned about the slow development of the case as it was complex.

It was a multi-state investigation that required a lot of attention and details in order to

prosecute it. He felt that his angle of the case was to locate Rico Jones by any means

necessary.

After some rest, Houston and Rico headed out on the road taking I-95 into New

Jersey and switching over to I-80 for a straight shot into Chicago. Houston avoided

all erratic driving, as Gaden told him too, he wanted to be sure that he drew no

attention considering that he did not know if Rico's description would generate any

attention. He was very focused on the task at hand and was quiet. "Frank, what is up

with this hide out where you guys are tucking my mother?" asked Rico. "Well, it was

protection because we knew that one of the first places that some of the investigators

would look is at your mother's house, as it was your last known address" said

Houston. "I get that, but what about my girlfriend? She doesn't know anything, but

do you think they paid her a visit?" "Of course, they did" said Houston, "as many

connections as we have, we can't stop those not in the know from doing their job.

Believe it or not, there are a lot of agents, cops, and others in law enforcement that

we can't buy off." "I could imagine. How do you guys get your missions? Does

Conley just contact you and send you out?" asked Rico. Houston began to laugh as

he found it funny that Rico would now inquire about the nature of their operation

after being thrust into one of their capers. "Basically, now the one that you went on

was sanctioned by us and only us, which explains the big payoff. Our next mission is

going to be in West Africa, a militia recently seized control of a diamond mine and

they need our assistance in securing weapons. Jennings was supposed to lead that team in, but now I might have to. Conley knows that we got a lot of shit going on, so he gave us a week to take care of things. I guess he put in the request while you were sleep, the Boss just told me about it before I woke you up" said Houston, who for the first time gave Rico some deep insight into the Organization's inner workings. If all goes well with this, Conley will truly run the world. But he isn't nothing without us, because his CIA 'tough guys' don't even have the balls to go into the places we go, not even North Korea." "So, I could imagine that he plans to keep you all around for a long time" said Rico. "Not necessarily, Conley has sent us out to cut the throats of some of his most his most longstanding business partners. The CIA has operatives all over the world so he was always paranoid that one of them would run into his customers and would expose his secrets. We never asked Conley what was the point of some of the hits he ordered us to do, but one thing for sure, we carried them out the fullest and we have never missed a mark" said Houston who sounded very proud of the of the dirty work for blood money that he and his cohorts had performed. "So, if Conley ever discovered that you guys went rogue on this mission to North Korea, what would happen? And how did you explain what happened to Jennings?" asked Rico who was trying to figure out his next move. "The Boss told him that Jennings went to Jamaica to talk to some of our members about their dealings in trafficking weed into Florida and they turned on him and killed him. He bought it hook, line, and sinker. As for North Korea, he would have some of his' super soldiers chop us up into little pieces and eat us" said Houston with no smile on his face. Rico stood there lost for a minute, he wasn't made aware that a sinister commander of the CIA who had unlimited power, resources, and militia wasn't let in on this. He began to worry, but then again, it could be his trump card if he needed to use this information to bail out of the mess that he was in. Meanwhile, he would just focus on getting home, seeing his mother and Jordan and explaining everything to them from start to finish. He just hoped that he wasn't hated by them for the decisions that he had made, but at the end of it all, he just wanted to do something that would help the people that he had hurt the most; even if he hurt himself in the process.

Chapter 24

"Alright, this is it!" said an excited Jankowski, as he and Shapiro spotted the car that they believe held Ricky Herrera. "This is going to be what determines how good we are. So much time and effort put into this case this is going to put the nail in the coffin. They pulled up behind the car and immediately cut the lights. They got out of the car and knocked on the door of the back-passenger side of the limo. No response, which prompted Shapiro to knock again. Once again, no response and this prompted him to reach for the door handle. The door opened and Herrera's body completely fell out of the car, covered in blood with a hole in his head and his brain and blood leaking on the pavement. "What the fuck!" screamed Jankowski as he instantaneously turned his head, so he didn't have to look at this grizzly sight. Herrera had obviously been killed only minutes before they arrived as his body was warm which Shapiro discovered after checking his pulse. While checking his pulse Shapiro found a note taped to his shirt. The note read:

Well I see that you guys are searching for some information, too bad
you cost this jackass his life. Poor Ricky, he didn't see it coming, he
must have thought that I was you because he had the doors unlocked,
I just simply opened the door and hit him in head with two quick
bullets. Now let's get to business, I know who you are, but you don't
know who I am. You're chasing something that you have no idea
about; this could lead you to the same fate that Ricky has faced, tell
you what pal just give up and go back to California where you belong.

If you hang around this city too long, you might disappear into thin

air"

After reading this letter Shapiro was in total and complete shock. On one hand who

had the drop on Herrera to know that he would be here? Then again, he could have

been followed and not have paid attention to what was going on. But another

problem that he was having was he didn't know how this person knew that Jankowski

and he were out from California. No one could have possibly known outside of the

agency which led him to believe one of two things: Either A, Jankowski or

McNamara had been using social media and their whereabouts were scattered

across the internet like fantasy football; or B, there was a mole in the agency who

was working for Martel, Stone, or whoever was behind this murder of Herrera.

Upon seeing the murder, Jankowski phoned NYPD to come and pick the

body up and they answered a few questions regarding what they had known about

Herrera. After both Shapiro and Jankowski talked to the local investigators, they

proceeded to get in their Tahoe and leave the scene. "That's it, when we come to

the brink of opening a major case and unearthing possibly one of the biggest crimes

in Corporate America, this fucking bullshit happens. This was going to be the game

changer Jack. I know it. But now look at us, heading back to the fucking hotel to go

and watch HBO. How do we report this to the director without looking like two

complete assholes? He's going to send us back to California on desk duty after this

one I know it" complained Jankowski who was very distraught by the whole

situation, even putting his head in his hands. "Cody, when have we ever been afraid of a little adversity in the time that we worked together? We need to first swing by the field office in Manhattan and make these fuckers answer some questions about possible dirty agents feeding information to lowlifes. Next, we contact Dir. Rogers and let him know that we lost our informant, then get ready for the morning. Don't forget that we have another objective to take care of" said Shapiro. "Well, I don't know how we will fair after all of this, but one thing for sure, I'm done after the meeting tomorrow. I just can't take any more of these let downs" said a defeated Jankowski. "If you do that, then you will definitely go on desk duty. You know the agency is all about your level of toughness so a knock down can't knock you down, it must inspire you to be successful. I think it's time for us to call McNamara and see how his investigation is going on locating Rico Jones" said Shapiro, who motivated Jankowski to lift his head up stay focused on their next newly added objective. As they drove down Grand Concourse heading back to Manhattan, Jankowski realized that this was not the time to quit but to be prepared for the climax of this investigation.

"Are you fucking kidding me?" asked McNamara, who had just been phoned by Jankowski about what had transpired with Herrera. "Well, we have to work a different angle then Cody. It sucks because that would have given us a mass conspiracy, but I will just keep searching for Jones out here and just go from there. I'm actually a block away from his girlfriend's house on the South Side of the city" said McNamara. He hung up the phone and had a bigger determination now to find where Rico Jones could possibly be. He knew that the last piece to connect the dots to Stone, Montana, and his jailbreak was through Jones himself. He pulled in front of the Jordan Riley's home a small bungalow about a block west of State Street off 94th street, not too far from Chicago State University. He approaches the door and notices a significant difference between her neighborhood and Rico's. Her neighborhood had symmetrically cut grass, as if the neighbors came together and agreed to a certain length. There were no people outside yelling or being obnoxious, he could tell that this was probably one of the nicer neighborhoods on the South Side of Chicago. He approached the door and rang the doorbell in hopes that someone was home. A Black man about average height wearing khakis and a casual button-up shirt answered the door. "Hi, may I help you?" asked the man. "Hello sir, I'm Agent Josh McNamara of the Federal Bureau of Investigation. I was hoping that Jordan Riley was home." "That's my daughter, could I ask what your business with her is?" asked Mr. Riley. "Sir, I wanted to ask her or even you per se, if anyone had corresponded with Rico Jones?" asked McNamara who noticed that Mr. Riley's face immediately frowned up at the mention of Rico's name. "Of course, what other reason would you have to be here but to look for that criminal. I told my daughter to stay away from that boy, he was trouble two years ago and he is still trouble. I found out about her going to visit him downtown. I was very disappointed. Jordan is a good girl and the last thing she needs is to be in the company of some con artist who is going to lead her astray" said Mr. Riley. As he was finishing that rant about his discontent for Rico, Jordan comes out of the kitchen to see what is going on. "Daddy, is everything ok?" "Yes, baby, this man wants to know have you heard from that ingrate Rico" "Ms. Riley, how are you, I'm Agent McNamara just wanted to do some follow up on Rico Jones. Has he tried to contact you? We are still unsuccessful at locating him." Jordan held her head down for a minute and folded her arms. The hurt that she felt from not hearing from Rico was eating at her, but she perked up swiftly as she did not want her father to know how she felt about him. "No sir, I still haven't; I honestly want you all to find him I know he is in a lot of trouble, but I would rather him be in jail in your care and not wandering the world possibly getting himself into more trouble" said Jordan. "What about his mother? Would you happen to know where she went off too?" "No, I talked to her about a week before all of this happened but then she had to go because some investigators had come to talk to her. "Possibly federal investigators looking into Rico's case?" asked McNamara. "Sure, but maybe they were actually conspirators coming to let her know of the plan to spring Rico and relocate her; just a thought" said Jordan, who had shocked McNamara with such a brash, and possible, theory. "Honey what would make you say something like that?" asked Mr. Riley. "Daddy, I said that it was just a thought. Think about it, how could he spring himself from jail and then she just mysteriously disappears?" "Here is my card, if you guys hear anything give me a call immediately and I will do the same" said McNamara who seemed to have all the information that he needed.

"Agent Shapiro, we will need you to calm down" said Agent Riordan, a short red-haired White man with freckles and green eyes, obviously of Irish or Scottish descent. "I want answers Riordan, right now!!!... A man is fucking dead because he was going to put Martel and all of his cohorts out of commission, when the director finds out about this he is going to send us back to California, but in the mean time we will get what we need" said Shapiro who was furious at the FBI agents in New York.

To him it seemed that they weren't doing their jobs in no shape, form, or fashion. "Shapiro, there is no proof that Herrera's murder had anything to do with Martel, we don't know what he was involved in" said Riordan. "This is true, but don't you find it strange that he is murdered at the spot that he was going to meet us?" asked Jankowski. "No, I think that whoever killed him had been following him and just waited for the right opportunity" said Riordan. "Fuck this, you just find out where Martel is and get back to us can you do that? Hell send the Marshals if you have to, they are pretty good at finding people" said Shapiro. "I can call my guys and get right to it, though Herrera's murder doesn't implement Martel in anything it does make him a person of interest for questioning" said Riordan. "Thank you" said Shapiro as he and Jankowski walked out of his office and out the FBI building. "These assholes aren't gonna find Martel I think they're on his payroll" said Shapiro. "So, what do you suggest Jack?" asked Jankowski trying to keep up with Shapiro's fast-paced walk. "I don't know yet, but somebody is going to tell us something" said Shapiro as they got into the Tahoe and almost immediately sped down the boulevard. Shapiro didn't know what he really wanted to do about the situation he would not only have to contact the director and Cpt. Nicholson back in San Francisco, but he would have to call Chicago and tell McNamara and the team there that the investigation had hit a dead end. He had to trust that Riordan and his team would locate Martel and that McNamara would catch a break in Chicago before the morning; he knew that if something good hadn't come in the case, they would dead the investigation.

Chapter 25

Gaden sat back in his chair at his office with Son-Li Kim handcuffed to the chair in front of his desk. He couldn't quite figure out what to do with Kim, on one hand Kim had betrayed the Organization and ordered the murder of Jennings and attempted to kill Frank and Rico. On the other hand, Kim was very useful before everything that had happened and could now be an intricate pawn to use in the possible fall out between, he, Stone, and Conley. "Ono, let me ask you a question, what would you do if you were in my shoes?" Gaden asked Ono because for once he didn't already have the solution to a problem that he was facing. "Honestly, I would have killed this piece of shit in the limo and dropped his body on the highway" said Ono who was disgusted at Kim for his disloyalty to the Organization and the attempt on his life. "I figured you would say that, but I need your undying loyalty and because of that I am giving this assignment to you" said Gaden as he handed Ono a knife that was nearly the size of a machete. "No, Gaden, please be rational we can work this out. I have more to offer..." said Kim as Ono sliced his throat from ear to ear. He nearly took his head off with the force that he put into the cut and pushed his body to the ground to let all the blood run out. "Have I proved myself to you?" asked Ono whose hair was now wild, and he was sweating profusely from the adrenaline of the act of murder. "Oh yes you have, because I will be honest Ono, if you didn't have the balls to kill a man then I would have had you and him shot. You can come out now Drake" said Gaden telling his top hit man Tony Drake to come out of a hidden closet in the office. Tony Drake was a 5'11, muscular, dark-skinned Black man who quite often wore suits with bow ties, fedora hats, and thick glasses to give off the impression that he was a man of religion. "Ono, this is Drake he is one of the top guys in the Organization but doesn't want many people to know that" said Gaden. "Now that you do know, it is nothing for me to put you on my shit list" said Drake who seemed annoyed about another person knowing his identity. "You two are going to take out the trash and I am heading to the W. I want confirmation that this motherfucker is six feet deep" said Gaden as he began to walk out of the office but then turned around. "Drake, remember we are shutting this fucker down tomorrow you will head the team to destroy everything." "You got it Boss I will be here first thing in the morning to make sure that it all goes well" said Drake. Gaden nodded and left Ono and Drake to clean up the mess. As he headed to the elevator, he decided to peek out of the window in the hallway. He had never been paranoid up until this point. He couldn't quite figure out what Stone was up to and he couldn't be too careful at this point. After he felt a little more secure, he stepped on the elevator to meet Bauer outside.

As he walked outside, he looked left and right, as well as across the street. Gaden was so nervous that he expected a hitman to be inside of the limo as well as Bauer to be dead; that probably would have been a better outcome then what happened when he got in. "Well, how nice of you to join us. I hear that you are on your way to frolic with some model whore" said Conley who really seemed very laid back and actually wasn't wearing a suit, but slacks and a Polo shirt. "Now what Conley? You have been really busting my balls lately" said Gaden who was really annoyed at seeing Conley. "It is not one of my highlights of the day to see you neither, but this is important. It's about Stone." "What about Stone?" asked Gaden who was wary about anything that had to do with Stone right about now. "Well, he's going to set you up in the morning" said Conley. "Are you fucking kidding me?" asked Gaden who had become very upset at the notion of Stone betraying him. "I wish I was making this up, both of you have been vital to this operation; Stone has cut a deal with the assistant director of the FBI. He is going to meet some agents before the meeting, get wired up, and get all of you trying to set up McKinley" said Conley, which had Gaden nervous because Conley wasn't supposed to get intel on this hit. As a matter of fact, the hit was supposed to be done without it coming back on Gaden or Stone. "Conley, I swear, this thing was put together simply to do a favor for DeLuna, having the mob on our side is very important" said Gaden. "Are you guys out of your fucking minds? You would hire DeLuna, the vilest of all criminals to do a hit on a man who could someday be the president? This isn't the 60s; it's been done and can't ever be replicated. I'm not only pissed at Stone for being willing to open about what you guys were doing but I am pissed that you of all people would authorize something that you knew that I wouldn't. But I forgive you, I just want to get rid of Stone. So, you and your guys are going to go down and wipe him, DeLuna, and everybody else out at the office" said Conley. "One problem, I got a team clearing the office out to avoid any heat coming down, plus I got Frank taking the kid Rico to Chicago to hide out" said Gaden. "You allowed that kid after his first mission fresh from springing him from prison out of your sight? Call Frank and tell him to turn that car around they can't be any further than Pennsylvania. As a matter of fact, because we don't know who we can trust other than the vets, I say you give the green light on him" said Conley who, with that one statement, proved his ruthlessness and lack of concern of human life. "Look I will just get in touch with Frank and have him brought back" said Gaden, "there is no need to kill the kid especially since he has so much use." "Suit yourself, I don't care how you do it, just make sure that meeting gets blown to hell tomorrow" said Conley who made that his exit statement, leaving the limo and slamming the door. Gaden had a few different dilemmas; Justin Stone his longtime partner would now be murdered, by him; not to mention contacting Frank to get Rico back to New York; And he still hadn't forgot about Martel who was hiding. With so much stress a release was necessary, and he wanted to get to the W to get his rocks off as quick as possible. "Bauer head to the hotel" said Gaden who switched his thoughts to Amber's sweet, soft body and how he was going to punish her with all his stress. How he couldn't wait to get to that room…

Stone had spent the entire day cooking up an immaculate double-cross; he would certainly get his revenge for being treated like a tool in an organization that he was the driving force in creating. Furthermore, these agents were from out of town were unknown and unseen by anyone, which was perfect just in case DeLuna got the drop on what he was doing. The agents had contacted him and instructed him to meet them at the docks at New York Harbor. Once they wired him up, he could gather all the information needed to put DeLuna down for a very long time. At the docks, he noticed a limousine sitting near the entrance. He was told that this would be an indicator of the agents. He pulled in front of the vehicle, parked, and waited for a phone call from the agents. Within 20 seconds, he got a call. "Mr. Stone, how are you? This is Agent Shapiro from the FBI, Dir. Rogers sent us to fulfill a request of his. We would really like for you to come get into our limousine so we can get to work" said Shapiro. "Ok, I am on my way" said Stone, hanging up before and exiting his vehicle. On his way to approaching the vehicle a small Bentley Coupe sped up beside him and fired five shots with three hitting him in the chest. The shooter proceeded to exit the Bentley and stand in front of Stone. "You motherfucker, I should have killed you when I had the chance" said the shooter before shooting him in the head point blank, "see you in hell you son of a bitch." The shooter then spits on Stone and jumps back into the passenger side of the vehicle before speeding off. In the process the "agents" jumped out of the limo and run to Stone's aid. "Stone, Stone, damn it don't die" said the imitator who perpetrated Shapiro over the phone. The plan was for Rogers to lure Stone in then be given the opportunity to go into witness protection if he gave up his own crimes. Shapiro was never there nor notified of what was going on simply because Rogers thought that this would have been a simple apprehension that no one would have known about. There was no back up and the shooting happened so quick that they were unable to stop or identify the shooter, as it was only two agents. "What the fuck, this was supposed to be something quick and easy Bruce we didn't sign up for this shit" said Agent Michael Thomas, a Harvard graduate who only joined to FBI so he could begin working on a career in politics. "Mike, shut the fuck up, get the Director on the phone I'll call the ambulance" said Agent Bruce Fuller, a blue-collar head cracker who the Director became very fond of. The director had promoted these two to be a part of his own special operations crew. When he needed a specific job done, he called his crew and they took care of it. Rogers was a man of the law, but sometimes he lied to get what he felt was justice. That same twisted

hypocrisy may have gotten Justin Stone murdered in cold blood.

On the way to the hotel, Gaden decided to call Houston and notify him of

Conley's request. To his disdain, Houston was not answering the phone and since

they moved in secrecy, he opted not to leave a voicemail knowing that he would

eventually get in touch. Perhaps there was something occupying his mind, perhaps

he was in the gas station putting gas in the car, or maybe he had some music on.

Maybe, he had put the phone on silent as to not distract him. Whatever the case was,

Gaden was sure that he would reach him in a decent amount of time to bring him

back. While that thought crossed his mind, he was pulling up in front of the the W,

one of New York's most prestigious hotels that certainly is a beauty right in the heart

of the city. A part of him may have even forgotten about the whole ordeal as he

stepped out of the limo and told his driver to be back at 6 a.m. He looked at the

beautiful hotel and decided to take it all in for a second before he put on his fedora

and sunglasses to seem like a chic New York socialite, though he was using this get-

up as a disguise from the cameras. He walked past security and the front desk,

flashing his key card to show that he was a guest and was just heading up to his

room. He approached the elevator and got an overwhelming feeling of paranoia.

He began to watch the bellhop, the security guards, even the front desk associates.

With it being so late he figured that the only ones that could even come close to

touching him were the employees. There weren't enough people in the lobby to kill

him. That is until he noticed a young woman approach the elevator. Now typically,

Gaden wouldn't feel threatened by a 5'6 slim-built Scarlett Johansson look alike, but then again who could he trust? Stone and Kim had both betrayed him and these were two men instrumental in growing the Organization. He kept his eyes on here through a peripheral view but all he could see was some rich man's wife, daughter, or whore going up a few levels just like he. The elevator door opened, and he proceeded to enter, negating the ladies-first philosophy so he could keep an eye on her, her hands, and motions. She looked annoyed but didn't make any comment about it. The door closed and the moment got more and more intense. He could never remember feeling his heartbeat this fast under any situation. He began sweating profusely and decided it was time to reach for his .40 caliber pistol he had resting in the holster over the right side of his chest. He stood there and watched her, but she was perfectly still the actions of a killer right before they make their move. She had pressed the "8" button meaning that she was getting off on his floor. If she was going to kill him, it would have been right then and there. He could not let her off first, by this time she could be around a corner waiting to knock his noodles out. No, he had to beat her out of the elevator so he can have leverage. When the elevator reached the eighth floor and the door opened, Gaden jumped out of it so fast that he shoved her into the wall. Before she could come out, Gaden had his weapon drawn and was ready to do what he had to do to survive. The woman, surprisingly, walked out, smiled at him and gave him a kiss. "Geez, papa, if you wanted to shoot something off all you had to do was ask" said the woman as she walked down the hall. Gaden stood there briefly confused, what was the meaning behind that? Was she an assassin who had gotten the drop on him? Or was she a whore who was not scared of guns? Whatever it was Gaden kept an eye on what was

going on and headed to his room.

Chapter 26

"So, you mean to tell me, that he lived? Thank God" said Dir. Rogers, who was woke out of his sleep in his luxurious home on the outskirts of Washington D.C. "Here is what's next, get him stabilized and remove the bullet. Disguise him and have him flown here. You guys are responsible for getting him to me. After that, we will finally open this case up. I will finally get in contact with those other agents to find out whom the hell shot him. And finally, you will move in silence. Don't tell your wives, mothers, or anyone about what is going on with this operation I am putting a gag order on this whole situation. You guys are representatives of me so it must be done right." "Yes sir, by all accounts, we will carry this out to perfection as you would like us to" said Agent Thomas. After hanging up the phone, Rogers sat back and thought briefly. This whole case was blowing up in his face. He was tempted to call Nicholson back in San Francisco and have him pull his agents off the case. They were the catalysts that brought Stone this close, but now they were chasing nothing. The bureau was investing a lot of money for these men to travel the country and investigate all the components of this case. However, it was all part of what he designed… Misdirection for the greater good of the country; because of this he had to make a phone call that was only inevitable.

"Oh shit, the boss called" said Houston as they were traveling down I-80. "I guess that damn phone was on silent. He probably wanted to see how things were going" said Rico. "We're running low on gas and we will be far into Ohio before we can catch another gas station" said Houston as he pulled into an oasis that had a gas station. He pulls up to a pump that is positioned out of sight of the camera and proceeds to go into the store to pay for the gas. Upon doing that Rico tilts his head back, enjoying the complete silence of the night. But that silence is interrupted by the sound of screeching tires and slamming car doors. Rico immediately rises and looks out of the window and notices two white men in black suits get out of the car. They approach the door of the gas station only to meet Houston at the door and snatch him up. However, Frank Houston was a trained soldier and quickly overpowered them, physically beating them both to a pulp by punching one square in the nose and knocking him to the ground. He then dodges a left hook from the other guy and puts his arm in a lock before slamming him into the ground face first. He looks at the men and look over at the car and notices that Rico has been pumping the gas while he was fighting the men. He also noticed that Rico had the Desert Eagle that was under the seat. He began to think to himself, "this kid really is a genius."

"What the fuck was that shit?" asked Houston, whose adrenaline was still pumping after the squabble. "I don't know, but I will say this, they were weak. It's like they were sent to test you or something. You think the boss would do something like that?" asked Rico. "Nah, that was somebody else who hired some assholes to do a job that they couldn't do. My question is this, who? Was it that faggot Stone? Nah I'm sure he would have hired some real hitmen, but I would've put their brains on the pavement instead of their face" said Houston who reflected for a moment of who would send men to attack him and but not kill him. Whatever the attack was about he was just going to take this trip to Chicago as a way of getting away from the madness for just a little while.

"So, you finally realized that you couldn't exist without me" said Conley who smoked a cigar sitting on the balcony of a CIA funded condo in Midtown Manhattan. "Call it what you want, but this is getting stupid and it is time for us to pull the plug" said Rogers, who had finally reached his breaking point with this case. He had always known of the Organization; he even gave intel to Conley so his guys could operate, but now things had gotten out of hand. "Well Mr. FBI, we have a problem, Frank Houston and Rico Jones are on the lam because Gaden sent them away after they hit Son-Li Kim. "Kim? He was still alive? Nevermind. Stone is on his way here and I am just going to have him open up on Gaden and send him away" said Rogers. "And who gave you that order? Your boss would never approve of that, Gaden has made all of us very rich men and has stimulated this piece of shit economy into something major. Without him, how could we have had a war on drugs, guns, or terrorism? He is what keeps our bureaus thriving; he creates mayhem and is very good at it" said Conley who had gotten irritated with Rogers' proposition. The CIA and FBI both alike could only survive if the world felt the need for them to survive. By bringing more guns, drugs, and other illegal rackets like prescription medications and counterfeit money, the FBI, ATF, and DEA could function at a high capacity and be able to continue to get huge bonuses from the government, which was obviously an incentive to Rogers. As for Conley, he needed terrorism to continue to be a threat so he could have eyes and ears all over the world to not only have an idea of what was going on, but also to work as ship points to move the illegal contraband to the country. From the outside looking in, it could seem that he was committing crimes to create this fear in Americans, but for the greater good, he felt that it was the only way. "So, what do you suggest?" asked Rogers who was puzzled by Conley's rant, but knew the truth and that the head of the FBI would never sign off on executing Gaden. "Simple, Gaden shuts down shop, slow the inflow of weapons and dope into the country for about a month and bring the people to ease. We will go into Mexico arrest a few top members of the Juarez Cartel, let Mexico prosecute them then come grab gangbangers in Chicago, LA, and New York. We will say we have stopped a major crime network from distributing 500 tons of cocaine into the country and your boys will look like heroes, as usual" said Conley who actually liked the sound of his own plan. "What about Stone?" asked Rogers. "Easy, Stone will testify against DeLuna, we put that fat bastard away for life on racketeering and murder and we will have Gaden handle our diamond mine operation in West Africa. Stone will go into witness protection and get a reality TV show or something" said Conley who had a huge grin on his face thinking about Justin Stone on television. "Jones and Houston?" asked Rogers who was really covering all his bases as he repositioned himself from the recliner in his study to the desk. "Find them and kill them, Houston is an easily replaceable mercenary and Jones is a liability. I never liked the idea of a tech geek with street knowledge, they can survive and outthink you; very dangerous combination. "That sounds good, when Stone gets here, I will tell him his objective."

After the debacle, Gaden continued towards his room nervously looking around to make sure the coast was clear. It was, until he finally entered the room and saw Amber tied up to the bed, gagged and blindfolded. To the left he saw a 6'7 300 lb. bald Russian with a scar across his face and cold blue eyes. To the right he saw another 6'4 bodyguard with curly blond hair and directly in front of him was David Martel with a .38 special pointed at Amber's head. Gaden surveyed the room and could see that they didn't necessarily want to hurt anyone, but most certainly would be willing to.

"Ok, let's talk" said Gaden who put his hands up and looked around at all parties, but focused in on Martel. "Yeah Rashan, let's do just that. Let's start with how you fuck friends over and throw them under the bus" said Martel. "What are you talking about?" asked Gaden. "I am talking about sending those fucking agents to look for me. I knew Ricky was too weak to handle that, so I iced him before they showed up. I knew I couldn't trust that cocksucker, but killing Stone was probably the most therapeutic. I knew that pussy would fold as soon as anyone asked him too much. You on the other hand, solid as a rock, maybe it's because you're a boss just like me and we all do what we must do to survive right? It's only right" said Martel who looked dirty as if he had been spending the last few days executing his plan to perfection. "So why are you here David? And why do you have her tied up? And what do you mean about Stone?" asked Gaden. "Because you are going to tell me why or I am going to fucking kill you, Mr. Big, Mr. Well-Connected, well that shit isn't going to help you or your trashy bitch. As for Stone, kiss him goodbye me and my boys whacked him a couple of hours ago" said Martel who had a sadistic look on his face as if he was enjoying killing these people. "David, if you calm down, I can explain to you that this is one big misunderstanding" said Gaden in a soft-conservative tone. "Fuck you Gaden you aren't the only tough guy in the city, you know I am under investigation for this fucking Montana shit, so you sell me out? I thought we were out for the big bucks, not to get messy" said Martel who now pointed the barrel at Gaden but pulled it down and thought for a minute. Gaden wanted to take this opportunity to get into Martel's mind so he could find a way to kill him. Martel was already on Gaden's shit list but to think that he killed Stone and was threatening him was unacceptable. In a split second he assessed the distance between the two bodyguards and who had their weapon drawn. To his surprise, neither one of the bodyguards did, so if he killed Martel, he might be able to knock off the two guards. "David, we made a lot of money in that deal I didn't want to do anything to jeopardize our operation; this had to have been all of Stone's set up. I just wanted to come and get my dick sucked and relax for the night. Now, I am hoping that you believe me. I don't have it in for you, I myself am running a sensitive operation so I understand, but do know that now that Stone is dead we can now run the business like we intended to" said Gaden, who noticed that Martel had relaxed his grip on the pistol and he quickly drew his weapon and shot Martel 3 times in the chest. He gave the bald guard one in the head, but before he knew it, he was getting bombarded by the other guard and they began to struggle for the gun. Amber was trying to free herself to help but to no avail. The struggle ensued, but Gaden managed to break free and punch the guard in the face several times before regaining control of the weapon and shooting him in the eye.

"Oh my God!!! What the fuck is going on?" screamed Amber after Gaden untied and pulled the gag out of her mouth. "Amber, I haven't been completely honest with you. Some of my business ventures are well..." "Illegal" said Amber

who was still frantic and leaning against the wall trying to catch her balance. "I

assure you that I will not let anything like that happen to you again. I was

untouchable for a long time, but now it seems that all my enemies are coming after

me at once. Your face has been associated with me, I will keep you safe, just come

with me" said Gaden softly caressing her back and embracing her as she leaned

into him. "You better, I have always liked assholes, but you take the cake. First,

problem is how do we get out of here?" asked Amber as she broke the embrace and

looked out of the window. "Easy, you see that taxi just sitting in front of the hotel?

We are going to simply take the service elevator down to it and go get in and get the

hell out of town" said Gaden. "I don't believe you, after all of this turmoil, no one is

going to notice?" asked Amber. "Open the door and you will see." Amber opened

the door and to her surprise noticed a swarm of police officers motioning them to

exit the room. "All is well Mr. Gaden, let's get you out here" said a police officer

who escorted them to the service elevator. Gaden always had a contingency plan

for matters such as this one. He had to always ensure that he could get out of any

situation in a matter of minutes and in case he had to kill some people in public, he

had a few officers of the municipality to always be first on the scene in case of any

problems. "Well now you see the luxury of accompanying me, never a dull

moment" said Gaden as they walked out of the service exit, hopped into the taxi,

and disappeared into the busy New York streets. Gaden couldn't help but to think

what would happen with the Martel situation. What would Conley think? What

would he do? The only thing that he knew was that there was about to be a serious overhaul of the entire operation. All he had to do was find out if Martel had really killed Stone.

Shapiro was now committing a crime to gather information. "This is not legal Jack, let's get out of here before…" "Before what Cody? Before we get assigned to desk duty back in California? Screw that" said Shapiro as he and Jankowski rummaged through Martel's office. Ricky Herrera had a set of keys in his pocket as he laid there bleeding to death. Shapiro felt that it was the perfect chance to do some snooping. Sure enough, after no other answers could be discovered. He walked right into the luxurious Manhattan office after giving the door man a few C-Notes. "What is this?" asked Jankowski, motioning Shapiro to come take a look at the documents he discovered. "This is perfect. This has Stone's signature on it" said Shapiro who now had found a document of a sale of a property with Martel and Stone's names both signed off on it. It also had another attorney who facilitated the agreement, Martin Horowitz. "If we can find this Horowitz character, we will be able to get to the bottom of all of this crap" said Shapiro. "What if he doesn't budge?" asked Jankowski. "Oh, he will, Martin Horowitz? He is probably so 5'2 Jewish nerd who fears his own shadow, I will kick the living shit out of him if doesn't talk" said Shapiro who kept snooping around the office for more evidence. "Holy smokes, this is an interesting picture" said Jankowski showing Shapiro a framed picture of Martel, Stone, and two other men who weren't identifiable. One was a Black man and the other was Asian of some sort. "If we could ID these other two guys in this pic, I bet that we can gather all of the information needed to put this Gresham deal together and show just how illegal it all was" said Shapiro. "Yeah it would be nice for those good men and women in Montana to have an explanation as to why this had to happen to their loved ones" said Jankowski who decided to dive into their computer documents. "Crap now would be a good time to have McNamara. I wonder what I can find." "See if you can find any removable disks or if we can see anything to help guide us in the right direction. Hurry, you never know who might decide to show up at these hours" said Shapiro who had become a little nervous as to the amount of time they had spent in the office where they certainly had no reason to be. "Oh my, I found a deed to the company. Martel isn't the owner per se, he doesn't even own the most stock in the company" said Jankowski. "Well, then who does?" asked Shapiro. "The International Organization of Health Wellness, the same assholes who tried to make a $250,000 deposit to the Fed back in San Francisco" said Jankowski who had a blank look on his face.

Cody, do you realize that this whole time whoever these people are have been pulling the strings to this case? They have been making uncanny fools out of all of us, and we couldn't see it because we were too focused on the surface, but not the root of the case" said Shapiro who had suddenly become enlightened to what was going on. "We have to get back to Chicago, McNamara is in danger. Rico Jones even for that matter, we are all pawns in this sick game that they are playing" said Jankowski. They both gathered whatever they needed and got out of the office as quick as possible. Shapiro thought that now that they had penetrated a certain aspect of the case that they would be attacked upon exiting the building. But to his surprise, nothing at all, just the same guard at the door waving them off. This was a wrinkle in the case that they weren't supposed to discover, yet they now had an advantage. The only thing that was left in New York was deception. Chicago had all the answers needed to figure out the rest of this case. Chicago is where the Rico Jones jailbreak happened, so there were many corrupt officers involved who might be willing to come forward and talk about some of the things they saw or heard. Due to the danger of what was going on, they opted not to go back to the hotel they were staying. Instead right to JFK, to board the next plane smoking back to Chicago.

Sitting in the cab driving through Times Square, Gaden began to contemplate what he really was looking to know about everything. On one hand, Martel was dead and Stone too, at least according to Martel. On the other hand, if Stone was dead, who would he replace to head up the long network of lawyers that he knew around the world. Gaden was no law expert, so to strategize operations and get around a lot of the legal wrangling of other countries when dealing weapons, Stone came in handy. However, how did he know that Stone was even dead? What if Martel was bluffing to get something out of Gaden. But what did he want? All these questions played through Gaden's head like a Ferris wheel; constantly turning with no end. He figured that in a little while he would get Conley on the phone but for now, he just wanted to hide out for a little while and put the pieces of everything together. He called up Tony Drake, to ensure that everything was safe at the Staten Island house that he had bought just for the fact that it was so quiet and distanced from all the madness.

"Is everything ok?" asked Gaden, who now felt a need to be more concerned about things that normally would have been a tiny piece of dust on a ceiling fan to him. "Everything is good, Bossman, just get up here with your lady we don't see any issues near the compound. Worst case scenario, if someone follows you, I will have to put them in the newspaper" said Drake, referring to the obituary section in the newspaper with his riddle. "On my way, but if anything is wrong, I will hold you personally responsible" said Gaden hanging up the phone, staring into the night angrily. "What's wrong?" asked Amber who laid her head on his shoulder and caressed his arm. "My dear, as much as I crave you and anxious to lay next to you, I feel that we are still in danger and that I can't come to grips with" said Gaden, who for once, reveals information about his emotional state to anyone. "Don't worry, worst case scenario, we will have to ride" said Amber pulling a small .22 caliber pistol out of her bra. "I would ask why the hell do you have that, but right now in this situation, it really doesn't matter" said Gaden, who decided to let the cards fall as they would. As they began to head to the bridge into Staten Island, Gaden thought to himself, this chick is not a damsel in distress, but a damsel of danger. She was hot, troubled, and carried a gun. In his line of work, this was the perfect type of female to accompany him everywhere they went. To the unknowing, they looked harmless; him in his suit and tie and her in her tight, elegant dress with diamonds and 6" heels. They looked like a power New York couple going to the opera, but they were a deadly duo ready to kill.

"So, let me get this straight, this organization is behind Gresham. It makes me wonder if they are a front company for Gresham to access the chemicals. Even more crazy is why would they leave themselves open to make a deposit into the Federal Reserve?" pondered McNamara, who had been called by Jankowski as he and

Shapiro stood in the airport waiting on their flight back to Chicago. "I don't know, but if I were to guess, I would say that it might have been some kind of government payoff" said Jankowski. "Cody, that's ridiculous. Even if it was a payoff why would they run it through the Fed?" asked McNamara. "Because, who could hack into it? Only some super geniuses like Rico Jones and Brandon Schultz, these guys had been waiting on a big transaction just to pull off their cyberheist" said Jankowski. "Yeah, but more than likely, it was some random information that they pulled out of cyberspace. More than likely they probably had hacked into every bank in the Palo Alto area and the Fed came up. When a transaction for $250,000 pulled through the pipeline they just grabbed it and pushed it into their own account" said McNamara, flexing his knowledge of hacking. "Well whatever the case is, I am really starting to think that this organization has something to do with Rico's disappearance. Hell, they might be the puppet masters in the whole thing" said Jankowski, who looked over at Shapiro in deep thought. "Let me know when you get in, I will come and pick you up from the airport." "Sounds good, be there soon," said Jankowski hanging up the phone. "So, McNamara thinks that all of this could be coincidental in regard to Rico Jones." "Yeah, well the good thing about McNamara is that he is still young and ambitious; the bad thing about him is that he is still young and ambitious" said Shapiro who was on the same page with Jankowski. To them they had figured that the organization had made a deposit, hired Rico and Brandon to hijack it, have red flags sent up everywhere and lead them on a wild goose chase to confuse them. All in the while, Rico Jones, Brandon Schultz, and this organization disappear into thin air without a trace. But if they could help it, it would be a little harder than that for their plan to be executed.

Chapter 27

Going past Fort Wayne, Indiana let Rico know that he was close to getting home. What Houston didn't know was that Rico had noticed a text message on the phone saying, "turn around now!" Rico couldn't let him do it. He had to get back to Chicago and see Jordan before the shit hit the fan. He knew that he didn't have much time before this whole case would go downhill. He sat back and wondered how he would be paid. He also wondered which direction he would run once Houston realized that the phone had been tossed. Whatever the case was, all he needed to do was make it to South Bend and he could take the Metra back into Chicago. He even plotted on ditching Houston in South Bend if he could get him to stop. The only problem was that Frank Houston would totally kick his ass. It left him in a bind, but the good thing was that he hadn't noticed the phone yet and it was possible for Rico to make it without incident. However, it played out, Rico would use his mind to process all scenarios and look at every variable in order to give him the best result in whatever situation he was in.

Pulling in front of Staten Island not far off New York Ave., Gaden realized that his success couldn't save him. He looked at the plush mini mansion secluded from the masses that he himself had purchased under the name of Dino Brown. He pulled up and noticed Drake standing outside waiting on his arrival. This was the time that he needed to figure out what was his next move. On one hand life was business as usual, there was always some adversity that he faced. But on the other hand, he realized that he could not continue to pretend that he was invulnerable to a double-cross or any attack against him. Tony Drake could be a conspirer, as well as Frank Houston, who he still couldn't get a hold of. He and Amber exited the taxi and he tossed him a knot with about $500. "You never were here, you don't know me, and I don't know you" said Gaden to the taxi driver who nodded at him to oblige what he said. As he and Amber approached Drake, his senses were on high. He searched every angle of the bushes, the perimeter; sure, he noticed that Drake had brought in his team and they secured the perimeter and roof armed with AK-47s, but he still had to be sure everything was safe. "Bossman, come on in, we got you all covered" said Drake who stood looking like a bodyguard. More sophisticated and detail-oriented, in certain situations Gaden certainly preferred him because he was more reserved and strategic. "Me and the lady are going in, you got my back, right?" asked Gaden before he went in. "Of course, just call me when you need me" said Drake pulling his phone out letting him know he was ready for his call.

Gaden liked seeing that Drake had his phone on him, but what was troubling him was Houston wasn't on the same page. What was going on with him and Rico out there on the road? Had he gotten distracted? According to his scouts, Frank was as sharp as ever, beating both to a pulp and getting out of there in minutes. So, he and Rico were still traveling to Chicago, but why no response from his calls and texts? Had Frank, the loyal soldier, gotten the inkling that he might be trying to yank him out of the operation? One thing for sure, he knew that he couldn't reach him, and he didn't know what to tell Conley. In the meantime, he and Amber headed up to the master bedroom which was set for a king. Beautiful artwork and a California king size bed with a golden headboard set for a king. She sees this, immediately undressed and went to shower. He watched her but continued to drift off into deep thought. Before he knew he was laying in the bed trying to devise a plan in which he would stay on top of the world. Those thoughts must have taken 20 minutes, because before he knew it, she reappeared naked. She crawled into the bed and on top of him and they began kissing. As he was caressing her bottom, he became erect. She pulled his pants down far enough to expose his penis, which she then climbed on top of and began to mount. As they started having sex, his worries faded and all he did was get caught in the moment, until he climaxed and fell asleep...

Looking around, Justin Stone was too weak to understand what was transpiring. He was basically on life support; IVs in his veins, oxygen mask on his face, and open cuts on his body. However, he was in a helicopter. He didn't know where he was being taken, but the last thing he remembers is seeing David Martel very angry, the look of a demon in his face as he relentlessly shot him over and over. He certainly wasn't strong enough to speak, he could barely see, but he knew he was alive and that feeling alone gave him a sense of peace as he looked at the world from the helicopter. "His eyes are open; I think he will be fine" said Agent Thomas to the paramedics who were servicing Stone. Rather he knew it or not, he was heading to a secret location in Washington DC to recover without anyone being able to see him. If Rogers had his way, the public wouldn't know about the shooting, for the fact that Stone is the star witness in a major federal case.

"South Bend, Indiana" said Houston who had become worn out from all the hours of driving. "Come on Frank, you know that the best thing to do is get some rest before you drive the rest of the way. You're going to kill yourself" said Rico, who was cooking up a scheme in his own mind. "Yeah I guess you're right. I guess

the Boss won't get too mad about us taking it easy for a few hours. But we are only

laying back til 10 am, after that we must get right back on the road" said Houston,

exiting I-90 to head to a motel right off US Route 31. While Houston ran into the office

to pay for the room, Rico began plotting on escaping right then and there. He

decided to play it cool but noticed a taxicab sitting in the motel parking lot. This

showed that it was probably waiting on a prostitute, john, or junkie. Either way he

wanted to get in on the action. The cab didn't have a number on the exterior, but it

was positioned in a spot that Rico could sneak in the back seat. As he snuck out of

the car and crept to the back seat, with the Desert Eagle, he jumped in quick and put

the gun to the head of the cab driver. "Motherfucker, you better take me to Chicago

right now" said Rico as he threw $1000 at him and waited for his reaction. "Will you

put the gun down sir?" asked the nervous Indian cab driver. "Whatever" said Rico

putting the gun down and waiting for the driver to count the money. Since they were

all hundreds, it didn't take long for the cab driver to start the car and head towards

the highway. Rico had made sure that he had raided the cash stashed in the vehicle.

It had to be at $10,000 and that would be enough to get him home. For all other

money, he now had the access codes to all the Organization's secret bank accounts,

as well as the North Koreans. One thing for sure, he knew that the government

wouldn't be too mad about robbing an enemy nation. The cab headed back towards

the Indiana Toll Road, I-80/90, and he was on his way back to Chicago. "Can I stop

for gas, sir?" asked the cab driver. "Sure", said Rico giving him another $100, "but

not until we get to Gary. "Let's get the fuck out of here."

For Conley, there was no sleeping. A man in his position couldn't help but to keep going and seeing how he would save the world this time around. Conley was a man from humble beginnings. Born and raised in a tiny suburb outside of Pittsburgh. Opted not to go to college but went to the Marines fresh out of high school. That stint landed him right in Vietnam near the end of the war in the early 70s. Once the war ended, he was approached by a man who would change his life forever. This man was a supervisor in the CIA's Black Ops. He offered Conley the opportunity to be a part of his team, who was doing espionage in the Soviet Union; particularly in Moscow working undercover in the Soviet government. He spent 15 years working as an undercover diplomat traveling the world, while the whole time reporting to his superiors and exposing Soviet secrets. Conley liked to think that he was part of the demise of the Soviet Union as he had partaken in the sabotage of its communist operation. He didn't believe in a world that was controlled by the government, not overtly at least. He liked democracy; though hypocritical because secretly democracy controlled the people as well; just not with an iron fist, but through fear. He pondered what would truly be the next move. Focusing on the diamond mines in West Africa sounded great because it would be a cash cow, but in his position he had access to all of the money and he himself held all of the power to dictate the state of not just the United States, but the world.

"Where the fuck did he go bitch?" asked Houston with his .38 caliber pistol to her head. "I don't know, but my cab is gone too" said the scared prostitute who had left the room of her john only to find that her cab was gone. She was a scrawny blond with green eyes standing about 5'7. "Get in the fucking car" said Houston forcing her to get into the vehicle. "What company did he work for? He is carrying a passenger that is very important to me" said Houston who had now put his gun away. "I don't know, but he drove me here from Hammond and I had planned on staying but..." But nothing, you're coming with me now, we're going to track this fucker down and you're going to tell me where I can find his dispatch" said Houston who was now full of energy. This was bad, with Rico on the loose there were numerous Organization secrets traveling down I-90 heading God knows where. What if he turned the story in to the media? Something of this magnitude would really cause a serious riff between he and Gaden. Therefore, he knew that he couldn't answer that phone until he found Rico, tied him up, and had him in the trunk. The hooker would lead him to the dispatch who would then tell him where the cab was headed. Houston already knew though, Chicago. Rico had raided the stash, so he had enough money to make anyone want to take him wherever he wanted. The one ace in the hole that Rico didn't count on was the intel on his mother. The Organization had stashed her away in a lavish apartment building on the Gold Coast on Chicago's North Shore. If he couldn't get to Rico, he would simply murder the mother and be done with this whole situation. But to avoid too much bloodshed, he would first find Rico. He would at least give it a hard effort before he murdered someone for no reason.

Traveling down the highway constantly checking the rearview and looking outside of the left and right window, Rico felt that he had gained some ground. Now, he wanted to get back to see his mother and Jordan, but he knew that in the grand scheme he had to figure out what was next. It would be nice to see everyone, but at the end of the tunnel there would be a shining light. That light would be the

Organization, with their CIA and FBI connections they would surely hunt him down

and kill him. His only chance was to expose this story to the media, even if it cost

him his life, he knew that exposing their wrong doings and telling the truth about

what was going on within the United States government this would be the only way

that corruption could be curved. Though Rico had been afforded many

opportunities to be a winner in life, he had made some poor choices. He felt that by

getting with the Organization, he could redeem himself and have his charges

dismissed so he could continue to be the winner that he was designed to be.

However, the only thing that this had done was cause him to throw out his moral

standards and do things that totally went against what he believed in. But by making

this next move, he knew that it would have to be the best move that he could ever

make in his life. How would the public react? How would Jordan and his mother

react to knowing what he had been a part of? More importantly, how would the

Organization come after him? These were men in very powerful positions who had

access to whatever they wanted. However, things ended, Rico knew that he had to

do what was necessary to clear his conscience and save himself. Not just from the

Organization, but he began to look back at his religious beliefs. He was raised in the

Apostolic Christian faith. He was taught that we as people should live with some

form of moral standard. If we are not living in that light, then why are we here on

Earth? We are here to serve a higher purpose, and he knew that he wasn't serving

that purpose. Not at Stanford, not doing business with Mookie, and not selling his

soul to the Organization to redeem himself. He now knew what was necessary to make things right. As he looked in the night, he noticed that the sun was beginning to creep up; indicating that it was probably about 4:30 in the morning in Chicago. As he and the cab driver headed up the highway, he had a sinking feeling that Houston was not too far behind him. He didn't know how well Houston knew Chicago, but he knew that once they got to 95th street off the Dan Ryan Highway, Houston would have a hard time finding him in the city. "Get off here" said Rico to the driver as they approached the Gary exit. "Why my friend, I thought that you were going to Chicago" said the driver. "We are but we're going to switch expressways. Gary had two Chicago expressways passing through it, I-90 and I-94. I-90 was the Indiana Toll Road, the more popular of the two expressways as it cuts out of Chicago first and is a quicker route into Indiana. I-94 curved further south of Chicago and hit Gary through Cline Ave. it also went to Detroit eastbound. Depending on how well Houston knew this area, it was a good place to throw him off, "you can get your gas on our way to Cline, from there we will get on I-94 and head into Chicago that way" said Rico who knew in his mind that he had put together a diabolical plan to escape Houston.

A little more time passed, and Stone noticed that the helicopter was landing. But it was landing on top of a building that was in a very discreet area. From what he could see there were other buildings and establishments around the place, but there was no show of where they were. "Let's move him out fellas, just follow the other agent to where we will have him set up" said Agent Thomas. "Are you sure there is a doctor waiting? If we slip up on this…" said the paramedic before Agent Thomas cut him off. "Everything is taken care of, just get him up there so we can get everything going." The paramedics carefully moved Stone through the rooftop entrance, down one flight of stairs and into the first door they could possibly go through. Once they did this, there was room set up with a bed, IVs, and doctors and nurses ready to get him back to health. Once the paramedics got him set up, they left, and Dir. Rogers walked in. "Justin, I don't know if you can hear me, but we are going to get you back to health. All of this will make sense once we get everything situated. Just sit tight" said Rogers as he nodded at the staff and walked out of the room. Stone had no clue where he was at, this big room had cloudy windows, so it was impossible to see outside. The staff immediately got to work getting him situated and set up for surgery. The paramedics, though trained to the highest degree, was unable to get all the bullets out of him so now the staff would have to prep him for surgery. As they were prepping him, he started thinking, who would be there to consult with DeLuna in order to make things happen with Rogers? He looked out of the window and he noticed that the sun was beginning to rise. This indicated to him that the meeting time was coming about. If he could talk or walk, he could have asked Rogers how he was going to handle that situation. For now, he would just take joy in the fact that he was still alive after being savagely shot by Martel.

Chapter 28

In New York, Tony DeLuna was getting ready for his big meeting. The only problem was this prick Stone wasn't answering the phone. No matter DeLuna knew of Stone's cocaine habit and figured that he had gotten hammered the night before. In his mind he figured that Stone worried too much, the life of a spoiled white kid from Eastern Pennsylvania who never been through 25% of the battles that he had been through. Truth is told DeLuna didn't have to continue this criminal lifestyle, hell he was a millionaire 15 years ago. But the sport of the lifestyle is what kept him engaged in it. He was a well-connected and respected man in his line of work. All the wise guys knew that if they needed anything, they could come to DeLuna. They knew that his family had the money, brains, and muscle to get whatever they wanted. It was that power that made him stay involved. As he continued to finish putting on his tailor-made Armani suit, he looked out of the window of his $5 million home in Long Island and prepared to head to Manhattan. But he began to have a weird feeling about everything. Though he had negotiated a conditional surrender, he felt why give the law the satisfaction of putting him away for the rest of his life. Not to say that he couldn't beat the case, but why not use his connections to go the other direction. Half of his fortune was tied up in offshore accounts any way. So, he picked up the phone and text a Massachusetts number a simple "SOS" message. Only he knew who was on the other end, and this was his ultimate escape from the lifestyle that nearly cost him his life.

"Please mister, I don't know how much help I can be to you" said the prostitute that had been left by the cab driver. "Shut up bitch, I'm not going to hurt you. I'm not a rapist or serial killer I just want you to take me to this dispatch that's all" said Houston who was getting upset that the woman would not relax even though he had reassured her that she was safe. "Hey, listen pal, all I know is that this place is in Gary." "That's cool, I was heading to Chicago anyway no biggie" said Houston who was now driving with a vengeance going 90 mph. "What? You don't know your way around?" asked the girl. "No, I don't actually. Indiana isn't exactly a place to come and just hang out" said Houston. "Well, if you spent more time in normal places like here maybe you would know how to treat people" said the girl, who to Houston's surprise, was quite intelligent. "Fuck that, when we find these cocksuckers, you're free to go I don't give a shit about none of that bullshit you're trying to feed me. Fuck this hick ass state, I'm on a mission" said Houston who was now doing 100 mph. Houston was on a mission. Rico had embarrassed him beyond belief, the fact that he had the balls to pull it off really infuriated because Houston really considered himself a tough guy. He had beaten the snot out of two guys back in Ohio to prove this. The fact that Rico still took off showed that he believed that his brain was stronger than Frank Houston's muscle. Either way, Rico had a hell of a battle on his hand and Houston was relentless. He wouldn't stop until he had Rico tied up in his trunk and on his way into Western Illinois to put his body 6' deep in a cornfield.

"Something is not sitting right with me right now; Frank always answers the phone" said Gaden who basically took a nap due to the stress of everything that was going on. "Don't worry I'm sure he is fine; he probably lost the phone along the way.

You know that he is a hot head he probably got into a fight and got himself arrested" said Drake, who felt that it was his time to ascend to Gaden's right hand man. "No, Frank is smarter than that, he would kick someone's ass for sure, but he would definitely get out of there before any cops showed up. Something has happened, I have to get to Chicago and see if our insurance policy knows something" said Gaden speaking of Rico's mother. He knew that if anything had gone sour, he held the upper hand by keeping Rico's mother tucked away under his watch. If Rico had just the slightest bit of decency, he wouldn't want his mother to be murdered in cold blood. "Yeah we should go and see what is going on exactly" said Drake. "I'll get the car ready while you get yourself together." "Hey, wait, make sure you get the AR-15 and AK-47. I get the feeling we will have to carry some heavy artillery for this" said Gaden. "You got it Boss" said an even more enthusiastic Drake. "Where am I going?" asked Amber who had lie motionless while Gaden and Drake talked but was woke the whole time. "My dear, you will stay here where it is safe. I wouldn't want anything to happen to you. I will get you an assistant and they will go and get whatever you need. If you feel the need to leave, I have a limo driver here, just make sure that you stay discreet until I get everything situated" said Gaden as Amber hesitated to respond. On one hand, here was exactly what she searched for years to find, a rich man giving her whatever she wanted with servants at her beckon call. On the other hand, there was the danger of being attacked in his absence, but she trusted him enough to know that he would leave protection for her. "Sure thing, but I need money" said Amber just to verify that this was all real. "Sure thing, here is $10,000. If you need more one of my assistants will get it for you" said Gaden as he got up and motioned one of his men to leave the room with him. Gaden had no true concern for money, it was just everything else that he had to make sure that he went out and took care of. As he got in the shower to prepare to leave, all he could think about was where the hell Stone was and what Conley's next move was.

30 minutes of driving like a maniac and Houston was in Gary getting off at 5th Ave. Passing through downtown Gary, he noticed just how much of a ran-down place it was. "This town is a fucking dump, where the hell is this place at anyway?" "Just make a right and it is the little shack on the left" said the prostitute. The little shack was so ran-down that it looked like an abandoned building. The whole neighborhood was majority vacant lots with 4 houses, including the shack, on the block. Houston pulls up into the lot right next to the house and pulls out his 9mm pistol, cocks it, and sits it on his lap. "Ok, so what you're gonna to do is knock on the door, they gonna open it, and I'm gonna ask them some real simple questions" said Houston, with a look of murder in his eyes. "Please just…" was all the prostitute could get out before Houston backhanded her like a pimp. "Bitch, get to walking." The prostitute gets out and Houston as well, he walked right behind her until she got to the front door. He then stepped to the side and allowed her to be the only one visible once the door was opened. When the door opened, she simply said "are you guys hiring?" Before they could reply, Houston drew his gun and told everybody to go in the house. "Buddy I have no money" said the Arab man who opened the door. "Cocksucker I don't won't none of yo fucking money I can wipe my ass with that little bit of shit" said Houston who commenced in pulling $1,000 out of his pocket and threw it at him. "Then what do you want?" asked the man. "Where is cab 48?" asked Houston, who surveyed the

abandoned house and realized that it was supposed to be a dispatch office, the walls were painted white, but the rest of the house, including what used to be the kitchen was filthy. "I don't know" said the man. "Let me tell you something, you better come up with an answer or I'm going to blow your brains all over that fat bitch at the desk" said Houston who was looking at the dispatcher. "Ok, he called me about 10 minutes ago and said that he was heading to Chicago off of I-94" said the scared man. "See was that so hard?" asked Houston who proceeded to shoot him in the knee. The man screamed in agony and Houston said to him "you should have told the truth when I asked you." He looked at the prostitute and the dispatcher, both in shock and silence, then proceeded to leave the filthy house. He got in the car and began to head back towards the Indiana Toll Road. Houston knew that all he had to do was go to Rico's mother and that would bring him back. He began to head to that location before Rico got wise. Houston being so angry now realized that he had wasted time. Had he just gone to Rico's mother in first place all of this could have been avoided, but then again, who was to say that Rico was headed to Chicago at least he knew for certain now.

On I-95 north, DeLuna and his accomplice who would allow him to rest in Switzerland rode in a tinted limo discussing terms of the arrangement. "So Tony, I can get you a new identity, apartment, car, and $1 million in cash. You would just have to do one thing for me" said the accomplice. "You name it, I'm sure there is nothing that I can't handle. Well I would need you to kill an important government official. He is not important as he would like to think he is. His name is Cmdr. Andrew Conley of the CIA. He has been a thorn in my ass for a long time and the sooner I can get rid of him the better. Then we can put our own guy to head up Black Ops." "Whoa that's a big job, how would I even get to him?" asked DeLuna who just wanted the safety and security of this high-ranking foreign diplomat. This man was the U.S. ambassador to Switzerland who could help him disappear if he needed to. This ambassador had made millions thanks to a contribution from DeLuna back in the mid-90s when DeLuna had a huge racket with fur coats. Truckloads of counterfeit fur coats would come in and DeLuna proudly gave this ambassador, who was a U.S. Representative at the time, millions of dollars just buying a friend in a high place. Now DeLuna just wanted to cash in but Conley somehow had rubbed this diplomat the wrong way and had to go. "Conley is a greedy man, he extorts third-world country leaders to do what he wants so he can get what he wants. How is it that a man who makes maybe $100,000 a year can buy a yacht and sail the Mediterranean Sea? Easy, he goes to Sierra Leone and hijack the diamond minds. He funds the insurgents in Afghanistan so he can get a kickback from OPEC on their oil profits. He goes to North Korea and when they don't cooperate, he blows up their establishment and make them think that South Koreans did it. There is much more, but I'd rather not say. Now, that you have the objective I will set you up with everything that you need to kill this man. Once it's done, you will disappear and live the rest of your life in peace in Switzerland. Understood?" "Yes, let me know what to do next since I am set to surrender myself today" said DeLuna who was now confused. "You will stay in my penthouse until we are ready to make the move. Once the call is made and we have him where we want him, you will do the job and be flown to Switzerland immediately on my private jet. I will accompany you; no one knows I am here, not even the president" said Ambassador Victor Amechi, a

Sicilian born man from the same neighborhood as DeLuna. When they were kids, Amechi could have gone down the same road as DeLuna, but Amechi had parents with good jobs and eventually was moved to New Jersey to finish high school. Upon finishing he went to Rutgers to study law and political science and worked in politics basically all the way until he moved back to Brooklyn and became a US Representative, later, he became the Ambassador to Switzerland. Now that he held so much power, he felt that it was necessary to help his old friend who kicked back millions of dollars to him.

After getting off on 95th street off the Dan Ryan expressway, Rico told the cab driver to drop him off 2 blocks from Jordan's house. At least now, he could watch to see if anyone was following him. He had to see her, there was no way that he could go without seeing her, through her, he understood the feeling of love. How it felt to be romantically involved with a person to the point that no decision you make can be made without her. He had on a hood, a scarf, sunglasses and a skull cap. He just knew no one noticed him, until he approached Jordan's block and was apprehended by the FBI. "Hands up Rico, it's over" said Jankowski who had his weapon drawn on him. "Gentlemen, you know I am not a threat, why so many guns?" asked Rico who surrendered with ease. "Can't be too safe Rico, there is no telling what can happen these days" said Shapiro. "We have been looking for you since the fiasco that happened at Stanford. How did you break out, what's going on?" asked Shapiro who looked at Rico and saw a young man with a cold stare and no fear. "I will tell you everything that you want to know, but how did you know I would show up here?" "We didn't" said McNamara, "but we been scoping out your old neighborhood and your mother was nowhere to be found, but we had reason to believe that your involvement with Justin Stone had something to do with your disappearance. "That's only part of the story" said Rico as the agents led him off. As he was taken to the black Tahoe, he could see Agent Brown talking to Jordan and her family and from the distance he could see her with a tear rolling down her eye watching him being apprehended. "I love you Jordan" he yelled as he was placed into the Tahoe.

As Gaden headed to the field to board his private jet, he began to think about what he would do to Rico's mother if things didn't go right. Just as he was getting deeper into the abyss of the morbid torture methods that he would use on her, his phone rings. "You've got to be fucking kidding me? Well someone better get to that little fucker and remind him that his mother will be getting gang raped and thrown from the 50th floor on Lake Shore Dr. if he utters a word" said Gaden as he takes his phone and slams it on the floor. "What's going on boss?" asked Drake who had never seen Gaden so upset. "They got the kid. The Feds got the kid!!!" screamed Gaden who for once was cracking under pressure. "No problem boss, we're going to go and remind them fuckers who we are, and all will be well." "It's not that simple, he was picked up by a special group hired directly by the director to investigate Stone, Gresham, and a whole bunch of shit that could get us all fucked over in the worst way. I have to call Conley" said Gaden, who for once, now was glad that he hadn't quite double-crossed him just yet. Usually Conley with all his government connections could fix this. In the meantime, Rico's mother was the key to all of this and would be the catalyst in pulling off another caper, this time against the same machine that had allowed him to operate for so long.

"It seems that you really got some stuff to sort out here. I am going to Langley to figure things out. We can't afford to have this situation stop what we are doing. We have worked too hard to have it all end because of this kid. Get to Chicago and kill the mother if you must. If this kid flips and speak on the North Korea mission, this will open the world to the CIA's Black Op missions that have been saving the world for a long time. Do what is necessary Gaden, this is not the time to flake out" said Conley, who was getting nervous at the idea of hearing about Rico being taken into custody. "I have this under control, we are just so used to the deck stacking in our favor, so for once we are working under pressure. Its fine Conley I am boarding the plane to sort all of this out" said a surprisingly confident Gaden. Rico couldn't dime them out it wouldn't make sense for him to go to that extreme, especially knowing that they had his mother. But other thoughts began to cross his mind, what if Rico had infiltrated them with the help of Stone.

Chapter 29

"So, Rico, let's start from scratch, you were broken out by T-Dog?" asked Jankowski, who didn't believe one word of what Rico was telling him. "No, that was an alias, he was actually an agent for this organization. I don't know what their connection to the CIA is, but they were privy to a lot of information and connections that only the government would have. It was surprising to me, we flew down to Miami, and I met with the guy who was like the boss of the whole operation..." said Rico, before he was cut off by Shapiro. "What was his name? This so-called "boss." "Gaden, that's all I ever got was that his name was Gaden" said Rico. "Run a search on this Gaden guy, see if anything comes up in the database" said Jankowski to another one of the agents who were in the room. The agent left the room and they continued to the interrogation. "So where is your hotshot lawyer when you need him Rico? Oh, that's right, he was in on the whole damn thing to set you up. Look at what good money buys these days" said Agent Brown who was still tense about what had happened at Rico's initial interrogation. "Rico, what made you agree to this madness? Do you know what kind of shitstorm you have created? This could send the world into a frenzy knowing that you were set free by some hoodlums that hide behind government protection" said Shapiro. "Well, it gets worse; they have my mother" said Rico who now felt the burden of the situation come to life. "Your mother? Rico, these men are dangerous psychopaths. If they have your mother, they got her for insurance. The fact that you're here now could put her in grave danger" said Jankowski. "We'll have some agents head over to his office to see if we can get our hands on some files or something, but Rico, this is big." "I know, I messed up and that's why I am trying to save the people that I love before this gets out of hand" said a sorrowful Rico who knew that this could lead to ramifications that he may not have been able to deal with. "There may be hope" said Rico, who suddenly got a bright idea. "Oh yeah? And what's that?" asked a curious Shapiro. "Frank Houston, Gaden's right hand man, has to be hot on my trail. He is going to scour the city looking for me, but if he can't find me, he will go right to the location that my mother can be found." "Let's run a search on Frank Houston and get some choppers on standby. I will bring back pictures to see if we can get a positive ID from you ok?" said Shapiro as he was about to exit the room. "Shapiro, one more thing, he was military at one point" said Rico remembering overhearing Frank bragging about it to one of the Korean prostitutes on private jet. "Ditto" said Shapiro as he exited the room.

Rico was now left in the room by himself to think about was he doing the right thing. On one hand he was trying to right his wrongs. On the other, he had ended the opportunity to be part of something that was potentially great. But what was great about terror? What was great about killing people and having secrets on government owned corporations? What could possibly be great about building wealth at the expense of people's sanity and well-being? Nothing. Rico knew that he had made the right decision about what he had done it was just a matter of the outcome. His mother's safety, the organization not finding him and killing him, and the connection that he felt with Jordan even though he wasn't next to her, he could feel her spirit consoling and comforting him. For him, there was upside to his decision; and that upside had no price tag.

"I just got intel that Conley plans to board a private jet out at 11:00 am. We will go there, and I will say that I too am boarding a jet. At which point, Conley's jet will pull out and you will have to exchange gunfire with him and his men. I will get a few extra men to go with you, this way they can target them, and you can target him" said Amechi letting DeLuna know exactly how everything was going to happen. "At that point, we will immediately leave and board a jet to Switzerland. When the smoke clears, they will wonder what happened to me. At that time, we will say that you were involved in the shooting and kidnapping of me. They will scatter the entire country, not knowing that we boarded a jet and took off. I already have the plans in the works." Amechi was so sure that this would work, but DeLuna was now finding himself paranoid. He didn't know if he could really trust Amechi or not. For one of the first times DeLuna was not in control of the situation and as much of a criminal mastermind as he was, he didn't have control of the situation to mastermind it and that didn't sit well with him. But, based on being in a situation was highly unfavored, he decided to roll the dice what was the worst that could happen? He was facing a life sentence and if there was a way out by doing something that he had done many times before, then why not see what it could bring him. Besides rubbing elbows with Amechi could lead him to places that he had never been. He could touch the power that he had always wanted but couldn't obtain because he didn't have a connection with such high rank that held him in such enough high regard to trust him to commit a crime that he orchestrated. In a sense, it was safe to say that DeLuna had moved up in the world.

"We got a hit on Frank Houston, he served in the Marines from 2000-2002. Highly touted recruit went into battle in Iraq and Afghanistan but was dishonorably discharged for being too violent against his commander's orders. In plain English, the guy was a bad ass and killed people at the drop of a hat. I mean he wasn't a sniper; he was a specialist in close combat. You name it he could do it and that's what makes him dangerous. Rico, would you agree?" asked Jankowski who was in awe on his Marine profile. "Yes, Frank could kick anyone's ass at any time and was like Quickdraw McGraw with a handgun." "Alright, the APB will go out as armed and dangerous" said Shapiro who listened in shock. "You know, the craziest part is that I being a military man find it hard to believe that men with that skill can be corrupted for what they can provide to an organization of punks. He is a soldier, getting wrapped up with the Organization was just like taking orders from Colonel, only difference was he got more money and praise. If we can get him, we may be able to flip him, but I'm not sure he could be a person that's prepared to be a POW out of loyalty."

9:30 am Central Time, Gaden steps off his private jet at the DuPage Airport, approximately 40 miles west of Chicago. There is a limo prepared for him, Drake, and a few other large sized men of the Organization. "First order of business, getting to Rita Jones and notifying her of her son's poor choices" said Gaden, who had a devious smile on his face. "She is not going to know what hit her. After that we got to find Frank, I know he is a traitor and a liar. An offense of that magnitude calls for death" said Drake, who had found his way to the top and was going to run with it. As they all got into the limo and began heading towards the city, Gaden noticed a letter on ice in the champagne bucket. Upon opening it, he was surprised by what he read:

> Hello Gaden,
>
> If you are reading this, that means you have made it to the Windy City. Welcome. Now let's get to business. I know who you are and what you are doing here. What you don't know, is that I will be the X-factor in stopping you. I am going to destroy you at what you think you do best. See you on Lake Shore Dr. I can't wait to dance with you. And as for Rita Jones, you might as well get out of your mind that you will do any harm to her because she is gone. Consider this a courtesy call.
>
> Your Worst Nightmare

"What the fuck is this?" asked Gaden looking confused and angry. "Looks like somebody got the drop on us, boss" said Drake. "Well we have never been ones to back down from a challenge. I think it's a bluff, it's cute that they found us, maybe Frank has turned on us" said Gaden angrily but sad at the same time. "Don't worry boss, after we take out Rita, we going to kill him too and throw their bodies on Lake Shore Dr. to put on display. That is front page news right there!" exclaimed Drake who had a new level of enthusiasm to get the job done, whatever that job may be. "Sounds good Tony, but we have to be smart about how we move. Give our friends over at the building a call to check everything out. I want to make sure that this is a bluff" said Gaden. Drake picked up the phone and immediately called one of the men watching the activity of Rita Jones to see what was going on.

"Gone? Never, I have been watching her like a hawk. There is no way something like that could happen" said Gordon, a member of the Organization with the task of watching Rita Jones' every move. Gordon was working under the guise of witness protection. To Rita Jones' knowledge, Rico had escaped and had men after him. To "protect" her Gordon and a few other Organization members posed as FBI agents and told her that she was in witness protection. She was forced to quit her job and was supplied with all the cash necessary to survive. She couldn't even go to the grocery store without these men in hot pursuit of her. "Well I'll go across the hall and see what's going on" said Gordon, who swiftly hung up the phone and beelined to the door to see what was going on across the hall.

Gordon made it there in less than 5 seconds and began to knock. "Ms. Jones are you there?" asked Gordon. Rita Jones, a very youthful looking Black woman in her early 40s with smooth brown skin and an invigorating voice responded. "Yes, give me a second." Rita opened the door wearing pajamas and a closed robe. She stared briefly before asking "can I help you?" "Yes, ma'am just making sure you were doing well this morning. Will you need to go anywhere?" asked Gordon. "No Agent Sharp, everything is fine. I will call when I will need to go anywhere" said Rita. "Ok, Ms. Jones enjoy the rest of your morning" said Gordon as she closed the door before, he could finish his sentence. Rita was quite upset at Rico; he had gotten himself in so deep that he couldn't get out. Moreover, he had gotten wrapped up with a group of undesirables who wished to use him to their advantage. Unbeknownst to the Organization, including Gordon, Rita had a visitor that morning.

About an hour and half prior to Gordon knocking on the door, McNamara had gained access to her apartment. He did it disguised as a maintenance man dispatched to her apartment to fix a leaking sink in the kitchen. The "feds" were aware of his arrival, but what they didn't know was that McNamara had stopped the guy in his tracks, paid him for a day of work and borrowed his uniform. He then eased up to the apartment, deactivated the audio to the bugs that were planted in the apartment, and gave Rita the rundown of everything that happened. He also let her know how he found her, by checking the IP address of all computers that she had used recently. The only computer that she can use is at the public library, since the "feds" confiscated her cell phone, laptop, and all other means of contact with the outside world unless it is from the landline that is bugged, inside of the apartment. There is only one in the area, narrowing down how many buildings they could have her holed up in. Once he had the information, he dressed as a teenage hipster and watched her until she left. Upon leaving he watched her walk down the street flanked by two "agents" to the building. McNamara with his hacking prowess got into the buildings database and noticed there were three vacant apartments. However, when he called the leasing agent, he was told that there were no vacancies. Odd, he thought so once he intercepted the maintenance call to one of the "vacant" apartments, he knew was at least was going to be in the area of the three apartments and was going to get to the bottom of the situation. However, he got lucky and landed right in Rita's apartment. So, while Rico was being questioned, McNamara was hard at work executing a plan that would either get him killed or help the case. But that wasn't the only reason he was in so deep with everything.

"So, you mean to tell me that you and my son stole a bunch of money while you were at school and now, you're trying to help him out? And you're impersonating a fed?" said Rita, who had just been notified that McNamara was really Brandon Schultz, Rico's college roommate. "How is that even possible?" "Ma'am, you would be surprised at the abilities that your son and I possess. If we had any good sense, we wouldn't be in this situation. After we stole the money we ran, he came back here, and I went to Vancouver. I stayed and partied for a few weeks but then I saw a report of Rico getting arrested. I figured I would try something to see if I could help him out. So, I got a fake ID, dyed my hair, started wearing contacts and got rid of my acne. I even had some stylist do something to my eyebrows so they could appear thinner than natural. I know the Feds are always looking for a talented hacker, so I hacked into UCLA's database and gave myself a Master's in Computer Science and headed to the Fed. They couldn't detect any fraud. That was my power, all the mistakes I made, that Rico told me not to make I didn't anymore. I took the gig to clean up the fact that we had stolen, but once I got inside I got swept up into this case as it became more focused on the fake government organization that sent it through, and I wanted it to stay that way" said McNamara/Schultz, who was actually a little surprised at how far he had come with the whole scheme. Still in disbelief, Rita just didn't know how to process the information. "I assure you; I will not let these animals hurt you. But I don't want an army of Feds storming the building either" said Schultz. "Are you crazy? That's what we want, I'm not going to tell them who you are, I want them to know who they are!" exclaimed Rita "Plus you will get merit or whatever you are actually looking for." Brandon thought about it, he was serving a purpose; he had single-handedly saved Rita's life. No one else would have had the intel that he had, though he was a rogue and not who he pretended to be, he had done something purposeful. He decided to make the call and have the troops head to his location without being spotted by the Organization hounds in across the hall.

10:45 Eastern Time, Victor Amechi and Tony DeLuna sit at the airfield awaiting Conley's arrival. If DeLuna can off Conley, he not only frees himself, he helps his friend. He watches the strip; it looks empty minus a few service workers unloading rich people's luggage into limos. That's the beauty of a private air strip, the privacy. He noticed the tower that air traffic control operated out of, and he didn't like how they could see the entire air strip. "Hey, maybe I should put on a mask Vic, I mean those guys can see me from a mile away" said DeLuna who had no problem expressing his concern with the whole situation. "Not a problem, let them see you, no one will ever see you again trust me" said Amechi who was sure of his plan. "Well just so you know I'm coming out blastin' soon as I see this guy, and where is our plane?" asked DeLuna. "Tony do you not trust me?" asked Amechi. "I trust you; I just don't trust the circumstances; this is a big thing that we're doing here" said DeLuna. "I understand Tony but let me ask you something. Do you believe in sacrifices?" asked Amechi. "Sure, sometimes sacrifices have to be made for business to continue to flourish. An example of this would be wacking out this Conley prick" said DeLuna. "Well in the life that you have chosen to live, sacrifices have to be made in order to keep the trillions of dollars flowing into Swiss banks. Tony, you have always been a good friend of mine I have used my influence to help you in so many ways. You have amassed great fortune and have brought no less than $1 billion to the Swiss accounts with your name on them. Unfortunately, there comes a time when the umbilical cord must be cut, and I must let you deal with the consequences of your actions. You have always been very hot-headed, meaning that you would kill a man over pride or respect or simply to reinforce your authority in the underworld. You never evolved; you still have the same mentality as we were raised around on the streets of Brooklyn. Because of that it has come to this" said Amechi, speaking cryptically. "Hey Vic, what are you talking about come to this? Is this why you have me wacking Conley? Because I have become too much of a liability, now you want me to do a piece of your dirty work and just disappear?" asked DeLuna, who had no idea that there was a hidden message in Amechi's statement. "No Tony, there is more to this story than I let on" said Amechi before the interior limo window rolled down and a man pointing a .38 with a silencer shot Tony DeLuna in the head twice. "Sarai sempre mio amico" said Amechi, letting a deceased DeLuna know that they will always be friends. Amechi picks up a cellphone and makes a call, simply saying to the person on the other line "it's done." At that time Amechi's jet was landing, the plan was never to have DeLuna kill Conley but to bring DeLuna to the airfield and kill him. Conley would board his flight to Chicago here and Amechi, alone, would board the flight to Switzerland. He had assessed the situation, DeLuna had put a lot of money into the Swiss accounts and with his recent legal troubles he had begun to draw too much attention to their operation. Amechi was DeLuna's contact to launder all his illegal gambling and drug money. Because of this he had access to well over $100 million of DeLuna's money. He rationalized his actions by planning to send $50 million to his wife and kids while keeping the other $50 million. Along with this he washed away the concern of DeLuna, facing a life sentence, flipping and implicating his cohorts in some of his operations. Him being dead also helped Conley because Stone was his attorney and had a lot of underhanded dealings with DeLuna in the cocaine trade. Plus, with Stone being shot that would bring more public attention to this whole ordeal. Stone was supposed to be the squeaky clean, high-powered attorney who defended cases worldwide. It wouldn't be favorable for the world to know that he had been shot just days before one of his most high-profile trials was set to begin. DeLuna's death was a benefit to all parties involved, including DeLuna himself, as he would certainly be convicted and sentenced to life in prison.

Conley showed up minutes after DeLuna's murder to examine everything. "Yeah, you got him good Mace, good job" said Conley to the shooter who was a member of the Organization. Amechi, pouring himself a shot of gin and downing it quickly, exits the limo and motions Conley over to talk. "Mace get rid of Mr. DeLuna here, they'll think he jumped bail or something" said Conley before closing the door and walking towards the back of the limo with Amechi, who was shaken up by the whole ordeal. "Conley, this is fucked up, Tony was a dear friend of mine. You know why I never reconnected with all my pals back in Brooklyn? Because I didn't want to be a part of anything like this, a gangland hit." "You done bellyaching yet?" asked Conley who looked at Amechi as if he was weak. Conley was significantly taller than Amechi, so he looked down at him with his hands on his hips. "Tony DeLuna was a piece of shit, he killed, dealed dope, and laundered money. One person he laundered money through is you Mr. Swiss Ambassador. How much money are you going to get from this deal again?" "It's not about that and you know it, this man was a friend of mine and I helped him as much as I could. But that's neither here nor there. I'm going back to Switzerland; I will do my work from there for the next few months. This is an unofficial visit, and no one is to know that I was here for anything. I guess what I'm saying is make all of this disappear, including Tony" said Amechi with real conviction in his voice. "Well, I guess you aren't so worried about him as you are yourself. Listen, my team is of the highest trained professionals in moving in silence. We are untraceable, so you go ahead back to Geneva in your cushy, plush penthouse and continue to live your cushy, plush life; my team and I will continue to do dirty work for all of you and keep you squeaky clean" said Conley, who let Amechi know that he despised men of his stature in the world; Privileged men who were compensated for their sheer existence and not for merit. While men like Conley who did the dirty work by serving the country in the military still couldn't be compensated properly without taking it. This was one of his main pillars in the bylaws of the Organization. They would continue to do the dirty work, but they would be compensated properly and in their own way, not waiting for the government to give them a handout. Sounds like a conflict of interest, but Conley always operated in favor of national security, which is why a lot of information couldn't get out and his team made sure of it. "Let's be sure of it, and don't forget, I handle money in Switzerland for you and your team as well. By the way, the quicker you can get to Chicago, the better. I hope your team can pull through this mess. It's not public knowledge yet, but your star attorney being shot, the bombing in Montana, and now this kid going rogue, you guys are some serious shit" said Amechi as he was escorted to his jet. Conley thought to say something but didn't bother. He knew that men in his position could never understand managing the operation that kept their stomachs full. He then walked over to his own jet heading to Chicago to clean up the mess in the Midwest.

Chapter 30

"We are heading there now, not sure how the hell you got this information but damnit, you're a fucking genius" said Jankowski talking to McNamara on the phone. He rode shotgun as Shapiro floored it with the lights on down Michigan Ave. Passing the Magnificent Mile would make you think about the finer things in life as you pass all the designer stores for fashion, furniture, jewelry, and more. There are army federal vehicles trailing, almost like a motorcade, but traveling 60 mph as if they are on a high-speed chase. They are missing accidents by the slightest bit, but once they cross Chicago Ave. and approach the Water Tower mall, they slow down and become inconspicuous. According to McNamara, the guys have the place covered and they need to approach in a way they won't see them coming. The way to do this will be park a block or two away, but with all cars parking on different blocks. Then they would enter and be ready to engage the so called "feds" at the building. "This is the ballsiest shit I think I have ever done" said Shapiro who began to approach slow as they approached the apartment building. "Yeah me too, it will be like an old gangland shootout and where better than Chicago, home of Al Capone. I wonder how Elliot Ness felt when he was in this situation" said Jankowski who was locking and loading his weapons as well as putting on his vest.

They parked the car about a block and a half away, along with another car of agents including Agent Brown. Jankowski and Brown both pulled shotguns out of the trunk and flanked Shapiro and the other agent who walked slightly ahead. From the block to the west they saw 5 agents coming, 2 with shotguns. From the North they saw 8 agents and from the South, there were 10 agents. They all converged on the block that the apartment sat on and entered from an open side door, possibly left open by an unsuspecting tenant making a quick run to the nearby convenience store. They entered and began to quietly move up the stairs. It was about 20 floors up so they had a good amount of time to make it up before they got there, but the element of surprise dictated that they shouldn't come through the elevators and give the "feds" the drop on them approaching.

At the same time, Gaden, Drake, and a few other Organization members approach the front desk. Somehow, they didn't notice the nearly 30 agents approaching the building, but their limo was turning down the block just as they all made it in. "Hello, I am one of the supervisors over at the Fed" said Gaden as he showed the receptionist his "FBI badge." It looked real and the woman called up to Gordon to notify him of Gaden's arrival. "You can head right up sir, floor 20." "Oh, I am aware ma'am, this is a highly sensitive case and I try to stay in the loop about everything that is going on. "Well you should know that some crazy man came here about 15 minutes ago saying that he was part of the federal team. He was unshaven and was highly upset, not sure where he went but I denied him access" said the receptionist. "Did he happen to leave a name?" asked Gaden. "Frank Houston" said the receptionist. Gaden looked at Drake and was confused, why would Frank be coming to the building that they are holding Rico's mother up at? "Did he have anyone else with him?" asked Gaden who was curious to know if he showed up with Rico to free his mother. "No, he was by himself, he looked pretty bad as if he hadn't slept in days" said the receptionist. "Thank you, I will have to contact that agent I believe he came here to check on things fresh off a stakeout. If he comes back, please call up to the apartment and let me know" said Gaden as he and his men approached the elevator.

Jankowski, Shapiro, and Brown all took lead slowly moving toward the 20th floor avoiding contact with anyone until they hit the 16th floor and someone decides to walk down the stairs. Shapiro motions him to go back in but he gets curious to what's going on, which forces Brown to hold his pistol up and threaten him before he ran back inside. As they begin to get closer to the 20th floor, they hear commotion. This causes the lead men to run up the stairs to see what is going on.

"You and this bitch about to be some dead motherfuckers if y'all don't tell me where Rico is right now!" yelled Houston as he had a gun aimed at McNamara/Schultz and Rita. "Put the gun down now!" yelled Jankowski with his shotgun drawn. "Oh, let me guess you're the Feds here to take us down. Well answer me this, where the fuck is Rico Jones, I'm going to put a bullet in his head the same way I did that motherfucker over there. This is where Frank Houston completely lost his mind, the misdirection of the Organization had led to the belief that they were untouchable and had infiltrated all aspects of law enforcement. This led to lawlessness so the fact that Houston had murdered a man in cold blood and notified federal agents didn't seem possible as they were supposed to be juiced in. "Listen, man, you just killed a man we can talk this out to save your life" said Shapiro. "My life? That's laughable, get the boss up here he'll straighten all this bullshit out. We got a hero over here, this little fuckin punk Brandon Schultz trying to run off with Rico's mother. I bet the little punk set all of this shit up himself. I had to ice Gordon, never trusted the motherfucker anyway" said Houston who believed that all of these federal agents were part of the Organization. "All of you guys must be part of the D.C. team, no worries all of this shit will be taken care of. First order of business is to get rid of this body and take out the trash. Don't kill the broad though, she'll lead us right to Rico. "We have Rico, just put the gun down we will get the boss right away" said Shapiro who realized what was going on. "Oh shit, must have been amped up" said Houston as he put his gun on his waist, at which time, two actual agents handcuffed him and placed him under arrest. "Man, what the fuck are you doing? Hey dumb ass it's me, Frank, you assholes are playing this shit too serious" said Houston. "This is serious, Frank Houston you're under arrest for murder" said Jankowski. "Get your hands off my associate" said Gaden as he, Drake, and their men stepped off the elevator. "Boss man, your guys are fucking up" said Houston. "No, Frank, you're fucking up. You should have called so I could have given you the rundown of what has happened over the last couple of days. Unfortunately for you, these men are the FBI and they aren't friends of ours" said Gaden, looking over at Rita and Schultz. "Brandon, did you tell your friends who you really were? Did you know that it was a federal crime to impersonate a federal agent? Did you also know that you were a fugitive of the law? Now just because you had a change of heart of your criminal behavior doesn't get you off the hook for the crimes that you have committed" said Gaden looking directly at Schultz before turning his attention to Shapiro and Jankowski. "You men seem to be reasonable, so here is the deal we will make right now. Let Frank Houston go right now and take this crook in, he has committed multiple felonies right under your watch. We would hate for all of this to get back to the media and expose the most powerful federal agency in the world as incapable of discovering a computer hacker in their own organization. And say for instance that this was the case, I'm sure the director would love to put water on this fire before it became too big of a deal. And if you don't believe me why don't you give him a call." Shapiro and Jankowski both listen to Gaden and take in what he says, but they both agree when Shapiro speaks. "It doesn't matter about appearances buddy, it's all about putting juiced in thugs like you and Houston in prison. We know who you are but the only person that could put you behind bars is dead, but I'm sure that you are aware of that. Frank Houston is going to jail, point blank. We are also going to take in Ms. Jones and Agent McNamara, for their protection as well possible charges being filed against McNamara. If the director has an issue with us doing our job as you say he would, he can come down to the MCC and we can discuss it." At this point multiple agents swoop in and take Houston, Rita, and

Brandon in cuffs and escort them to the elevator. "Let me and my men take them out boss, we'll kill these punks" said Drake who was highly upset by the whole ordeal, even though he was glad to see Houston taken out in cuffs. "No worries Tony, we have to call Conley, if Stone isn't available as he hasn't been, then we will get some new lawyers to get Frank off. Brandon Schultz is lucky to be in jail, but we will kill him before it's all said and done. Rita Jones, I will send in someone that is perfect for the job to torture her nice and slow before throwing her out of a window" said Gaden with a smile on his face. "Let's go men, we're heading to the penthouse to strategize." They all waited until the elevator was available again and headed downstairs to the limos that were parked out front. Gaden knew that this was one that was out of his control and knew that Conley could easily step in and diffuse the whole situation. There might be some strong arming involved, but he was prepared to do whatever was necessary to put this situation to rest.

Chapter 31

"Calm down, we will get all of them. No Frank isn't going to die in prison. No, just calm down. I've got all of this under control. The director is on his way out, these tough guy G-men wannabes are going to get assigned to desk duty for 30 years. I'm going to take care of everything" said Conley as he was trying to calm an overzealous Gaden. Conley knew that no matter how much the game is rigged, there will still be logistical errors that will cause everything to look bad. Rico Jones was that logistical error. All he could think about was how many times he had told Gaden and Stone to not deal with the kid, but they were hell bent on scoring all that money from the North Koreans. Conley knew that a man who hadn't walked through fire would crack as soon as the heat hit him, but these guys thought that Conley's way of thinking was outdated. Well, in the grand scheme, everyone came running to him in trouble. Kind of shows that the old way of doing things is the right way of doing things. As the flight landed and he stepped off the plane, he knew that there were some things that would never be the same on the way the Organization operated. They would lose a lot of connections based on these events and their power in the U.S. would deteriorate. In his mind it was worth it as most of their money came from Europe, Africa, and Asia. But in keeping true to that old-fashioned way of thinking, there is no place like home. As he stepped off the plane and started heading down the stairs to his limo that was waiting, he had a strange feeling. That strange feeling was confirmed when he opened the door and saw the director of the FBI sitting in the limo smoking a cigar. All he could do was smack himself in the forehead and acknowledge the "Big Cheese" as he was called to people that knew him.

"Director, good to see you" said Conley as he stepped into the limo. The Big Cheese was none other than the director of the FBI Hamilton Schlister. Schlister had been a major player in law enforcement for years, he was one who lived by the old school code of law; get the bad guys off the street by any means necessary. But he also understood politics. He was a major part in the war on drugs in the '80s, as well as bringing down gang chiefs in the '90s such as Larry Hoover and Jeff Fort. But his biggest claim to fame was personally slapping the cuffs on the most powerful caporegime of the now DeLuna family Paul DeLuna, Tony DeLuna's father in 1991 and putting him away for the rest of his life. "So, I hear that this mess in Chicago are your men. A shame, I always thought that your connections would surely keep all things like this under the radar" said Schlister. "Sir, with all due respect, this is a few of your men. Some guys who are operating without clearance" said Conley as he lit a cigar of his own. "What you have to understand is that not all of our business is going to mesh well with your business. You must make sure that the right people are in place and understand everything that is going on. What do you expect me to do? Go in here and tell my men not to do their job? This is what they are paid to do. Now if you couldn't connect with them and set up an arrangement, in all fairness, all bets are off. If we don't take care of things using some form of proper procedure then all hell would break loose, and that is something we can't afford" said Schlister. "This is understood, but these guys have been going from state to state following this case. Sounds great

right? But here is the problem, they got their nose too deep into Gresham and

got some local yokels blown up in Montana, then they went to New York and

got a VP of Gresham killed. I'd say it's high time they pump the brakes and

let all of this get off the grid before some more bad things happen" said

Conley, who at this point was beginning to worry about the overall health of

his operation. Schlister stared off into the sky for a short period of time. This

is where he usually shines as it was just some politically correct mambo jumbo

that he could say to get things to go his way. In this case, things were a bit

more sensitive. Gresham was a corporation that he was highly familiar with.

Over the years he had taken massive kickbacks from this corporation to keep

the SEC and FDA off their ass for some underhanded things that they were

doing. More importantly, it kept the IRS from jumping down their throats for

the multitudes of tax fraud they had executed. Reason being is that Gaden

and Stone were silent partners and would do whatever they needed to do to

keep everything quiet. Schlister was very familiar with these men and the

way they operated. He figured that if they were doing their dirt in the name of

the CIA, then his bureau was safe. But now was the time when too many men

had too much information about his wrongdoings and that he couldn't have

getting out. "What is needed of me when we get down to the MCC?" asked

Schlister who, after assessing the severity of the situation, had decided it was

time to get this quiet before it made any noise. "Walk in, exonerate whoever

we need to and decide who will be imprisoned for their wrongdoings" said

Conley who felt a bit of relief. "Make no mistakes Conley, I am still going to do the right thing, I just want to do it with no heat" said Schlister. At this point, Conley knew that he would need Stone. Conley knew of Stone's plans to double-cross the Organization and it might just be needed for the ultimate plan to save his own ass.

"This is bullshit" said Houston in interrogation. "Frank, it's just us here now, the tough guy act can go away. Tell us a little bit about the guys that you work for, was Justin Stone involved? Where is he? He was Tony DeLuna's attorney, DeLuna skipped bail, did they run off together? What is Stone's true connections? We know that you know something" said Jankowski as he interrogated Houston to no avail. Frank Houston would not turn on the Organization. It was just not going to happen in that manner. If anything, they would have to turn on him first. "Damnit Frank, I can do this all day, why don't I step out of the room turn up the A/C and see what you have to say in about 2 hours." "Yeah you do that and bring in my lawyer while you're at it" said Houston who had his arms crossed with no intention of giving any detail. In his mind he knew that he would get out, but there was some doubt. He doubted he'd get out anytime soon, maybe he would have to sit for a day, a month, a year. He didn't care he wasn't going to help the Feds prosecute him for something he felt he was doing for the benefit of the government.

"I don't think the guy is going to budge" said Jankowski to Shapiro. "He doesn't have to, he admitted to killing that guy, we have him hook, line, and sinker" said Shapiro who stared at Houston through the interrogation room glass. "But what secrets lie with him? I bet they have so much dirt that could get all of them the electric chair" said Jankowski. "Yeah, but all that matter is that if Rico IDs him, he's done he almost isn't necessary. But he isn't who we really want, sure he has rank but Gaden is the guy and he is the one that we don't have a case against and that doesn't sit well with me" said Shapiro who was getting mad at the fact that not only did Houston admit to killing the fake agent, but he also admitted that Gaden was the head man in charge but there was nothing that could be done. Ricky Herrera would love to see this man face justice as he was the one that was pulling the strings to have him killed. It was Shapiro's theory that he was the one that had Stone killed as well. All to tie up the loose ends of Gresham. And what was so significant about this company? It had ties to money laundering but nothing that was admissible in court, and anything they did have died with Herrera. As Shapiro contemplated all of this, he felt a tap on his shoulder...

"Jack how are you today?" asked Schlister, flanked by Conley and a few other FBI agents. "Director, how are you? It's an honor that you would come down and see the body of work that I put together. I hope Captain Nicholson doesn't get too much credit" said Shapiro with a non-chalant chuckle. "Jack, I'd like you to meet Cmdr. Andrew Conley, head of the CIA special forces task force and he has some information that he would like you, Agent Brown, Agent Jankowski, Captain Shaughnessy of the Chicago field office as well as Captain Nicholson. Captain Nicholson will join us via video conference, and I have a meet time set up for all of us in 15 minutes. Don't be late!" said the Schlister knowing that this is when he would spring the news that would catapult this entire operation into orbit. Keep it quiet and all suspects that you are holding regarding this please keep them detained and calm, all will be explained in this meeting." Schlister, Conley, and the rest of their group began to head down the hall towards that conference room. Shapiro was more shocked that he would be keyed in to such a high-level meeting. Was it promotions for he and Jankowski? How and why were they in Chicago so fast? It was amazing to see hard work paying off. Whatever would be said in that meeting, Shapiro knew that it would change his career with the FBI forever.

As he finally began to come back to consciousness, Stone realized that he had been shot multiple times by David Martel. The only problem was why? "Justin are you ok? asked Dir. Rogers. "I think so, but I'm alive that's important right? I got to get out of here, DeLuna's case starts today" said Stone who was really groggy, and vision was still blurry. "Justin, DeLuna's case was 2 days ago and from what I can see he jumped bail. They're looking for him now, don't worry about it just get back to health, I'm sure you will be needed soon" said Rogers. "For what? Does anyone know where Tony is right now? I know this guy we do a line of blow and he'll be back focused" said Stone who was lucky to only have the bullet graze his head and take a piece of his ear off. "DeLuna is dead Justin, but no one knows, and we're going to keep it that way. Things are moving, the Organization is going to be reshuffled and there will be new leadership. You will be given your life as you are so useful, but you won't be involved in the day-to-day. Gaden is going to be executed I hate to tell you this, but you are on the upper echelon part of life now no more underhanded bullshit. You have been selected but Gaden, Houston, and all those guys will get rolled over. What do you think of this information?" asked Rogers who had a sinister smirk on his face. "All I can ask is when does the new life get started and when will we know Gaden is dead" asked Stone who wanted to double-cross Gaden anyway, so all of this was great news, the men in power finally saw the problem with Gaden and was going to take care of business the way he wanted to. "We will know within the next hour, get your rest and I will keep you posted" said Rogers as he walked out of the room and headed into the war room with Captain Nicholson as they awaited news of the new regime.

"Thank you" said Agent Brown speaking to Rico. "What are you thanking me for?" asked a curious Rico. "I'm thanking you because this thing that you got in the middle of just made my career. Did you think that this was it? Did you think that you were done taking orders?" Agent Brown had become convinced that he would be a part of the new regime. He had knowledge of all that was going on beforehand which led to his disdain for Justin Stone as he knew that he was a key player in all of it. But with Rico's information this would lead to a shuffle of the deck. "Agent Brown, listen I'm sorry for my arrogance before, but I promise I just want the right thing to happen." "Oh, the right thing will happen, trust that" said Agent Brown as he got up and walked out.

Rico sat and thought for a second, was he being set up? Was the government stringing him along? What if this was a hoax and he was the fall guy? So many questions, so few answers. Around this time, he began to think of his mother and wonder was she okay. Though he could be a cunning thief and even a killer when necessary, Rico was still a kid at heart. He wasn't ready for the responsibility that had fell into his lap. If he could turn back the hands of time and just stay at the MCC and serve his time, he would be at peace a lot more. This is when he realized what he wanted, the opportunity to just stay in jail and live out what was going to happen in his wire fraud case. If this opportunity was presented in return for his silence for what he had seen over the last few days, he would run with it and not look back.

Chapter 32

Gaden and Drake sit in the limo in front of the MCC prepared to go in and post bail for Frank Houston. "I have a feeling Tony; I think they will assassinate me today" said Gaden who was in deep thought. Gaden prided himself in staying two steps ahead of everyone. Right now, he was only one step ahead and the heat was closing in on him. He could feel people plotting to take him out as he had gotten too powerful to control. After all the money and all the success, it didn't matter. He was still being controlled by the CIA. After years of service, he had gotten many men rich. This includes high ranking law enforcement officials such as Conley, Schlister, and Rogers. He also had millions of dollars of kickbacks going to politicians, judges, and the wealthiest of businessmen. He started thinking, what his next move? This was war, but he already knew how to win. His best strategy was to retreat and hide, without letting anyone know that he was retreating or hiding. The only way this was possible was for the world to think that he was dead. From this ideology, he knew what he had to do next. "They can try, but I promise you, I won't let anything happen to you" said Drake, the loyal soldier just as much as Houston. "Our next move is going to be a big one, they don't want you, so you will have to tell them that you killed me" said Gaden looking Drake square in the eye and notifying him of his duty. "Boss, what are you saying? I'm not going to kill you" said Drake. "You will have to tell the big wigs i.e. Schlister, that you did. Once they think that I'm dead they will be comfortable. And for your actions, you will be awarded, you might be the new head of the Organization" said Gaden brainstorming as the plot began unravel. "Where will you be?" asked Drake who finally began to understand. "The less you know is better, what we are going to do is video tape you 'killing' me and showing my body being burnt in a building. This will be a cadaver and I will get off the grid for a little while until things quiet down. Remember, don't get too caught up in Conley's garbage and I want you to brief Frank on what's going on. But before this could be viewed as legitimate, we must go now with you resurfacing later. Frank may think that he will go to prison, but you will come in and save the day as I always did" said Gaden who eerily sounded like he was speaking from the grave. "Boss whatever your plan is, let's get it done and I will execute to the 'T'" said Drake who was eager to think that he would now be the man in charge. Their limo pulls off and they head to a distant location to film Gaden's 'death.' Drake shot him with blanks and rambled off the words that would legitimize this ordeal, "Boss, your way of doing things are over, I am taking this operation and whatever those above us wants to do, I will get it done, better than you could have ever done." In the video Drake shoots Gaden 5 times in the chest and films him taking his last breath. He then chops off his head as a souvenir for Conley and all the higher ups. All in a plot to save Gaden's life he had to be 'killed.' Gaden knew that he had gotten too powerful so while Drake was filming this with the cadaver, Gaden was escaping out the back door. He had never run from his problems, but this was the one opportunity that he had to get away and not deal with repercussions. In a sense he felt free as he drove in a Chevy Malibu heading to an unknown destination. All he wanted to do was get back to New York, get Amber, and head out to a distant island to plan his next move. As for the Organization, for once, he had let it go. His conscious was clear, he had left all accesses to Drake to pay for Frank Houston's legal defense/bail money and could only hope for the best. For once, he was no longer responsible.

"Gentlemen, I'm glad we could all be here today to discuss some new direction" said Schlister. On video conference was Capt. Nicholson in San Francisco and Rogers from Washington D.C. "First, I will ask Director Rogers if all his plans are on the horizon." "Director Schlister everything is ready, Justin Stone is ready to talk in court and he is recovering well." "Excellent" said Schlister who wanted Stone to bury the men that he had been working with the last few years. "The next order of business is Rico Jones. Do we imprison him, or do we leave him on the streets to work off his debts?" "Sir, if I may interject" said Shapiro who was surprisingly invited to this meeting. "I don't think that Jones was given much of a choice. Sure, he is a hacker, but he is not a gangster by a long stretch. I think we make him stay silent, but imprisonment is not necessary." "Shapiro, I like the way you think, but what if he talks?" asked Schlister. "Then we kill him" said Conley who had no problem letting it be known where he stood. "Sounds good, we put him and the mother somewhere where they can be watched, and we make sure not a word leaks. I'm in agreement" said Schlister as he was going through the subjects rather fast. "Rashan Gaden, he is a problem, how do we solve it? We all know the answer but now is the time for objection" said Schlister as he scrolled the room and saw no objection. "Alright well there is our answer." "Next we need to reassign all of you men here, this case has gotten too out of hand and the media is starting to catch wind. Shapiro and Jankowski, you two are no longer based out of the San Francisco office, you are now based right out of DC and you will co-anchor the special investigation force. Shaughnessy, you will see no change to your position, but you will lose Agent Marcus Brown as he will go to San Francisco and replace Shapiro as lead agent. Conley, you will continue your post with the CIA, but I have cleared with your superiors for you to become our new liaison. We need to know what's going on nationally and internationally. Are there any questions or concerns?" asked Schlister as he opened the floor to all in attendance. All the men were astonished. All agents asked to attend were promoted, including Agent Brown who had worked so hard and was now a player in the FBI grand scheme. Shapiro and Jankowski had done such a great job running around the country that they had earned a spot as the director's personal investigation team. They would be the guys that had the inside information to all investigations and would lead the charge in stopping crime. But of course, Shapiro had questions about Gaden. "I think we are letting him off too easy, I believe he should be imprisoned for his actions, then he will see what it's like to be on the other side of destruction. "Jack, we risk exposure from that move, sure we can discredit him, but he knows too much and could easily utilize the information that he has. I know, we weren't logical in ever giving him enough power to bury us, but now is the time to bury him before he gets too out of hand" said Schlister. Shapiro weighed it in his mind for a little while and then realized that it wasn't worth it to let information leak. The American people needed facts, but some facts were certainly not needed in order to keep everyone on the same page. "Finally, there is the biggest threat of them all, Brandon Schultz, aka, Agent Josh McNamara. How the hell did we get so sloppy to allow this bozo to infiltrate us to save his friend? We got to put this kid out of commission, but I have a plan for that. Our boys inside can handle him once we lock him up for impersonating a federal agent. We have to show all of these tech junkies that we won't be fucked with!" said Schlister, who seemed more hostile over this situation than any of the others. "But, in all honesty, we own him and can use him however we see fit. I believe that will be the bigger power play" said Conley, who always wanted to use all resources available. "Commander, what were you thinking?" asked Schlister. "Well first we could use his help out in Montana..." said Conley, with a smirk on his face. The look on Schlister's face showed that he knew exactly what Conley was thinking.

"I demand to get out of here right now! I have done nothing wrong; I didn't know what my son and his friend put together" said Rita Jones sitting in a cold interrogation room. "Ma'am, you have nothing to worry about. The preliminary word here is that the higher-ups are finalizing some things to send you home with no more guards. Your son will deal with his original charges and that's it" said Agent O'Donnell who was told to keep her at bay while Schlister got all of the details in order. "Well I'd say that y'all have really done enough today" said Rita. At that moment, Agent Brown walked in and motioned Agent O'Donnell to leave the room. Once he left the room, Agent Brown focused on Rita and she focused right back. After an intense stare-down for about 10 seconds, Agent Brown sat down, folded his hands, and let Rita know what the future would look like. "Rita, you have been a doll for this investigation, and we thank you. We no longer need you, so on behalf of the Bureau, you are free to get up and leave right now." Brown knew that she would have questions and there was a 5 second silence before she started them. "What about Rico?" asked Rita. "Well, he still has that wire fraud case, but I think that there will be some NDAs that he will be presented, and he will be free to go as well. In the grand scheme, what he has done isn't worth us worrying too much if he abides by his NDAs" said Agent Brown. "What will be in these Non-Disclosure Agreements, Agent Brown? Is it because there was some misconduct by the FBI and now if he shuts up, he walks free?" asked Rita, who at this point was kind of seeing what was unfolding. "Ms. Jones, however, you want to dissect this situation is up to you, regardless, there will be NDAs" said Agent Brown. "So, will I have to sign them as well?" asked Rita who couldn't believe the information that she was getting. "Not at all, however, since Rico can't tell you what happened, what will you know? Except when we put you in witness protection to save your life as Rico was in the mix with dangerous gangsters? Now is that really something that you would want to go public with. Your genius son, who just perpetuated the stereotype of gangbanging and drug dealing?" asked Agent Brown who was sure that he would get her silence. "The biggest mistake Rico made was believing that he was circumventing the justice system. He was merely getting in too deep with you demons, and now he must decide to stay silent or die. I may not be in with your crowd Agent Brown, but I know that you all control the world and because of that, I will retreat. I am no one that you must worry about, but God is watching, and you remember that. Am I free to go now?" asked Rita as she was hoping to reach Agent Brown's conscious, his soul. However, her words went in one ear and out of the other. Agent Brown simply replied, "Yes ma'am" and escorted her to the door. "Do you need a ride to your home?" "No sir, I will find a way" said Rita as she walked out of the interrogation room and headed through the main lobby. Her means of getting home was the CTA. She would take the bus back to her home and try to put all of this behind her. She understood that though she wouldn't sign any NDAs, her silence was expected. She would simply jump back into her old life and forget any of this had happened. As she walked, she thought to herself that she could literally write a book to what she had seen over the last few weeks. However, a glance back and she saw Agent Brown standing at the doorway waving and smiling almost as if he was a good officer of the law. The whole situation had opened her mind up, and it woke her up to the innerworkings of the FBI and law enforcement in general. They will protect their own even if it means letting a criminal out to keep them quiet or killing someone to keep that same silence. For years she had been an advocate in the police's cause, but from this point on, she knew that she couldn't trust them. She just prayed that after some time in the day, Rico would join her at home as Agent Brown had made it seem.

"Conley just wanted you to know that Gaden is gone" said Drake on a cellphone sitting in the limo after he had helped Gaden get off the grid. "What the fuck do you mean he's dead, who killed him?" asked Conley, still with Schlister "You got some explaining to do Drake, do you know how many pieces I have to move in order to make this thing overseas work?" "No worries that's what you have me for, I haven't been in the States for a long time. I have been in North Korea, Ghana, Sierra Leone, China, Turkey, Australia, and anywhere else in the world heading up the day-to-day for The Organization. I am fully capable of running the entire operation and I know who to put in key positions to keep this ship sailing smooth" said Drake, who was confident in what he was saying. This illustration helped Conley put 2 and 2 together and figure out that Drake was the one to kill Gaden. "So, what made you do it Tony? He was always good to you. Anytime something went wrong, he'd get on the phone with you and you would get it handled. You seemed to be a loyalist, so how could you step up this way?" Conley was curious and had to ask this question. "Easy, he got greedy. After a while, the same men we were doing business with began to question the piece of the pie that we were taking. Example, in Sierra Leone, we would cut them into the diamonds that we put on the black market 50/50 split. But, the cut for them got smaller and smaller and I didn't want to do this, but I did what was necessary. The man in charge questioned our actions, and when I consulted

Gaden, his response was simply 'kill him.' I couldn't believe what my new mission was, a man that had been good to us and let us in their country to steal ended up getting his head chopped off" said Drake, who sounded sincere in what he was saying putting it off on Gaden when it was actually his idea. Conley listened to this and remembered this and was simply told by Gaden that there was a threat made and they had to murder in self-defense. "Well, I will say I had no idea about that and I'm sure that was by his design. Tony, I'm going to trust you for now, but I need you to find a lawyer like Stone to keep in the loop and to keep all our guys out of the shits. His first order of business is to represent Frank Houston, he will be your right-hand man, and that is non-negotiable. Frank can handle things that you won't believe, but we must set the stage right to have him out soon. He is a soldier and he can easily do a year, but he must get out. This lawyer that you find has to be ruthless, willing to get his hands dirty and have a track record of getting shit done" said Conley who figured that if Drake could handle this mission, he could be a suitable replacement for Gaden. "Tony, if the guy that you bring us is not worthy of our time, you will die" said Conley who hung up the phone in that instant and let Drake stew over what he had said. Drake on the other hand put the phone down with a smile and popped open a bottle of champagne. He grabbed a flute and poured a glass and drank it as fast as he poured it. He let the privacy window down to notify the driver of the next destination. "Hello sir" said the driver, "off to Executive Airport, correct?" "No, let's take the scenic route, I love Chicago, let's go to DuPage and please, take the streets" said Drake who would enjoy his champagne while he watched the city of Chicago operate. Traveling the world had allowed Drake to enjoy some luxuries that the average person would love to have access but hadn't been afforded the opportunity. As he rolled the window up, he turned on the stereo and turned on satellite radio, in which he found his favorite song "My Ambitionz Az A Ridah" by 2Pac. He played the music drank champagne and mentally got prepared for this big step he was taking. The only thing he could think about was Gaden, who could potentially could come back to life but if everything went well, he would take him out for real this time.

Chapter 33

"Rico, good news, you're going home!" exclaimed Jankowski, he might have been happy to know about the big money promotion he and Shapiro had just got, but either way, he was very direct. "Interesting, what do I have to do?" asked Rico. "Sign some forms and you're out" said Shapiro who promptly brought out the NDAs. "These are Non-Disclosure Agreements, basically, you promise us in writing that you won't speak of what happened and you're free to go" said Shapiro. "So, the shootings, the stealing, the injustices, I just agree to not speak on and I'm free" said Rico who was very apprehensive. "That's it, look, we fucked up, we should have taken better care of you in here and you would have never been in the situation that you were in. We are going to take care of everything, you don't have to worry about anyone coming after you" said Jankowski. "I'm sure Gaden wants me dead, what do you do with him? What is your plan? I could easily step out of here and take a bullet to the head" said Rico who was sincerely concerned about his safety. "Don't worry about Gaden, we are tracking him right now" said Jankowski, as an agent came and notified Shapiro and Jankowski that there was something that they needed to see right away. "Excuse us Rico, we will be right back. Look at those documents, all you have to do is sign and you're out" said Shapiro, as he and Jankowski stepped out to see what the agent had that was so important. After a few minutes and a few looks at one another, Shapiro and Jankowski stepped back into the interrogation room. "Your biggest concern isn't a problem anymore" said Shapiro to Rico. "What does that mean?" asked Rico, who was confused as both agents looking at him looked sick or confused. "Gaden is dead" said Jankowski who was just blunt and spit it out. "Wait, what?" said Rico, before all men in the room went silent for about a minute. "Well, he was your biggest concern, but I just watched that man be brutally murdered by Tony Drake and that ends the whole ordeal" said Shapiro who was not only shocked but confused as well. The Bureau was going to kill him any way but the way he died and had his head chopped off was graphic and had sent he and Jankowski into a depression almost. "Look Rico, just sign the forms and go home. Stay out of trouble from this point on" said Jankowski. "What about Brandon?" asked Rico who was concerned for his friend. "Don't worry about him, he will be processed in for impersonating a federal agent" said Shapiro as he seemed to shake off the memories of the video from his mind. "Well, I just want you guys to take it easy on him, he only did what he did to protect me, and he had nothing to do with Montana" said Rico as Brandon was implicated a suspect in all of the incidents happened in Montana. "How do you know about Montana?" asked Jankowski. "Gaden told me, he said that he sent a couple of hitmen out to blow up the manufacturer and their cover was blown so some more people had to be killed" said Rico, who even himself realized that he said it too casually for comfort. "Well, the Bureau is taking care of everyone who was hurt in Montana and Brandon will be cleared of that as he obviously is alive and has a good alibi, as Josh McNamara" said Shapiro who knew that he would need to make an appearance in the next couple of days to pay respects to Henry Wallace. "So, what's it going to be Rico, signed silence and no jail time. If you can't agree to that, you go down and you see how these guys are plugged into the prison system. They are like a virus; they infect everything and there is no limit to what they will do" said Jankowski. "Well, let's get it done, my lady is waiting on me" said Rico, who proceeded to sign the NDAs. "You've done a good thing, you're a smart kid. You will go far and probably put some good into this crooked world that we live in" said Shapiro who took the forms and placed them in his folder. At that moment, they shook hands and the guards outside of the interrogation room were called in to take Rico to an outbound cell. On his way out, Rico asked "Where is my mother?" "She is headed home; she has been released. Tell Mom not to worry about the mortgage, the bank has been paid in full" said Shapiro. "Wow, thanks, I think you guys need to fuck up more often" said a smiling Rico who was escorted to the cell to be processed out. As great as all of this was, he couldn't help but worry about his buddy Brandon. He had gone so far to impersonate an agent to help his friend out that Rico wouldn't feel right letting him rot in jail. But Rico would use his God given talent of hacking to situate him upon processing. He knew that he would not leave his friend to rot and he had a plan to spring him.

Amber sat in her plush apartment in Manhattan doing her makeup. As beautiful as she was, she would never have any issues making money rather it be in bars or a high-profile escort. As she didn't want to give her body away too much, she opted to work as a hostess at the hottest club in Manhattan. Her looks would bring a man in to spend $100 at the bar and that was all that was needed. Before she could get to the mascara, there was a knock at the door. She asked, "Who is it?" but got no answer. She decided to look through the peephole, saw that it was Gaden, opened the door, then immediately headed back to her vanity table without speaking. "Nice to see you too" said Gaden who couldn't believe the cold shoulder that he had gotten. "I'm glad that you could fit me into your busy schedule" said Amber as she rolled her eyes as if to say, 'I can't believe you're here.' "Amber, I know that you are upset that I haven't checked in, but there has been a lot going on" said Gaden, who came in and sat in chair that was next to her vanity. "Oh, like what Rashan? Some of your other whores who need your time and affection?" asked Amber who had actually fell in love with the man that she looked at. "No, I'm dead" said Gaden, who watched Amber stop doing her makeup to watch him for 10 seconds and say, "You really are an idiot." "No, I'm serious me showing up here puts me and you in danger. I had to fake my death so I can escape to my mansion in the Bahamas. I want you to come with me, I need you" said Gaden who was sincere in his words. "Mansion? In the Bahamas? Am I still going to look beautiful? I'm high maintenance. I need a lot" said Amber who took more time to look him in the eyes. As much as a high-priced woman as Amber was, she didn't mind danger and that made her perfect for laying low in the Bahamas as Gaden planned to do. "Yes, everything that you need, I will fly them out and hell this house is so big, they can stay too. They just can't talk about what is going on" said Gaden. "Not a problem, and you know I love my

Gucci, Prada, Louis Vutton…" said Amber, who a sane mand would turn away. "Amber, if that is what you want, I will have that shit come off the production line and flown to us on a private jet. Hell, if you want Donatella Versace or Vera Wang themselves to come make you clothes on site, I'm ok with it. I just need you to say yes" said Gaden, who was done with her and all of her complaining about what she may or may not get. "OK, well, when do we go?" asked Amber who was still getting ready for work. "Tonight, right now, call wherever you're going and tell them you won't be coming tonight or ever" said Gaden. Amber looked at him and was shocked at the turnaround. She had spent her whole life in New York, how could this be possible? But it didn't take long for her to say "OK!!!" she began packing some clothes and Gaden told her "pack light, anything that you think you might need we can buy once we are down there. You got 30 minutes, any liquor here?" said Gaden who figured that if they were abandoning ship, might as well drink up. "Yeah, there is some Patron in the freezer, drink up!" shouted Amber, who was in her room packing up at this point. Gaden figured, take a hot chick down to the Bahamas and restructure. Drake might be running in his place for now, but Gaden still had his connections and he did the best thing he could, get away from Conley. In 15 minutes, Amber was packed and ready to go to whatever adventure waited for them. Gaden helped her with the bag, got them downstairs to the waiting limo, and headed for the airport to fly to the Bahamas on a private jet. It might be crazy, but he knew that this was for the best. He was happy that Amber was ready to rock and roll with him, and for once, he could be a normal person.

Justin Stone finally gotten close to full strength and Rogers got word to take good care of him. "How are you Justin?" asked Rogers. "Great" said Stone, "I think this is the best rehab you can go through. Hell, I haven't even fiended for coke and I usually can't go more than 4 hours" said Stone. "Good, I'm glad we can provide this service to you Justin. Rest up, we have a big day tomorrow" said Rogers, who was flanked by two men in black suits and sunglasses. Stone thought it was strange when the two men who came in with Rogers didn't walk out to his pace, only enough to close the door before they riddled him with bullets. Originally, it was planned to use Stone as a key witness and kill him afterwards, but with the new ordeal it wasn't needed. Therefore, he wasn't needed and Schlister wanted him dead before they proceeded to the next phase of the operation. It important for Drake to find a new lawyer, they knew that Stone could never be what he used to be and that he was no longer trusted. Lawyers come a dime a dozen but finding one who fit Stone's profile would be hard. Either way, it was best for the business going forward. Now that Stone was dead, Rogers knew that he had to get in line. That means, shut up or die, how would he handle it? His only choice was to shut up at this moment in time. But him being a by-the-book lawman, he would figure out a way to bring Schlister and the whole old-time brigade down. He just needed more time.

"Great work men see you Monday at headquarters" said Schlister talking to Jankowski and Shapiro. "Sir, we need to go to California to get our lives situated for the moves, I believe Cody and I would both like 2 weeks off for the transition" said Shapiro, knowing that he would have to do some heavy loading to get all of the stuff that he needed. "Not me boss, I'll throw all of my shit in storage and be to DC on Tuesday" said Jankowski who was already trying to upstage Shapiro for another promotion down the line. "Alright, Jack, you got 2 weeks off report on that Monday. As for Cody, the day you report, I got some interesting things for you to investigate" said Schlister, who was almost disappointed that Shapiro couldn't make the move as soon as Jankowski could. "Have fun with that Cody" as Shapiro walked off almost into the abyss and headed for the vehicle that they both shared. Instead of going back to the hotel to stay, Shapiro simply grabbed his items and headed for O'Hare airport, he would first fly back to San Francisco and then head to Washington D.C. He didn't see the need in rushing what was next. However, he was upset at how Jankowski, an agent he had trained could be so overzealous in the decision-making process. However, he decided to just take some time away and upon his return, maybe he could figure it all out.

As Amber and Gaden settle at mansion outside of Nassau, he struggles at wondering how long all the peachiness will remain. She can take a dive in the pool, as she does regularly. She can eat the best of food, which his private chef prepares. She can have all the best fashion delivered to her, and she can walk through the richest area of Nassau and hobnob with all high society. But that isn't his only concern with Amber, she had seen too much. This mean that she knew too much, and if anyone found out he was alive, they'd surely target her to get information to kill or arrest him. Either way, this is the route that he was going and there was no turning back. More than anything, he had to assess rather he would kill her if needed, and the answer to that was hell yeah. There was no piece of ass so significant that Gaden wouldn't do what he needed to do in order to not lose his own life or status. The thought simmered his worried and he began to smile. He then lit a Cuban cigar on the balcony outside of the master bedroom and looked over the sunset. "This is paradise" said Amber who had just returned from a swim. "I'm going to take you to real paradise" said Gaden who grabbed her and led her into the shower for some fun.

Rico and Jordan sat on the front porch that night embracing one another. He knew that he loved her, but his youth would not allow him to express this. She understood and embraced him for who he was. "It's so peaceful, I feel like nothing in the world could destroy what we have as long as we are here for each other" said Rico. Jordan looked up at him and kissed him deeply. She loved his presence, his scent, his aura around her. She wasn't sure what it was about Rico Jones, but she couldn't get enough. "Do you promise that you won't do anything crazy like that without me knowing?" asked Jordan. "Of course, not baby, I need you here with me to keep me from making the worst decisions of my life." He realized that this is what he needed to sustain his inner peace, but there was still a part of him that desired the cash and influence he had as part of the Organization. But he would take a piece of their playbook and form his own organization clouded in secrecy. Not many knew how far his influence could reach, but he now had connections to some of the Organization's outliers, and that would lead him to make a lot of money if he could keep everything that he was doing under wraps.

"Agent McNamara" said Schlister, who finally had a chance to interview Brandon Schultz after navigating through the sea of confusion that was this day. "I'd say, I think I did pretty good, I was able to pull off one of the biggest infiltrations ever, I liken myself to the Great Gatsby…" said Brandon before Conley put him in a headlock. "Tell me something kid, if I killed you right now, don't you know that I could make you disappear? Where do you get the balls to say something stupid like that" said Conley who was running out of breath squeezing so hard. "Let him go Conley, you're going to kill the kid" said Schlister who didn't flinch at anything that he had seen. "Besides, this kid is our golden ticket." "What…what, what does that mean?" asked Brandon who was gasping for air and trying not to pass out from nearly being killed. "I mean, we got a big mess to clean up in Montana and since you like impersonating people, we'll have you do it again. You'll change your hair and we'll send you to a surgeon to restructure your face a little bit, with it being so messed up and all" said Schlister before punching him right in the nose and knocking him out of his seat. "Geesh Schlister, and you said I was rough housing him" said Conley who let out a chuckle. "You are now part of the Organization kid, you're good at infiltrating deep security clearances and we will start with using you as a good Samaritan to clean up the town of Billings. More than anything, we want you to gather intel to see who is talking about Gresham. We need that whole thing swept under the rug" said Conley who had a genius way to utilize Brandon to his advantage. "What if I decline the offer?" asked Brandon, causing the room to go silent. After the silence was laughter. Lots of laughter, sick, twisted, morbid laughter. Finally, Schlister said "what makes you think this is an offer, a choice? Your only other alternative is death son." "I drew Gaden here, which drew Frank Houston. I did a lot of good things for the FBI" said Brandon who was pouring blood at this point. "As an imposter! Now look, I'm trying to clean this shit show up, but rest assured that the two Neanderthals that were the catalysts of this mess is dead. And you're going to join them if you don't smarten up" said Conley who tossed him a rag to clean himself up. "Alright, when do I get started?" asked Brandon who knew that he would again outsmart these idiots but would play along. "As soon as you stop bleeding everywhere, I'll get you another rag and you will be escorted out" said Schlister, as he and Conley left the room. As Brandon continued to clean himself up, he began to come up with his grand plan of escape, but he knew that he would need Rico to get in on it. He would have to send a smoke signal to him from Montana. The good thing was that he and Rico had developed a secret, coded language to communicate with each other. They were just messing around one day on one of their hack missions and made the coding to send to each other and only the other could understand. He knew that by taking this mission he would be heavily watched and would have surveillance, wiretapping, and all the

technology in the world monitoring his every move. But he knew that the

code was untraceable and wouldn't get picked by anyone other than Rico.

Chapter 34

<u>One Month Later...</u>

"Damn Tony, I never thought that you would pull it off, but you did.

Acquitted of all charges at the preliminary hearing?" said Houston, who had

beat the murder charge simply because there was no evidence, because no

officers showed up and all of the evidence simply disappeared. "Frank, I told

you that I have all of the same connections as Gaden and more" said Drake, as

he popped the cork on a bottle of Dom Perignon. "Well, time to get back to

New York, right? Our operation will still be based out of there I'm assuming"

said Houston who toasted his flute to Drake's and others in the room. "It was

one of the quickest dismissals in the history of the Dirksen. Chicago has

always been a gangland city, but this takes the cake" said the Organization's

new attorney, Derrick Underwood, whose nickname was Derrick Underworld

in his hometown of Los Angeles. He was a lawyer like Justin Stone, crooked,

intelligent, connected, and could get dirt at the snap of a finger. One of his

first cases in private practice was getting a major drug dealer off on a

technicality, illegal search and seizure. He noticed that the address was

written wrong, the defendant lived in apartment 426 and apartment 425 was

written on the warrant. He exposed this and the case was thrown out after a

haul of 5 kilos for the LAPD. The drug dealer was so grateful that he not only

paid him $40,000 in cash but gave him a kilo of cocaine. Instead of snorting it,

Derrick put it on the streets and made a cool $100,000 off it. He was a legend in the LA streets and all gang members of all races gave him the utmost respect, there was rumor that he had gotten involved in a murder or two as well, but no confirmation, not even from Derrick himself. He used a team of investigators known as the Mod Squad to intimidate witnesses, bribe jurors, and a long list of other nefarious acts. Underwood stood 6' weighed about 200 lbs. and had a boxer's training regiment, he would spend a whole weekend running, sparring, lifting, hitting the gun range, and being generally prepared for anything to come his way from Monday through Friday. He took on the role because Drake had sought him out. Tony had been to LA a few times and Underwood would act as his tour guide in showing him where he needed to go avoid exposure when they were conducting Organization business. He had even filled in for Stone in court when he got too coked up to wake up in time to catch a flight to the West Coast for a deposition. Luckily, Underwood was a solid litigator and garnered a favorable outcome. "No Frank, I think I want to take the Organization in a new direction. Starting today, we will be based out of LA, I talked with Conley and he think it's genius. Even though we blended in with the New York population, in LA, we can reinvent ourselves. Hell, we can become movie stars if we want" joked Drake, who garnered some laughter from the room. Everyone except for Houston, who had grown up in New York and really enjoyed being part of the chaos that is the city. "Tony, we have to be careful, we can't go out there and be Hollywood. We must move in silence, maybe buying a building in downtown LA and operating as a real estate company. It was easy to be an empty shell in New York because nobody really cared. In LA, I think the spotlight will be all over us" said Houston who had some general concern about the move. "You're right Frank, that's why Derrick is going to run point on getting us all set up and connecting us with the right people. In the meantime, I think we all must go back to New York to shut down any obligations that we have and be ready to head out when the time is right. Derrick, how long will it take?" asked Drake. "No longer than a week, I got some real estate friends who will get us set up and we shouldn't have any problems. I also have some friends with the chamber of commerce so there will be no need to worry about having a shell company, it just has to make sense" said Underwood, whose wheels were spinning in his mind. Not only was he The Organization's new attorney and de facto right-hand man, but his city was now the base of operation. He could literally here cash registers going off in his head. "Well get on that, in one week the team will be coming down and we must move swiftly" said Drake who was taking in his new role as leader of The Organization as if it wasn't fake. But what if it wasn't? In his mind, even if Gaden tried to come back and reclaim his place, he has burned the bridges of Conley and they would no longer be based out of New York and with him being on the outs, he would have no way to find the new base of operation. Even if he could, Drake would simply kill him and that would be the end of the story. What a time to be alive! This is what Drake thought as he noticed Gaden trying to call him on his untraceable phone, but Drake looked at it and silenced it. The Organization was his now, and there was no turning back.

Houston knew something wasn't right, but he played along. He could not get a bond, so he had spent the whole month behind bars waiting on his preliminary hearing. In that month, his best friend had been "killed," according to Drake. But Houston had heard rumors that Drake was the one who killed him and there was a video. Houston would play the game; Drake was obviously appointed to the head of The Organization because he was a yes man to Conley. Conley had even had him kill Gaden because he was growing bigger than the games that Conley liked to play. If Houston had his way, he'd kill Drake right there in front of everybody in the room. But he knew that if Gaden was around, he would advise against it. Drake was a powerful man now but knew that he couldn't handle the pressures that would come with it. Even though it wouldn't happen at this very second, he knew that he would have to kill Drake and take over The Organization. He would move methodically and make sure that it was done to perfection.

Cooper was sad, she had taken some time off work to try and gather her thoughts. After all the bloodshed, the friends that she graduated the academy with dying, she was not in the right state of mind. She was next in line for a promotion since Lee had begun his campaign to run for Sheriff but wasn't in mental condition to do so. She sat on a park bench drinking a bottle of vodka, when a calm figured appeared to comfort her. "Don't look so sad, you're such a beautiful woman" said the stranger who was a shorter, slim dark-haired man. She immediately was turned on to his presence. "Hey bud, you don't know my troubles" said Cooper to the stranger who motioned for her to pass the bottle of vodka. Instead of being a self-righteous person and throwing the bottle away, he took a swig and passed it back to her. "I have some of my own, but who knows, maybe we are each other's solution" said the stranger staring deep into Cooper's eyes. Cooper was an attractive woman; she just never took time to date as she was always working around the clock. For once, maybe she would indulge in something that solely benefitted her. "You know what, I think you're right" she said with a smile taking another swig and passing it back to him. They continued to talk and would become good friends and more as the weeks went on...

The Godfather's blood was boiling knowing what Gaden and Drake pulled off. Yes, it got Gaden out off the grid, but what about his money? Drake had never been trusted by the Godfather and he knew that it was time for him to come and let Drake know who really ran the show. He would not reveal to the rest of The Organization that Gaden was still alive, but he would tear Drake into pieces if he messed up the flow of the operation. Gaden was loyal to the man who had once carried the torch of running the original incarnation of The Organization, but he hated Conley who had taken over for the original CIA point man. Conley was greedy and was also a snake, a man of no honor. The Godfather had to come out of the shadows and let him and the CIA know that they had no authority and Gaden would return to reclaim what he had built up. But he was not upset that Gaden used such a strategic move, he was more upset that it happened without his authorization. Either way, it was time to shuffle the deck and the key to this was Rico Jones...

7 Deadly Sins (Beginning) ...

As Rico sat in his cell, he decided that the decision that he had to make to advance himself was to agree to The Organization's offer and pull off one of the greatest acts of disregard for the American Justice System since 2Pac's "death." How else could a man that is designed to lose ever win? If he didn't jump on this offer, he'd be another statistic, another Black man rotting away in prison with rapists and thieves, and that couldn't be his legacy. For those who couldn't understand, they probably never had much to begin with so it's easy for them to judge him for his decision. But in order to have riches in this life, you must make sacrifices, physical and mental. Rico had a plan, and it was to be rich, the thing was, he had every intention of playing the Organization like a fiddle until he couldn't anymore. At that point, he would begin to operate on his own.

Excerpt from The Organization

Volume 2: Conspiracy Theory

"Yes, oh God yes, fuck me harder!!!" yelled Amber as Gaden put in
major work on this sexual escapade. He wasn't sure if it was the relaxation or
just the fact that he really enjoyed having sex with Amber, but he had become
legendary in his sexual prowess as of late. Amber had recently even
recruited one of the island beauties to engage in a threesome. As Gaden
climaxed and nearly fell trying to pull out before he ejaculated inside of her,
he noticed a shadowy figure standing on the balcony. He immediately
reached for his gun and yelled out "Who the fuck wants to die tonight."
Though they tried to maintain a low profile, the mansion was the talk of the
island, even noticed by the president of the Bahamas. They still drove nice
cars and still dressed in thousand-dollar outfits. To the unseeing eye, they
were some rich couple that would be easy marks. Unbeknownst to the
unseeing eye, Gaden was still sharp as ever and ready to kill. "Put some
damn clothes on, you got a hard dick and your ass is exposed" said the raspy
voice shadow figure. Gaden, instantly knowing who was on the balcony
quickly hid and yelled out "I'll be out shortly." "Don't keep me waiting" said
the shadow. "Who the hell is that babe?" asked Amber hiding on the side of
the bed with a sheet wrapped around her naked body. "If I told you, you
might think that I'm crazy" said Gaden. "I think that it's crazy that some
strange man was watching us fuck!" said an angry Amber, who wasn't too sure

how long this strange man had been outside. "Amber, that's the Godfather, the man who put me where I am" said Gaden. He found some shorts on the side of the bed and then grabbed a robe. "I'll be back, I have to see what's going on" he said to Amber as he got up and walked out to the balcony. "Ok, but tell your father or whoever that I would prefer if he didn't stand outside and watch me, I'd be a porn star if I wanted an audience" said a still upset Amber as she got up and ran into the master bathroom. Gaden was a little weirded out by the situation too, but he knew the Godfather too well to question when and where he appears. He knew that it had to be important, almost laughing on his way out to the balcony, as he did find humor in the situation.

"Godfather, how are you?" asked Gaden as he attempted to give him a hug but was rejected. "No, that's alright, don't want your sweat all over my Armani suit" said the Godfather. The Godfather was a wise man, a 5'11 tough guy who had endured it all over the years. He had seen death time and time again, the hardness of his face and the fact that nothing seemed to bother him gave him an ice-cold disposition. He was the ultimate decision maker, but 15 years ago he began to feel age catching up to him, so he recruited Gaden as his trainee. 10 years ago, he completely got off the grid only communicating with Gaden and leaving leadership of The Organization to him. "Where the hell do you and Drake get off pulling this shit, so he is now running what I built, and I never ordained him to do that" said the Godfather. "I know, but it was supposed to only be until I resurfaced. The problem is, I can't, Drake ran off with everything I gave him. He even moved the team out of New York" said Gaden, who for once, seemed empty without the world in his hands. "Yeah, they're in LA, I got the drop on all of them. People forget that I exist and that's how I like it. I told you years ago that Drake had some ideas that I didn't like, but you loved him because he was a killing machine" said the Godfather who knew that they were in a real jam with Drake at the helm. "I didn't know that he was power hungry, but I have a plan so it's good that you're here" said Gaden before his idea got shot down. "No way, you and your antics got us into this shit, I'll go and fix it. Since Jennings is dead, the only other member that I am still familiar with is Bauer. I'll get in touch with him and track down Rico Jones" said the Godfather. "Jones? He is the reason we're in this shit. If you get him, I'll have to kill him" said Gaden. "You're not killing anything but that hot piece of ass you got in there, you understand? I am coming out of retirement to reclaim what belongs to me. I will then think about relinquishing it back to you once I'm done. I need Jones to infiltrate the FBI system and plant some viruses. The Big Cheese will be exposed once this is all said and done" said the Godfather. "The Big Cheese? Schlister? What the hell does he have to do with anything?" asked Gaden. "Just know that once he sees what I have on him, he will make Conley turn power back over to me. I will then personally kill Drake myself" said the Godfather, who was hell bent on his plan. "Ok, so I understand your plan, but make sure you get Frank Houston involved" said Gaden. "I like Frank, he has been solid since you brought him in. I definitely planned to use him for the major takeover" said the Godfather who put Gaden's mind to rest. "Can I do anything?" asked Gaden, who hated to be left out of the plan. "Lay low, and stop drawing attention, the locals are plotting on you" said the Godfather. "Let me walk you down to your car" said Gaden, being polite. "It won't be necessary" said the Godfather who pointed to a hook and rope he used to climb up the side of the balcony. "I still got it!!!" yelled the Godfather to Gaden as he slid down the rope and headed to a waiting Black Town Car with the lights off. This was the man who taught Gaden the key to knowing every detail without being seen. For all he knew, the Godfather may have been watching him for days, waiting on the right time to strike. If he was an enemy, Gaden would be dead as he appeared at his most vulnerable. A lesson to be learned. Then again, every conversation Gaden ever had with his mentor was a lesson.